BLOOD STONES

Gerald Kearny

AuthorHouse™
1663 Liberty Drive, Suite 200
Bloomington, IN 47403
www.authorhouse.com
Phone: 1-800-839-8640

© 2008 Gerald Kearny. All rights reserved.

No part of this book may be reproduced, stored in a retrieval system, or transmitted by any means without the written permission of the author.

First published by AuthorHouse 9/2/2008

ISBN: 978-1-4343-9976-2 (sc)

Library of Congress Control Number: 2008907980

Printed in the United States of America
Bloomington, Indiana

This book is printed on acid-free paper.

PROLOGUE

August 3, 2116

A crisp morning breeze rushed through the lush green forest of towering pines. Their branches swayed gently to its will and their thin peaked tops bowed respectfully.

The cool rush continued out across Bear Island Lake, chased by a fan of rippling water that sparkled under the rising sun. On the deck of a small north-woods cabin, the wind rustled a newspaper propped upright by a pair of young hands.

'That's impossible.' Gib Larkin thought as he quarter folded the paper to hold it more firmly against the breeze. He was caught up in one specific headline: <u>Last Native of Old Ely Dies at Age 102</u>.

It wasn't the death of Mrs. Virginia Morton that he questioned. It was the implication that the town of Ely, the place where his family had been vacationing all his life, was ever anywhere else but where it now sat. From the vast experience of his fourteen years, he just assumed he knew all of Ely's most interesting secrets.

Next to him in the second of two slatted wooden chairs was his father Sam. With one leg crossed sharply over the other and a mug of steaming coffee on the arm of the chair, he also had his face buried in a paper and he was also fighting to keep it upright against the breeze. The weekly fishing report was out and he wanted to see which of the area lakes was producing well enough to warrant a trip.

Gib finished reading the article then lowered the paper and stared into the distance. Also with his leg crossed, and also with a cup of coffee, he looked like a teenaged carbon copy of his father. "Dad, where was Old Ely and why was it moved?" He asked.

Sam laid down his paper and reached for his mug. "The original town was about twenty or so miles north of here." He answered. "Along the southern shore of Shagawa Lake."

Gib's brow furrowed and his gaze drifted out across the water. He looked past the group of tiny rock islands just off their shore, through the giant island that named the lake, and farther still to an image of the distant northern shore. *That* was the edge. *That* was the gateway to a vast and completely undeveloped forest. *That* was the federally protected Boundary Waters Canoe Area - two million acres of nothing but thick forest and endless waterways. No motors were allowed on its many lakes, no roads crossed its border, and certainly there were no towns. It had always been this way, as far as he knew.

He thought maybe his dad was teasing him, but the casual, passing manner in which he said it, as if it was some ordinary bit of information known by everyone, suggested otherwise. An entire town was just moved – end of story, no big deal, and what kind of idiot doesn't know that?

The dying breeze still held enough bite to make Gib's eyes water. As he blinked away the excess tears, his shock eased enough for him to speak. "Really?" He scoffed.

"Mmm-hmm." Sam confirmed, swallowing a sip of hot coffee. "A century ago this whole area looked very different and Minnesota's Boundary Waters were significantly smaller."

Sam stole a sly sideways glance at his son's face and saw the intrigue growing there. His oldest child rarely deferred to his wisdom anymore. This was a momentous occasion and he intended to revel in it for as long as possible.

"Are you sure you have time for a history lesson?" Sam asked. "I thought you were going fishing with the Hoaglunds this morning? They'll be heading out soon."

"I've got time." Gib pleaded. "Mrs. Hoaglund takes forever to get ready. They won't be leaving for another hour."

Sam sighed and shrugged indifferently, "Well, actually I'm not sure what else to tell you. The town used to be up there and now it's down here. They just picked up everything and left."

"DAD!" Gib shouted out. "Why was it moved?!"

Sam smiled behind another slow sip as he let Gib stew in his frustration a moment longer. "Well, at the turn of the twentieth century, environmental pollution rose to alarmingly dangerous levels."

"Yeah, thanks dad." Gib interrupted sarcastically. He'd seen the secret smile and he couldn't let such gloating go unanswered. "I learned that in the fifth grade. You got anything useful for me?"

"Oh…well. I didn't realize you were so enlightened. Maybe it would be better if you went to the Ely library and found out about the old town from a book?" Sam threatened lightly.

Gib's sarcasm quickly subsided and he shed his condescending attitude to make up for his rude remark. "Okay, okay. I'm sorry. I'll stop interrupting."

"Alright then." Sam said then took up his story once again. "In 2015, all countries that were part of the United Nations held a two week summit to determine what could be done to slow the effects of global warming. They gathered theories and recommendations from the world's leading environmental scientists. One of the solutions was to significantly increase the size of already existing natural habitats. As a sign of unity in fighting the global threat, the United States and Canada made a joint agreement to use land surrounding the BWCA and the Quetico Park."

"Was this the only place they changed in America?" Gib asked.

"No. I don't know all of them, but I do know that Wyoming, Colorado, Washington and Minnesota were the states most affected by it. The government paid billions of dollars to either buy out or relocate entire towns. Ely was the only town in this area that chose to relocate. In 2025, the town was picked up and moved here, between Bear Head and Bear Island Lakes."

'Picked up?' Gib thought quietly as a rush of logistical questions raced through his head. How could a whole town be moved? Did his dad mean they rebuilt it? What was left of the old town now and was it really possible to just erase something so permanent?

Those burning questions would have to wait. Right now he was still trying to digest this sudden twist of reality. Most of Gib's knowledge of the boundary waters was from bits and pieces he remembered of his grandfather's stories. Somehow this monumental fact had been left out. "Was grandpa around when it happened? Why didn't he tell me about it?"

Sam spotted another opportunity to reiterate his point about respecting the wisdom of one's elders. "He was born not too long after it happened. His father told him about it and even took him to the place where the family cabin used to be. Maybe you didn't show enough interest in his stories for him to think you'd care?"

Sam's patronizing remark worked and Gib recalled several occasions when he had rushed out of the room as soon as his had grandfather tried to entertain him with the less interesting details of his life. Unless it was about some great fishing adventure deep in the woods, he never paid much attention to what his grandfather had to say. Now that chance had passed him by.

Gib sat in quiet regret until something his father said clicked in his head. "*Your* grandfather had a cabin somewhere in there?"

"Oh yes, all of his childhood vacations were spent on a lake that is now deep inside the boundary waters and his family was right in the middle of its transformation. The cabin actually belonged to *his* grandparents and the whole family got together there several times a year. In fact, his two uncles loved it up here so much that they even moved up to this area."

As the story deepened, Gib found himself more and more caught up in its implications. Until now, he had never given the word "family" much consideration beyond his parents and younger sisters. Ancestors were nothing more than dead relatives he didn't know, nor ever really cared to know. But there was a connection to them now. They too had grown up vacationing here and they too had enjoyed these waters. Their lives, over a century ago, were eerily similar to his own.

"What happened to grandpa and his family after the town moved?" He asked. "Is that when they started coming here?"

"Well they didn't come here, but they continued to come up north. One of the uncles, Gerald, was a craftsman and writer. He built a cabin on the north shore of Lake Superior so the family started going there when everything was moved. Wasn't the same, but they were together."

"Have you ever been there? To the cabin? Why haven't we gone?"

"My father showed it to me once, but we couldn't stay there. For some reason, Gerald made a deal with the state to have them take it over after he died. Once that happened, they opened it up for the general public to rent."

"Why?" Gib asked. "Why not pass it on through the family?"

"I don't know." Sam answered thoughtfully. "No one knows. It's a pretty amazing place, very rustic with a main cabin and a guesthouse. A small river runs right through the property forming several small waterfalls. Because of its location and the fact that Uncle Gerald was a moderately successful author, it instantly became a popular tourist attraction. We've never gone because there is a five-year waiting list. Anyway, the next generation of our family came back here; to this new Ely."

In this bonding moment, Sam wanted to tell his son that he had already put their name on the list and that they would indeed be vacationing there next summer. He wanted to, but it was meant to be a Christmas surprise and he decided he could wait.

"A writer?" Gib asked, though he guessed it was another one of those fascinating facts that he never bothered to hear. "Why didn't anybody tell me we had a writer in the family?".

"I'm sure we've talked about it before. You weren't old enough to read his work - hold on." Sam got up and disappeared into the cabin. Gib barely noticed that he had left. His mind was still whirling.

A few minutes later, Sam stepped back out onto the deck. In his hand, he carried a small leather bound book. "Here. You might like this. It's a book written by your..." He paused for a moment to think through the correct order of lineage, "great, great, great uncle. It's about a young man that goes in search of two magical stones crafted by one of his ancestors."

Gib took the book and looked at the cover. It was titled *Blood Stones* and he flipped it open to the first page.

Their legend doubted by all but the faithful, dismissed with time as the wild imaginings of the superstitious, the power of the stones yet waits to be recovered...

Five minutes later he was twisted sideways in the chair with one leg slung over its arm. He held open the book with one hand while the other eagerly waited to turn the page. A boy close to Gib's age yelled up to him from the dock at the bottom of the hill. Mrs. Hoaglund was finally ready to go fishing. Gib tore his attention away from the book just long enough to tell his friend that he had changed his mind. Instead, he spent this summer vacation reading and asking his father questions about the history of his family.

CHAPTER 1

Gib eyed up the modest two-story house in front of him before deciding to make his way up the snow-covered sidewalk. The icy January wind stung his face, but he wanted to remember this moment. It had taken him a mere six hours to drive from his home in Illinois to where he now stood in Cloquet, Minnesota, but it had taken eleven years of tenacity and patience before his research had uncovered this last critical piece. This was the beginning.

He climbed the stairs, rang the doorbell and waited anxiously. The inside door opened almost immediately, answered by young woman with a stone-faced scowl. "Yes?" She snapped rudely.

The abruptness of her response, the terseness of it, started Gib fumbling for words. "Uh, hi. I'm, um, Gib Larkin."

She gave a quick look back into the house then spoke in a bare whisper. "Can I help you?"

"I'm here to see Alise Gethold." He said, pulling his coat tighter to protect from a sudden stronger gust of the biting air. "I called last week."

The young woman shifted her stance and planted herself sideways against the door jamb. She reached up to a thin strap of leather tied close around her neck and began rubbing the two reddish agates that rested tight against the hollow of her throat. The greener outer ring of her hazel eyes burned with fiery resentment and defiance. He was younger than she expected, but that didn't make his presence any less intrusive, or unwanted. "She's sleeping."

"Oh, um, sorry. It's just I came all this way. I thought she was expecting me."

"She's a hundred and seven years old." The young woman shot back. She rebounded off the doorway and stood ready to close the door. "She needs her rest."

From deeper in the house the cracked and withered voice of Alise Gethold asked, "Who's at the door, Addy?" She was one of only a handful of people that were allowed to use this pet name for her great granddaughter. Everyone else called her Addison.

Addison swung her head around to answer. A tightly pulled pony tail of honey-brown hair whipped over her shoulder and now there was a sweetness to her voice that sharply contrasted her tone with Gib. "It's that guy about the book – the one that called the other day." She faced him straight on again with the same hard and accusing eyes and with the same accusing tone. "What did you say your name was?"

"Gib Larkin." He answered trying to sound as innocent and non-threatening as he could.

"Let him in. Let him in." The old woman ordered. She eagerly welcomed the opportunity to socialize with someone other than family.

Addison unlatched the door and hesitantly stepped back to allow him in. Gib offered a pleasant smile against her suspicious and defensive look. He hoped she would let up a little once she found out who he was.

For now, Addison kept her guard and refused to entertain any more conversation as she escorted him to her great grandmother's bedroom. She left him to enter on his own, but stood right outside the door just in case. Some of these men could be incredibly rude and she had thrown out more than her share of pushy fortune seekers in the past.

The room that housed the mostly bedridden woman was a throw-back to a late nineteenth century north woods décor. The bed frame was made of thick pine logs. Beside it, an old fashioned oil lamp burned softly on a green country-style night table. Its soft glow warmed the pale yellow walls and cast gentle shadows of various nick-knacks around the room. The frail looking woman in the bed was covered with a cozy bear and moose patterned quilt. Gib was swept up in a wave of nostalgia that deepened even more when he saw the woodland

Gerald Kearny

scenes depicted in two old, but vibrantly colored pictures hanging on the wall beside her bed.

"Hello young man." Alise Gethold greeted. She waved him to bring over a small wooden chair by the door. "How can I help you?"

Gib snapped out of his little escape and pulled the chair over to the side of her bed. "My name is Gib Larkin. I am the great-great grandnephew of Gerald Kearny."

Alise cocked her head to the side with a curious tilt as she took a long study of his look. His short dark hair was thick with shallow waves and half curls. His sharply arched brows, while distinctly bold and prominent, seemed contrary to the softness of his brown eyes. A gentle half-smile rounded his cheeks and wrinkled the corners of his eyes. It was a kind face, and pleasant, and she recognized it. "You are." Her fragile voice confirmed. "I see pieces of him in you."

"Really?" Gib asked proudly. It was perhaps the greatest compliment he'd ever gotten. Since his introduction to his uncle's life, he had developed a deep appreciation for the things he accomplished. It encouraged his ego to hear such a comparison from the only living relative that had actually known him. He would have loved to explore the similarities further, but he set aside his vanity and turned the conversation to his reason for coming. "For the last ten years or so, I have been researching our family tree and seeking out the people in our bloodline. I'm very happy to finally find you."

"Oh, thank you, dear." She said sweetly. Then her tone became more challenging. "But I don't think that's the only reason you're here. I recognize that fire burning in your eyes. I've seen it before. You're searching for the blood stones and you're here to ask me questions."

He appreciated her candor and admitted to his intentions with a bashful grimace. "Well, that too, but I really am glad to meet you. I have been interested in genealogy since I was in high school. My dad says heritage is one of the greatest gifts we have of the past. I can't tell you how hard it's been to find you. Why isn't there a record of your marriage to Mason Gethold?"

"Oh…him." She sighed with slight annoyance. "I almost forgot about that old fool. I followed him up to Canada so he could take some big guiding job at a resort. I was young and my parents were against it. They were right of course, and it didn't last long. I got pregnant with my daughter, Autumn and he got a case of the catch-ya-laters when he realized the responsibility."

She paused then looked at him solemnly and sternly. "Men oughtn't be making promises 'til they know for sure they can keep 'em."

Gib smiled at her berating comment. "Should any young man ever be making promises?"

She wanted to laugh, but she wouldn't; not in his presence when she didn't quite have a read on him yet. Still, she couldn't keep her face from brightening a little. "Didn't let my daughter make the same mistake, though.

No marriage til he's thirty and no children til he's certain – I drummed that into her head every single day from the second she came into this world. She listened well and she taught her own daughter the same. Made good choices, both of them; God rest their gentle souls. They both found good men who knew how to honor a commitment. And so far Addison's following that sound logic pretty darn well, too!"

Gib sat quietly embarrassed knowing that this life lesson was less about her family history and more about expressing her feelings on the intentions of young men. Specifically, she was trying to impress them upon him.

Alise shifted in her bed, propped herself up a little straighter, and pulled the quilt higher up on her chest. "A lot of other people were able to track me down easily enough. Why did it take you so long?"

"Well, I'm only twenty-five." Gib defended. "I've been a little busy with grad school and work. And I don't have the money for private investigators or research specialists."

She dismissed his excuses with a condescending snicker.

"Will you help me?" Gib asked.

"Who are your parents?" She asked coyly. "How are we related?"

She was testing him, Gib realized, but he didn't mind. In fact, he rather enjoyed it. She seemed feisty and good-natured. He hoped he would have as much spunk when he was her age. "My father is Samuel Larkin. His grandfather was Michael Larkin; the grandson of Gerald's sister Christine. You are the granddaughter of Gerald's brother, Steven."

"Hmmm" Alise distantly acknowledged. "And Gerald's other sister Kelly? What of their line?"

"Many are still in the Midwest. In fact, Kelly's great, great grandson is coming with me to help look for the stones. I met him three years ago when I tracked down his parents. He actually grew up less than sixty miles away from my home town in Illinois."

Alise wandered through the images of her past. The most vivid one was of the four siblings, together with their families, at Gerald's cabin on the north shore of Lake Superior. She was very young then and if she remembered correctly, it was the last time they were all able to be together. The pleasant memory had been long forgotten. She was glad to have it again.

"Well, you've certainly done your homework. I'll give you that much." She teased, returning to her mild brow-beating. "And what does your family know of this area now?"

"Actually, my family went back to new Ely after the north shore cabin went to the state. We've got our own cabin there and most in our line still go back every year."

Now Alise couldn't help smiling. She was glad that the tradition started by Gerald Kearny's parents hadn't been completely lost. "And Kelly's line? Do they still come?"

"Some still do - a pretty small group, but we're hoping to get all of us there at the same time in the next couple years. We're only missing Steve's line..." His last words hinted at the hope of brining them back as well.

"Oh you won't find many of them." She quickly corrected. "Other than me and Addison, of course. I think the restructuring hit Steve harder than any than other in the original family. He stayed long enough for his children to grow, but eventually left and he never did come back. Just wasn't the same place anymore. The forest didn't hold the same mystery it once did. My aunt and uncles followed after, scattering across the state, at first, then throughout the country as they got older. Only my mother kept her family in the area. The rest of Steve's line has forgotten it. Pity, really. I've lost touch with so many." Her words had trailed off at the end and she turned her face away from him.

Gib picked up on the distant sadness she was trying to hide. "I could help you. I've actually already located some of those in your line living in California"

It was an appealing offer and she would probably take him up on it later, but she wasn't ready to give in to his charm quite yet. "What got you so interested in the business of families and long deceased relatives?"

"Well...Ely, I guess. I was fourteen when I first found out that Ely had been moved. There was an article in the paper about the last native of Old Ely. That's when my dad told me how long our family had been going there. At least, that's the first time I listened when he told me."

"Virginia Morton?" She asked peculiarly.

"Excuse me."

"That article – the last native. Was it a woman named Virginia Morton?"

"Um, maybe." Gib said, not quite sure why it mattered, but certain she was about to tell him. "Yeah, I think that's right. Did you know her?"

"Just an acquaintance. She was a fair bit older than I, but she sure liked to be known. Heh, last native of Old Ely, Ginny rode that pony long after it had died and turned to dust; always spouting off about being the last."

Alise's voice suddenly turned quieter as if she was about to reveal some closely guarded secret. "Truth be told, she wasn't. She may have been the last one conceived in Old Ely, but Old Ginny was born in the city of Virginia. Just about every old-timer knew it. For some reason no one ever could produce a birth certificate to prove she was Ely's last. The powers that be just accepted her word without question. And, her parents were pack-sackers to boot!"

"Pack-sackers?" Gib asked.

"Transplants. People moving in from somewhere else. My own mother wouldn't even be considered a native and she was born there. You don't lose that label til a couple generations pass. Ginny Morton was about as native to Old Ely as a koala bear."

Gib dropped his head and laughed softly. "Well, I guess we're both a couple of pack-sackers then."

"Guess so." She agreed. "So what makes you think you can find the blood stones, if they even exist? Most people gave up searching for them years ago - and they had a lot more money than you!"

From the pocket of his coat, Gib pulled out his faded copy of the book. Stuffed between the pages were clippings from tattered old newspapers and magazines. "I've studied everything about Gerald, including every interview he's ever given. I've also read everything there is on the Kearny family. And," He said, sliding out an old photograph from the very front of the book. "I found this."

Alise took the yellowed picture he held over to her and let out a soft little gasp. It showed the Kearny parents holding a large ornately carved cedar box. She remembered it well. It was a family memory box Gerald had made for them as a Christmas present. All sides of the box were covered in a hand carved pattern of crawling ivy. She remembered marveling at that as a child. The leaves grew up from the sides and onto the outside edges of the lid creating a frame for an enlarged portrait of the Kearny family sealed under glass.

She was in it, though just a baby, and she flashed back to a time not too many years later when she and her own father had sifted through the pictures concealed within. This memory had also been completely forgotten and Alise tried to recall the last time she had seen the old keep sake box.

Finally her impish attitude faded and her words were filled with wonder. "Where did you find it?"

"It went to Christine after the Kearny parents passed away and went down through my line. Various aunts and uncles received it, but a year and a half ago it came to my parents."

Gib recognized the hopeful look in Alise's face and answered the question he knew she was about to ask. "The photos are still intact and at my apartment in Illinois. I'd be happy to bring them to you when I come back in the summer."

A tingling excitement washed over Alise as she anticipated seeing the lost pictures. With each passing year, the memories of her childhood had grown ever distant and lost. The chance to relive them again overwhelmed her. Her thin, brown spotted hand reached over to rest on Gib's shoulder and she gave him a teary-eyed smile.

It was a tender moment that touched Gib just as deeply and he was happy that he was able to give her that gift. He watched as she looked back to the photo and he waited for her to regain her composure. "I have a theory and I'm hoping you can help me verify it. There is a tray that sits half way down inside the box. There are two four inch holes side by side with veiny lines of gold flowing from them. Their size suggests that two round stones would rest perfectly inside."

Alise pulled a tissue from the box on the night stand and dabbed at the corner of her eyes. "Yes, of course I remember the tray." She said cryptically.

Despite her failing memory, the image of the tray was stuck clearly in her mind. She too had taken an interest in the blood stones when she was younger and, like Gib, she connected the flowing gold lines to those on the legendary stones. To her, it proved their existence. But, like everyone else, she was unable to decipher the clues that identified the first step of the journey.

"Did anything ever sit in those holes, or do you know of some special purpose for them?" Gib asked.

"No." She responded, staring into his eyes intently. "Nothing ever sat in there and the holes served no useful purpose."

Even in their short time together, she had already decided that she liked this boy. She could feel that his interest in their heritage was sincere. In fact, she believed it was every bit as important to him as finding the stones. After years of people seeking her out for answers in greedy hopes of striking it rich, finally there was someone with the right mindset to succeed in the quest. Young love and single motherhood forced her to abandon her search for the stones. Maybe he would have better luck.

"Addy." Alise called out as she took hold of Gib's hand. "If you're going into the boundary waters, you'd better have an excellent guide. Nature has completely reclaimed the area and it is very dangerous if you don't know what you're doing. My granddaughter might be willing to help you. I'd bet there's not another living soul that knows the forest as well as she. It'll cost you though."

Half way through their conversation, Addison had felt secure enough to leave her post by the door. She had been listening when her grandmother began toying with the young man and she decided he was no threat. She wasn't too far though, and returned when the call came. "Yes, nana."

"I think this boy might be onto something. You might want to consider helping him."

Addison was impressed. This was the first time her grandmother had ever spoken so favorably about anyone undertaking what she considered to be a colossal waste of time.

"Are you really that familiar with the area?" Gib asked Addison doubtfully. Their residence here in Cloquet was a good hour from the Boundary Waters. His research suggested that only locals knew the canoe wilderness well enough to navigate it. He was planning to hire someone from Tower or Ely, border towns famed as entry points into the national forest, to guide him through.

Addison took immediate offense at his lack of confidence. She assumed he was judging her because of her gender, as many other men had done before, and she began listing off her impressive credentials. "My father worked out of Ely as a guide. He took me on my first camping trip into the boundary waters when I was just five years old. By the age of ten I was going with him to the inner forest; beyond Old Ely, forty miles away from the closest town. I began portaging canoes at the age of thirteen and was guiding my own trips by sixteen. He made a ton of money off of wackos like you and after he passed away I took over his guiding business."

"I - I'm sorry, I didn't realize…" Gib fumbled. "This is just so far from where we're going. I was under the impression that I needed to find someone from the iron range."

He had already found one other Kearny descendent to join him; it was only logical that he have another to guide him. She was the one and already they were off to a bad start. "Do you have the time to help us?"

Addison maintained her cold demeanor but inside she was dying for the opportunity. Not to find the stones, of course, but to get back into the woods. Her guiding trips were on hold for this summer so she could complete another semester of college and take care of her grandmother. Already she was depressed about not having the chance to do a long trip this year.

"I don't know. It depends on when you're going and how long you plan to be there." She answered.

"We'll be coming up in the middle of June." Gib said hopefully. "But I'm not sure how long we'll be in there. Probably not more than two weeks."

"Hmmm, too bad." Addison responded. "My summer classes won't be done by then."

"Oh just skip the classes this summer, Addy." Alise spoke up, deciding it was time for a little interference. "You're young and you need to have a little adventure before you head out into the real world. I'll be fine until you get back. One of those nurses from the agency can check in on me."

That was telling, Addison thought. Her grandmother hated having strangers taking care of her. She stood in the doorway, pretending to be thinking, but her mind was already made up. She just wanted Gib to sweat it out.

"Well, you're gonna have to pay. I'm not giving you a break just because you're some cousin's, brother's, mother's, son."

Gib looked back at Alise with a conspicuous wink. Despite their rough start, he was glad to have Addison along.

CHAPTER 2

The heels of his shiny three-hundred dollar shoes clicked a rapid beat against the shiny teak floor as Harris Montgomery scurried down the long dark hallway. His heart beat furiously in his chest, though not from his aerobic pace. 'Why would he have called for me at this time of night?' He wondered anxiously.

Meetings with his boss always made him anxious. Being called for a special meeting, at night, was cause for even greater concern. It didn't help that this wing of the mansion held an eerie quality that completely unnerved him. The rich brown mahogany wall on his left was decorated with exaggerated geometric molding and evenly spaced sconces that cast only dim light. On his right, a continuous row of windows lined the upper half of the wall reflecting both the pale lights and the muted shadows they created. Sinister shapes appeared to jump out at him as he walked and his eyes shifted nervously each time they did. The few friends Harris had time for often heard him refer to the hallway as "The tunnel of terror".

After nine years of employment, he should have been accustomed to the anxiety that overcame him when attending these meetings. He wasn't though, and his employer liked it that way. Temple Marston ruled by fear and Harris Montgomery was ripe for scaring.

Harris came to the end of the haunting hallway, but stopped before opening the door to the library. He smoothed out his blue suit coat against his wiry torso, straightened his tie, and curled back the sides of his fine blond hair behind his ears.

"Relax." He whispered to himself, though part of him still hoped that maybe his boss wouldn't be there. Perhaps some other urgent matter had come up since he'd called forty-five minutes ago.

A quick glance downward showed him just how foolish that hope was. A yellow strip of light glowed from under the door; disheartening, but not surprising. His luck had never been that good. He'd given up on good fortune a long time ago. One deep breath and he grabbed onto the door knob, turning it slowly at first then resolving to be stronger. He swung the door open and walked confidently into the room.

Rows of book cases sprawled across the narrow room, meeting both the yellowed marble floor and the white stamped ceiling twenty feet above. He forced his steps to fall slower as he made a determined effort to demonstrate his composure.

A brilliantly colored Persian rug marked his course through the middle of the library. Woven caricatures of tribal people frolicking among native animals escorted him along the way. Gold plated pedestals lined the sides of the elegant pathway. Each one was topped with a glass case to protect whatever valuable artifact sat inside. Ancient pots, gold statues and jade figurines were just a few of the things that had captured Temple's interest in the past. All held great value and all had been obtained by what Harris secretly referred to as "questionable practices".

Harris had been there when most of these treasures were found, though he only got to see them when he came for these wretched meetings. In truth, he had found most of them. He might not have done the hard labor, but it was his knowledge of history that had unraveled the clues to their location. If not for him, most of these things would not be here.

The very last pedestal, the one that used to hold a set of Indian Rudraksha beads, was now empty. Harris stopped to look at it and understood why he had been called.

"Come here." A commanding voice boomed from above.

Five steps above him, upon a rounded split-level platform, sat his boss, or Sir, as Harris usually addressed him. His immense oaken desk was positioned between two slender windows that stretched from floor to ceiling - a throne between two columns, Harris had realized a long time ago. There, Temple shuffled through business documents and scribbled out notes on each. He didn't even bother to look up when he addressed his subordinate.

Harris started up the stairs, stumbling a little when the tip of his shoe caught on the first step then trying to cover it by running up the rest. Temple had noticed. Studying a page reporting last quarter's fiscal gains, he smirked to himself a little. It was his presence that caused it.

"Sit down, Harris." Temple ordered curtly, still giving his attention only to the reports.

Harris dropped into a leather wing-backed chair feeling resentful that he was so obligated to appease this man so obediently. Temple was terminally cruel and unreasonably demanding, but Harris valued his employment enough to tolerate it. The esteem of working for one of the most successful entrepreneurs in the country was worth the abuse. Of course, the money helped too.

However, there were times when the demands were too much. Temple's desire to make everyone accommodate him always strained the threshold of Harris' dignity, but there were times when it went too far. One day that next order would be the last. Harris would tell him, in a most eloquent manner that he no longer needed his employment then he would close his resignation with some inappropriately crude street gesture. That threshold hadn't been crossed yet, but it could be and just thinking about telling Temple off somehow softened his discontent. It gave him control.

Temple still hadn't looked at him and Harris waited in silence as he watched him write - business as usual. Over the years, Harris had come to know the top of Temple's head very well. Heavy, black hair hung several inches from his forehead, well groomed always and easily whisked back into the perfect place with one pass of the hand. The age in his face suggested he was in his late twenties, though he was actually within months of turning forty - three years younger than Harris and another minor source of resentment. His sharp angled features, high cheek bones and defined jaw line created a strong and devilishly handsome look.

Temple sat upright, though still not too interested in Harris' presence and still not giving any eye contact. In his hand, he held the gold plated pen he'd been using. Now he rolled it back and forth between his thumb and forefinger as he studied the shiny patina. "Are you familiar with the blood stones?" He asked, finally breaking the long silence.

"Um, yes." Harris answered at once. "They are the subject of a fictional fantasy book written around the turn of the millennium by a man named Gerald Kearny. They are two perfectly round, emerald stones with gold filled grooves running along the surface. The twisting pattern of the grooves looks like rivers flowing on a map."

Harris beamed with pride as he spoke. He'd anticipated this years ago. He knew Temple's attention would eventually turn to the mythical stones and he was glad that his foresight could be put to use. "As described in the book, each stone is said to be five inches in diameter and they were created to provide protection for an ancient clan."

"Very good, Harris." Temple conceded, though with a distinct hint of condescension. "I am always fascinated by the depth of your knowledge in all things historical."

"Thank you, sir." Harris replied, pretending not to catch the patronizing undertone of the compliment. "While obscure when it was first released, the book gained wide spread popularity in the late 2050's. The main character, Archer, learns about the legend of the stones from a book said to be written by their craftsman. He later learns that he is a distant descendent of the author. These facts lead him to believe the stones are real. His determination takes him on an adventure in search of them. During this journey he meets new friends and faces many dangers before eventually succeeding."

"This revelation defines the theme of the book. The stones are actually a symbol for the value of heritage and family. His journey was an exercise in learning to appreciate these things."

Gerald Kearny

"Like Archer's ancestor, Gerald Kearny was also a craftsman and writer. This fact convinced many people that Kearny actually did create stones of this manner and that his book was a type of map they could use to find them."

Harris stopped, drew his breath and put forth his most haughty intellectualism to quote the appropriate passage that defined Kearny's myth. "…And the trees with all their strength and with all their majesty would not grow for they had been beaten, the path will lead you."

"Yes." Temple interrupted. "Kearny's pedantic ramblings."

Harris thought that assessment a bit unfair, though he certainly would never say so. "This line is believed to be the starting point; the 'beaten path' that everyone has looked for – obviously without success."

"Fifty-Seven years ago, the first person started searching for the stones." He continued. "I believe his name was Charles Reardon. He followed the same clues that Archer followed in the book, but he was unable to find anything substantial."

"Many others have searched, trying to find the fabled path so heavily referenced. Each followed different interpretations of the book and its clues. To this day there are still a few people trying to figure out the location. Most, however, have generally concluded that the stones do not exist and that Gerald Kearny was a plausible story teller with an effective imagination."

"Correct." Temple stated, ending his obsession with the expensive pen and now giving Harris his full attention. "Except that Charles Reardon did find something. Something that became available after his recent death. Something I was able to acquire at the estate sale."

Harris shifted uneasily in his chair. He wasn't aware of Reardon's passing and that was a poor reflection on his performance. He chastised himself for not catching the important detail, but beyond that he felt more. There was a spark of excitement he hadn't experienced in years. His father had shared the book with him when he was younger and, like so many other kids, the story had filled him with the wonders of adventure. If Temple was bringing up the subject, he must have something concrete.

Temple opened one of his desk drawers, pulled out a folder, and handed it over to Harris. "Last year Reardon came across an interesting find in the computer archives of an old and defunct insurance company. Fortunately for us, age caught up with him before he could follow up on it."

Harris opened the folder and saw two old photographs attached to a narrative form. The pictures showed an outside and inside view of a carved cedar box and an intriguing tray set within. The narrative included detailed descriptions of the box and an estimate of its value. The implications did not need to be explained.

"Imagine their worth, Harris. Two emerald stones of that size alone would be worth billions. The crafting of them, with gold and by Kearny's hand, would make them invaluable."

As Harris continued to study the picture, Temple walked over to one of the book cases and pulled out his own copy of the book. He fanned quickly through the pages knowing the clues were there waiting to be found. "I want you to study Reardon's work. The blood stones do exist and this summer we're going to find them."

CHAPTER 3

He had to wait almost six months to begin searching for his prize, and nothing frustrated Temple more than waiting. But the remnants of Minnesota's cold winters hold strong well through the spring and those unaccustomed to the climate wisely plan their trips no earlier than mid-June.

Sprays of water doused the passengers of the eighteen foot motor boat as it broke through the choppy waves tumbling across Bear Island Lake. Temple sat in front, rigidly upright and staring straight ahead. His stiff, darkly clothed body swayed back and forth each time they bounced over a trough in the water, but he never lost his forward focus. Harris was next to him wearing only a blue fleece jacket. His arms were crossed tightly around his chest to conserve as much body heat as possible. It was still too early in the season for him.

Three other men were in the boat as well. Ben Jurick, the local outfitter contracted to provide their canoes, drove them to their last stop before heading into the boundary waters. The weather didn't bother him at all. In fact, he rather enjoyed the breeze flowing through his flimsy short-sleeved shirt and he even had the top two buttons open. The other two were what Temple called "requisite muscle". Both were dressed in brown, green and tan clothing that seemed more appropriate for the fall hunting season rather than a late spring canoe trip. Another boat followed behind them and contained three more of Temple's camouflaged men, another driver and several large back packs.

The driver of the second boat, the sixteen year old son of the outfitter, tried to pass the ride with a little small talk. "What lakes 'ya headed to." Jordy shouted cheerily over the roar of the motor.

None of the men bothered to respond verbally, but one did answer with a stern look that clearly meant they were in no mood to talk. That message came through loud and clear and not another word was spoken by Jordy for the rest of the ride.

Both boats slowed to a crawl as they approached a long wooden dock extending forty feet from shore. Temple's men quickly heaved their gear onto the dock while Ben impatiently waited for them to finish. The social interaction in his boat had been just as minimal.

There was no camaraderie between them, Ben thought, certainly not between he and them, but more importantly, not even among them - strange really, and suspicious. They were about to enter the deep wilderness where they had to rely on each other, and put up with each other. They would be with each other constantly in the tight, cramped confines of a canoe and the only slightly more spacious room of a tent. If you didn't even like each other going in, you'd be just about ready to kill each other by the time you came out.

Temple had claimed this was a fishing expedition when he reserved the canoes, but Ben had a hard time believing that. He counted only three fishing poles for the seven of them and he only saw one tackle box. He wanted to question them, to find out their real reason for being here, but it crossed his mind that they could be running drugs down from Canada. If that was the case, he was better off not knowing.

"The canoes are back up in the woods a bit." Ben said grimly as he started to stand. "We'll get them out for you."

"There's no need for that." Temple answered. He pulled out a stack of bills from the chest pocket of his vintage-style hunter green shooting jacket and handed them to Ben. "My friends can handle them."

'Friends?' Ben scoffed silently. He looked back and motioned to his son. "Go with 'em Jordy and unlock the shed with the paddles."

Jordy hopped out of his boat and hurried down the dock after the group of hulking men. He boldly and roughly pushed his way through the mass of giants to lead them to the right place. He wasn't as intimidated by them as he should have been. He wasn't as aware of the possible danger as his father was and he foolishly took this opportunity to hold his own against the big boys.

Temple noticed the boy's youthful transgression and turned back to his father. "Brave boy." He said. "But he should learn to be more careful. My friends would not be so forgiving if he was a couple years older." His words lingered on with a slight, ominous smile.

Ben was about to argue because he certainly didn't care for these men either, but that malicious grimace on Temple's face told him it was better to just send them on their way and be done with them. He kept a careful eye on Jordy and he made a mental note to be more prepared when it came time to pick these men up. One or two of the other outfitters would come with him to bring them back, not his own son.

Ben pointed to the end of the dock where a small tree stump stood amid a patch of high reedy grass. "There's a little door on the side of that stump. Inside it is a linkphone. Give us a beep when you get back and we'll come get you."

Jordy came trotting down the dock a moment later and jumped back into his boat. Ben waited until he heard the firing of his son's motor before starting his own. Usually he would wait around to make sure the group got off alright, but not this time - not for this group. He motioned for Jordy to follow and they sped back across the lake even before Temple's group got their gear loaded into the canoes. Back home, the two of them spent an hour guessing what kind of illegal activities the men were up to.

CHAPTER 4

Standing at the counter, waiting for the Rent-A-Ride lady to finish entering his information into the computer, Gib stared blankly at a sheer white curtain that almost completely surrounded the check-out station. On it, in big sweeping letters that sprawled from one side to the other, were the words "Welcome to Duluth!" The letters faded away after a few seconds and a burst of colors began to fill the fabric's fiber optic threading until it showed a complete panoramic view of Enger Tower Park.

The scene held for forty-five seconds then dissolved into a different view of the downtown area. Each image held amazing clarity and actually played in real-time video. Cars could be seen passing by, birds flew overhead and people hurried along the streets. The glass floor tiles were also incorporated and changed to look like grass or cement, depending on the scene. It was as if they were standing right in the middle of it all and an overhead vent even simulated a gentle breeze to further enhance the illusion. The most realistic view was of Lake Superior. The tall rolling waves heaving up and down actually made Gib feel like he was on a boat.

It was a beautiful way to show airport visitors the best parts of the city, but Gib didn't see it that way. To him it was a tragic sign that the current wave of technological advancement was washing up too far into his beloved and remote northern wilderness. He worried how much further north it would go. Part of him wanted Minnesota's arrowhead region to stay just the same as he'd always known. Technology had its benefits, but as far as he was concerned, not up here.

"Sir?" The lady asked with doubting curiosity. "Are you sure you want the gas powered truck? I mean, there are plenty of hydrogen models available. The gas ones are really only used for very rugged terrain and there aren't many fuel stations around any more. It might be quite an inconvenience."

"I'm sure." Gib replied. "We're heading to Ely."

With that one bit of information, the lady at the counter completely understood why he requested it and why he would need it.

Coming up behind Gib a short and stocky young man was pulling along two small brown suitcases. In front of him, he was kicking along a large green duffle bag. Curly tufts of light brown hair poked out from under the bill of his faded blue ball cap; his favorite hat, judging by the wear of it. His fishing hat, he'd told Gib earlier. He was younger than Gib by three years, but the stern look of his face made him look much older and the hardness of it contradicted his truly gregarious nature.

With one last harder kick, Josh Bertram's duffle bag slid into Gib's right leg.

Gib didn't need to look to know it was him. "What, did you have to unload them off the plane yourself, Josh?"

Josh dropped one of the suitcases and slid it over to Gib. "Well that would have been a hell of a lot faster. Two hundred years of service and the airline industry still can't figure out a faster way to handle luggage."

Gib thanked the attendant for her help as she handed him the keys. He turned and pointed Josh to the exit. "You better get used to inconveniences. Once we're in the BWCA the land of automation will be far behind us."

Josh paid little attention to Gib's comment as he followed him outside. This was his first time visiting Minnesota and though Gib had told him again and again what to expect, he didn't really believe it would be any different than the recreational parks his family camped at in Illinois. Trees, water and fishing, it was pretty much the same everywhere and that was all an avid outdoorsman needed, in his eyes anyway.

Gib led the way over to the lot of rental vehicles. Sitting at the end of the first row, towering over a line of sleek and compact vehicles, was a large, steel blue, box-shaped truck. Josh's steps slowed to a shuffle when he saw it and he stopped completely when he realized Gib was heading straight for it. His eyes widened and his jaw dropped open. "We've got a real truck." He said, sounding a little dumb-struck with surprise.

He'd seen them before, though not often. There wasn't much need for them in the flat lands of Illinois. Almost no one drove them anymore, except to flaunt them. His father had taken him to a car show once, where over a dozen truck owners had come to show them off. Josh remembered running from one truck to the next, giving each one a quick once-over before going back for a more careful inspection. That was more than ten years ago and that was the last time the car show was in town.

"Sure is." Gib replied as he heaved his suitcase into the truck bed. "I thought you'd like it."

"Can I drive?" Josh asked in his most charming tone.

"Sure…" Gib replied with a dry smile as he opened the driver's side door. "on the way back."

Josh wasn't too disappointed. He couldn't be. Just knowing they'd be riding in it was enough for him. He walked around to admire every angle of the body's design and he even knelt down to the ground to check out the axle. His friends back home would never believe it.

From his shirt pocket, he pulled out a thin silver card and clicked a tiny button on the upper left corner. Four telescoping legs split the card apart and a small screen unfolded from the top half; the very latest in micro technology - a video-capable digiphone with all the accessories.

He slowly walked around the entire truck filming every part of the chassis, even the door of the gas cap - especially that, just to make sure there was no question when his friends saw it. He even filmed each of the four tires, their rims and the deep tread they held.

"You might as well pack that away when you're done there, Josh." Gib said, trying to get Josh moving. "Digiphones don't work where we're going. Well...the phone won't, anyway."

"Send, all contacts." Josh said into a small microphone in the lower right corner. The camera lens faded to a blue screen that asked if he wanted a voice intro to the video. "Now this is traveling in style." He said and waited for the confirmation prompt.

He hopped into the truck with Gib, but he didn't pack the camera away yet. As they drove, he continued his documentary of the interior and this time he added commentary.

"The acceleration is a little slower, and the ride isn't nearly as smooth, but just listen to the sound of that engine. That's power, boys - raw and A-live." He held the digiphone up and moved it around the cabin as he tried to find the place where the hum of the engine was the loudest.

He filmed for ten more minutes, until they were beyond the city limits. Josh's attention suddenly turned to the abundance of tall pine trees lining both sides of the four lane highway. He couldn't believe they were already outside of town. The boasting to his friends was officially over. "Send, group five." He ordered the phone. No introduction this time. He returned the device back to its compact card shape and slipped it into his pants pocket.

The trees went on forever with only a few occasional breaks, but the road was what really intrigued him. Its surface looked different than regular roads, darker than normal concrete and slicker. He looked to the sky for any hint of rain, but there was none. He looked to the shoulder for any puddles, but there were none of those either. In fact, they were dusty with dirt and gravel. "What is all over the road?"

Gib had already noticed and dismissed the discoloration. He'd seen it before. It was one of the less pleasant, yet totally amazing sites of the area he loved so much. "It's covered with the guts of tent caterpillars."

Josh leaned closer to the windshield for a better look. It wasn't just patches that were covered, the whole road was one long sheet of slick goo. "You can't be serious. What are they?"

"Little blue and black caterpillars that are infesting the area and eating all the leaves from the trees. Some people call them army worms because of the relentless way the move through and feed."

"And there are so many of them that they actually cover the entire road?"

"Billions probably." Gib answered. "Every ten years or so they start an intense cycle of feeding and breeding. They strip the trees bare. This should be the peak year for them."

"Oh…what luck." Josh said glibly. He looked out at the abundance of green still surrounding them. "They must not be too bad yet. They haven't really done much to these trees."

"They only eat leaves." Gib corrected. "They don't do much to the pines, thankfully. At least there's still some green. I think that's the only thing that makes it bearable at this time of year."

'Some green?' Josh questioned silently. There was far more green here than he ever remembered seeing. He picked out the leafing trees as they sped by and noticed that not only were they bare, but they were also covered in nests of white webbing. "Do they kill the trees?"

"No. They only last for about a month and a half, but during that time they're everywhere. Houses and garages get covered by them. You can't walk outside without stepping on them. They huddle so close together and in such great numbers that you can barely see any of the bark on the trees they're eating. And the roads can get so greasy with their guts that they sometimes have to spread sand for traction."

Josh couldn't deny that it was an awesome spectacle, but his foremost thought was the mess they created. "I suppose it never crossed your mind to plan this trip after they were gone?"

Gib croaked out a little laugh. "Uncle Gerald wasn't too fond of them either. In one interview he referred to them as the bane of nature. He said the only productive use he could find for them was that some people use them to make wine."

Josh cringed as he imagined a happy lumberjack in a plaid shirt and red suspenders greedily gulping down oozing caterpillar guts. For the three years he had known Gib, he was always spouting off about the beauty of Minnesota. This first experience with its nature already had Josh somewhat cynical.

Still, he remained excited for the adventure they were about to begin. In May he had finished his degree in political science. Next fall he would start at the police academy. This trip was his last hoorah before carrying on the tradition of his fathers for the last three generations. This was just the break he needed before diving into his career.

———

Their hour and a half drive passed quickly, especially for Josh. Thirty minutes into it, he had his hat tilted down over his face to catch a quick nap. With night already coming on, Gib wondered how he'd be able to sleep later. He didn't say anything though, because it gave him some quiet time to enjoy the transition from the fast pace of everyday life into the more serene and peaceful world of the boreal forest. A few tiny towns popped up along the way, but for the most part all traces of urbanization had disappeared and the woods grew thicker the farther north they drove.

The welcome monotony of sprawling forest allowed him to drift back to when he was young and his family would make this very same drive. No one vacation stood out specifically. They were all pretty much the same. It was the ritual that mattered and the expectation of being available to one another. He thought fondly of long lazy days swimming off the end of the dock and countless hours spent floating in the lake. He thought of the fishing trips he'd taken with his parents and even those rare occasions when one or both of his younger sisters would come along. The girls never did fish really, but they would go along for the company. He remembered laughing a lot more when they were there.

The evening fires at the pit by the lake were his favorite times. His father always made sure there was an evening fire, even if no one else intended to enjoy it. That was how he wanted to end his day while he was on vacation. And even when no one intended to enjoy it, they all eventually came down and did so any way. At the end of the night, as he lay in bed, Gib would fall asleep to the smell of smoky pine on his skin and in his hair.

They always seemed to be doing something on their trips up north, though he never remembered doing anything overly exciting. There wasn't the thrill of an amusement park, the fascinating sites of historical landmarks, or the fast pace of an exciting and bustling city. It was utter quiet and peacefulness in the simplicity of nature.

It wasn't always perfect or without a few family squabbles, but right now he couldn't remember a single one. In the absence of outside influences like work or school, parents were available for quality time and sibling rivalries were usually forgotten - at least until they returned home.

Josh woke from his nap as the truck made the last turn onto the road that would take them into Ely. He was struck again by the overwhelming amount of trees, only now they were darker. The sun had dropped just below their tops leaving a jagged outline of the spruces, balsams and pines. They held much stronger against the two lane road they were now traveling and it seemed to him that even a brief break in traffic flow would allow them to reclaim the road. Without the full light of day, the trees looked like a mysterious wall of shadowy black lining the road.

"So what can I expect from Addison?" He asked turning his attention away from the daunting, dark forest. "You haven't really said much about her."

Gib thought for a moment on how best to describe her and when he finally did answer, he still struggled to find the right words. "Guarded...tough, and kind of standoffish – when you first meet her. Don't expect a warm welcome. We've talked on the phone four times since I met her back in January, vid-conferenced twice, and she's only now starting to warm up to me."

"Hmm. She sounds like a real treat. No wonder you've kept so quiet about her."

Gib didn't answer. That actually was the reason he hadn't mentioned much about her. Josh might not have been so willing to come if he knew there would be tension. "Give her a chance. I think you'll like her."

"Yeah, but is she going to like me?"

"Of course she will." Gib answered right back. Then, after a slight pause and a little softer, "You just might not realize it right away."

"Oh, goodie." Josh said sarcastically. "A treat with sweet little sprinkles on top."

When they got to the outskirts of Ely, Gib became more caught up in their arrival than in trying to ease Josh's concerns. There was a water tower sitting on top of a hill as a beacon to let him know he was almost there. His stomach tingled with excitement and anticipation, just as it always did when he was younger.

The town popped up out of the forest soon after. Rows of tourist shops and restaurants lined both sides of the streets. Each one was named and fashioned with a north woods theme and some variation of a log cabin façade. There were no annoying flashing lights to catch the eye or giant glowing signs of advertisement. There was a raucous night life, Gib knew, but it was understated and only casually announced. At this time of night, the streets were already quieting down from the day's activities.

This is how Gib had always known Ely and he was not at all surprised when he learned that the old town had looked much the same. He'd found pictures of the original site in the Ely library. Everything was kept as it was before the move. The layout of the streets was the same, as were their names. Historic buildings were perfectly recreated or, in some cases, actually had been moved. The main street, Sheridan, was still the primary artery of the town only now it ended abruptly two miles outside the city limits instead of leading off to the small town of Winton as it had long ago.

Gib made his way through the minor traffic and turned east just before Sheridan Street ended. Five minutes later they were curving around the shores of Bear Island Lake looking for the drive that led to Addison's cabin. There were no distinguishing landmarks and the signs that marked the addresses for each drive were small and mostly hidden among the trees. Had it been completely dark, he doubted he would have found the turn at all, even with Addison's exact directions. When he pulled in, the truck's headlights flashed on her kneeling over organized piles of gear in the driveway.

"Hey, Addison." Gib greeted as he stepped out of the truck. "How's everything coming along?"

Addison stayed bent over and held up her hand to stop his interruption as she finished counting packages of noodles. Josh gave Gib a doubtful, silent stare from behind.

She finished a moment later and finally stood to meet them. "Pretty well. I've got everything together. You guys must have made pretty good time or did your flight get in early?"

"I was bending the law a bit." Gib confessed, holding up his thumb and fore finger with a tiny space between to suggest he was only speeding a little. "I tried to keep to the speed limit, but it's just too tempting on such a lonely road."

Josh lagged behind to allow them a chance to say hello. After unloading the bags from the back of the truck he crossed over to where they were talking and waited for Gib to introduce him. Gib kept going on about their trip up until he noticed both Josh and Addison shifting awkward glances at each other.

"Oh, sorry." Gib apologized. "Addison, Josh Bertram. Josh this is Addison Gethold."

Gib had told her about him and how he fell into the family tree which made their formal meeting a bit uncomfortable. Technically they were family and both felt as though they should hug or something. But Addison didn't give out hugs that easily and Josh was also wary. They settled on a tentative handshake.

"So, is everything ready?" Gib asked, peeking around her at the gear on the ground.

Addison stepped aside to allow them a full view of what they needed for the trip. There were only three packs. A pretty light load, Gib thought, for a possible two week trip. "Is that everything?" He asked questionably.

"Gib, don't start with me." She said under a forced smile. "We'll be having fish a lot, but there is enough food in there to have three meals a day with snacks if our luck isn't good. The tents are in that pack, sleeping bags in there, and there's still room for your clothes and stuff."

She continued listing things she had packed to further demonstrate her thoroughness. Some of them Gib wouldn't have thought to bring. As she went on reassuring him, his doubts quickly disappeared.

"That's it." She finished. "Let's go inside."

The cabin was made entirely of large, dark brown logs and the cracks between were sealed with grayish tan mortar. The porch, if it could be called such, consisted of a small overhang jutting out from the roof supported by two thinner, more spindly logs. It was humble and plain looking, but completely in step with the rural surroundings.

The inside was even more modest. There wasn't a single thing that looked new or modern. It was crowded with oversized cushiony furniture and though the rooms were rather small, Gib and Josh still found it invitingly warm and comforting. They had entered into a small kitchen. In the corner, next to a white porcelain sink, a black wood burning stove gave off a dim glow from the burning coals within. Further in, on an end table in the living room, a large candle provided the only other light.

"Wow." Gib uttered as he headed to the living room. "Great place."

Josh was drawn to the antique stove. Through the small open door he saw the orange embers. He was amazed that the ancient appliance was still usable. "I didn't think they even made these things anymore." He said as he studied the iron castings of the legs.

"They don't." Addison answered, walking around the kitchen lighting oil lamps. "This cabin has been in my dad's side of the family for generations. It was moved over here from Moose Lake after the restructuring of the forest. The stove came with it. I love cooking on it. It makes everything taste better."

"You actually cook on this thing?" Josh asked skeptically.

"Of course." Addison replied. "I don't need many modern conveniences up here. That's not what this place is about."

This philosophy was completely foreign to Josh. In a world where meals could be prepared in five minutes and houses could be cleaned through the use of a simple computer program, why would anyone waste time doing such menial tasks themselves.

"No computer, no virtuvision?" He asked.

"Who would you want those things up here?" Addison scoffed, now fishing in the refrigerator for three cans of beer. "You can do that at home. All they do is keep you tied to the everyday world. I come up here to get away from all that."

Josh, still not getting her reasons for living in the dark ages, blurted out the only possible explanation for her choices. "So...what? Are you like a hermit or something?"

The comment sounded a little rude, but Addison sensed his intentions were sincere enough. He related with humor. She appreciated that and she tossed him a beer. "Gib told me you were a city boy - through and through aren't you?" She teased.

The full can slipped through Josh's hand and bounced across the wood floor. Her assessment cut him a little. He actually prided himself on being an outdoorsman. Looking now, at all this and what he'd seen of the area so far, his perspective was beginning to change. This was much more remote and much more wild than what he'd ever experienced. Gib was serious when he said they'd be roughing it. There would be no showering facilities or power hook ups like the campgrounds he frequented in Illinois. And there would probably be no indoor toilets. They would have to be totally self-sufficient. The thought of it was intimidating, and thrilling.

"Well, I wouldn't really consider myself a 'city boy'. I've done some camping and I love fishing." Josh defended.

"As long as you have a comfortable place to sleep at night?" Addison added before he even finished speaking.

In the living room, Gib could hear them, but he was far removed from their conversation. He slowly walked around marveling at the simplicity of the structure. It was as if somebody had invaded his most cherished fantasies and pulled out this place. Nothing here was built for energy efficiency or convenience. The couch and chairs were made of bulky bare logs that were somehow still light in color even in their apparent age. They were placed at awkward angles that made the room seem smaller, but cozier. The dark burgundy cushions that adorned them gave the room an air of subtle sophistication without pretense.

Various collages of family photos hung on the lightly stained tung and grooved walls and Gib studied each of them closely. Many were of Addison when she was younger along with two people that he guessed were her parents. Each year of her life was chronicled on these walls, though it seemed that the pictures stopped when she was around seventeen or so. He thought of his family's cabin and how his mother did the same.

He and Addison had grown up vacationing on this same lake. The two of them had figured that out when they first began planning this trip. Gib saw it as an amazing coincidence. She did not.

Perhaps they had seen each other before; passed each other on boat, or maybe at the supermarket in town. Addison wrote it off to the fact that Bear Island was the biggest and most popular lake in the area. Standing here now, looking at a wall of memories so much like the one in his family's cabin, he saw it differently. Addison was right. It wasn't that great of a coincidence, although not for the reasons she gave. It was simply the fruit of seeds sown generations ago by the original Kearny family.

On the far wall a large window overlooked the lake. It was dark now, but the bright three-quarter moon reflected off the water's surface and outlined the dim silhouettes of trees in the still night. There were no city lights or passing cars to ruin this view. Not even the lights from the neighboring cabins could be seen. It was utterly peaceful and isolated.

"…Believe me, I'm no stranger to roughing it." Josh said, still protesting the "city boy" label Addison had given him. He was about to list several childhood experiences as evidence of his woodsman qualities when he spotted a large map folded out across the kitchen table. His focus shifted solely to it and his pride wasn't so important anymore.

The map, with waterways instead of highways, captivated him. It was a condensed version of the all the lakes from Bear Island in the south, to Lake Vermillion in the west and Basswood in the north. All water was shown in light blue and all land in yellow. To Josh it seemed that there was just as much blue water on the map as there were yellow patches of land. "It's like one giant lake with thousands of islands." He said in a soft awed voice.

"Pretty close." Addison commented.

As he looked over the map, he noticed many of the lakes had black dotted lines connecting them to others close by. "What are these?"

"Portages." She answered. "Trails to get from one lake to the next. The numbers next to them is their length."

Her explanation gave the map a whole new meaning and Josh studied it more intently. Anything not connected by river was accessible by trail and the trails jumped all across the map. The possibilities for travel were endless.

Some of the numbers were quite big; one-hundred, two-hundred, and more. But even the smaller numbers seemed big as far as he understood them. "Are these in miles?" He gawked.

"No." Addison laughed. "That would be impossible. The numbers are in rods – about sixteen feet or so. Roadways of the Voyageur."

"What?" Josh asked.

"French/Canadian fur traders who traveled the lakes by canoe in the eighteenth and nineteenth centuries. The native Ojibwe people used the lakes before them. The pictographs they painted on some rock faces are still visible today."

Josh perked up. "Will we see any of them?"

"Not on Gib's route, I'm afraid. But maybe, if things don't work out."

A red line had been drawn through several of the lakes and rivers leading deep into the forest. "Is this where we're going?" He asked.

Gib heard Josh's comment and tore himself away from the window view to join their conversation. At the table, Addison pushed a beer over to him as he took a seat beside Josh.

"In the morning, we'll boat over to Log Bay where the canoes are stored." Addison started as she ran her finger along the red line. "After that, we paddle down to Bear Island River. Some parts are pretty shallow so we'll have some short portages to go through. And," Addison stopped and gently placed her hand on Josh's shoulder. "We'll have to wade the canoe through some spots. I hope your dainty city boy feet can handle getting a little wet."

Josh was far too interested in the map to really even hear what Addison said, but he could tell she was teasing him again and he gave her an exasperated glance before she went on.

"Tomorrow night we'll camp on One Pine Lake. From there, we'll follow the river to White Iron and paddle to the other end of the lake. That's where the old resort site is that you wanted to see, Gib."

Gib studied the first part of their journey carefully. He had never done a full blown boundary waters trip, at least not so far in and not for so many days. The distance she covered seemed extremely long. "Are you sure we can make that in two days?"

"I do it all the time, Gib." Addison assured. "We'll be paddling with the flow of the river so we'll make good time. Getting across White Iron will take a while, but we'll be able to set up camp and do some fishing before dinner."

"Then we'll get to the site of the old Kearny cabin the day after?" Gib asked.

"Yeah, it's an easy paddle over to Garden Lake. We'll have just about the whole day to look around before night fall."

The highlighted route ended at the body of water labeled Garden Lake, but Addison's finger continued along the map. "After Garden, we are pretty free to go anywhere we want. If you guys don't mind, I would like to head north and try fishing the…"

"Uh…what?" Josh interrupted. "I thought we'd be following this beaten path that Gerald Kearny wrote about."

Though he didn't know it, his question tipped off the biggest source of contention between the other two.

Addison and Gib looked at each other hesitantly. The issue had been debated during most of their previous conversations and both were waiting for the other to start in. Gib started first.

"We will be. Addison's not a big believer in what we're doing and she hopes to turn this into a fishing expedition."

"Gib, it's not that I want to doubt you," She protested. "but I've been to the old cabin site dozens of times and have never found any 'path' that leads anywhere. I'm just asking that we keep our plans open in case we come up empty. We can head up to Jackfish Bay on Basswood, go over and hit Fourtown Lake and then maybe swing over to the Hegman Lakes to show Josh the pictographs. He wants to see them."

Gib smirked and dropped his head down, slowly shaking it from side to side. "If we don't find anything then you can take us where ever you want. But I don't think you should get your hopes up."

"You don't believe in the blood stones?" Josh asked her.

"Well, let's just say I'm skeptical. I would like to think they're real and it would be great if we could find them, but I've seen too many people try and not one of them has ever turned up anything even close to a real clue. This beaten path that everyone's been looking for is nowhere around the site. Believe me, it would have been found a long time ago."

Gib wasn't at all disturbed by Addison's lack of faith. In fact, he kind of enjoyed her relentless pragmatism. He couldn't wait to see the look on her face when she was proven wrong.

CHAPTER 5

"Almost there." Addison beamed as she directed Gib to turn down a small dirt road. She was unusually chipper, Gib thought, giddy even.

She hadn't woken up that way. For the last two hours Gib and Josh had been obeying the orders she doled out with her direct, borderline rude, approach. She didn't even allow them to sit for breakfast. The scrambled eggs with cheese she'd made were sandwiched between two pieces of toast for an easy meal on the go.

When they finally came to the end of the twisting drive, Gib realized what was inspiring her good mood. A large, portly man was ambling down a grassy hill toward the lake below. Gib noticed how Addison's eyes lit up when she saw him and a big smile brightened her face. She jumped out of the truck before either of the others and ran down to greet Ben.

Her running steps caught Ben's attention before she got to him. "Well good morning, Addy." He called out with a cheery half-laugh and wide open arms.

She slowed down and fell into his warm, strong hug. He rocked her back and forth a couple times before letting her go and she kissed him sweetly on the cheek. "Hey, Ben. How are things up in the great green north?"

"No quite as green with those damn army worms moving in, but pretty good otherwise." He answered. "Connie and the kids just left for the cities for the week so I'm going to be enjoying the bachelor's life for a while."

Addison had known Ben her entire life and probably knew him better than anyone outside of his family. He talked as though he'd enjoy the time alone, but she knew the truth. After a day or two, he'd be missing his family and bugging the neighbors for some company.

"Is business doing alright?" She asked. She didn't need to. She could tell that it was from just a look. His kind face had already developed the dark tan that only the busiest guides got this early in the season. Spending the day in a canoe for weeks at a time was rough on the skin, even with the use of sun block. He was only forty-five years old, but his graying hair and the deep lines in his face gave the illusion that he was well into his fifties.

"Not bad." He replied. "Just sent out a group of seven the other day; equipment rental only…fortunately. Bunch of jack-asses. Give 'em a wide birth if you run into them. Roughnecks mostly, the orneriest lookin' group I've ever seen."

"Fishing?'" She asked.

"That's what they said, but I have my doubts. Jordy's convinced their running drugs down from Canada. I didn't tell him so, but I wouldn't be surprised if that was the case. Your group is going to make better time. There's a good chance you'll catch up to them if you're on the same route."

She appreciated the concern much more than she let on. After the loss of her parents to a car accident four years ago, Ben and his wife had become her surrogate parents. "When did they go in?"

"Thursday." He answered then switched the topic to something more pleasant. "So, you fishing this time or fortune hunting?"

Addison answered him with a cocked brow and a secret smile understood among local outfitters to mean the latter. They generally avoided voicing opinions against those that searched for the stones. It wasn't good business. Addison was the only guide who ever verbalized her frustration with those engaging in the futile effort. All the others just took the money and kept their doubts to themselves.

"Fortune hunting, but this trip might be a little more interesting."

"Oh yeah." He responded curiously. "What makes you think that?"

Addison pointed up the hill to the parking area where Gib and Josh were unloading the truck. "They're descendents of the Kearny's. They have a lot of inside information."

Ben sized up the two young men as they started down the hill. The shorter one started a light trot down the steep incline. With a pack loosely slung over his shoulder and a handful of fishing rods, Ben half-expected to see him take a tumble. He had a good strong face, but Ben guessed he didn't know much about the woods.

The denim shorts he was wearing were a poor choice for this kind of trip; inconvenient in the woods, slow to dry if they got wet, and everyone knows that the color blue attracts the early season bugs especially bad. The brand new tan construction boots weren't a good choice either nor was the sweatshirt he had on to fight off morning's cool bite. He would shed that in about an hour when the sun started coming on high and he'd be looking for a place to store it. Most likely, it'd end up soaking in water on the bottom of the canoe. Ben had seen his kind too often before; people trying too hard to look the part. But the kid had a sturdy, rugged frame and Ben knew Addy would whip him into shape pretty easily.

The other guy looked more thoughtful and self-assured. He didn't have the same pep in his step as he came down. His excitement showed only in his eyes. There was a maturity to him that kept him contained and he wasn't trying to look the part at all. In only a cream colored t-shirt and mid-ankle hikers, he certainly knew what to expect and how to be best prepared. The nylon pants he was wearing had the zip off legs that could be easily shed in the hot sun and just as easily replaced for the bug-infested portages.

"Family, huh." He said. "From round here?"

"Naw, I just hooked up with them a couple months ago. They're from the Kearny sisters. Those families stayed down south. I got a good feeling about them though. The taller one is really into family history. He spent hours talking with nana about our relatives."

As they approached, Ben offered a generous and sincere smile. It wasn't often that Addy spoke favorably about people searching for the blood stones. In fact, he couldn't ever remember her saying that she had a good feeling about someone involved with the adventure. He often thought she resented having strangers prying into her family history, that they had no business looking for something that really didn't belong to them.

The introductions were quick and short as Addison moved things along to keep them on schedule. During their trip across the lake, Gib and Josh listened intently while Addison and Ben continued discussing the stones over the loud hum of the motor. Ben had his own thoughts on their possible location and he was more than willing to share his opinion with almost anyone that had an ear to bend. Of course, he would never search for them himself, but if they did turn out to be real, he hoped they would be found by someone who followed his advice, just so he could say he was right.

"…I don't know, Addy. Hundreds of people used to come through here every summer looking for those darn things. I think it needs to be looked at in a different way. To my knowledge, no one has ever tried looking during the winter months. The whole landscape is different then. Any secret paths might be easier seen in a more barren landscape. Then again, I suppose not too many people are willing to brave the elements out in the wild when it's thirty below."

Addison had heard this conjecture many times before, but she never bothered to disagree with him until now. "I'm not so sure, Ben. I've given your theory some thought and I don't believe he would have done that. Norm and Mary Kearny started bringing the kids here when they were very young and always during the summer. They fell in love with the remoteness and beauty of the area and that's why they continued to come back. It wasn't until years later that they started coming up in the winter months."

"I think Kearny set this whole thing up so that more people would come up here and learn to appreciate nature in the same way his family did. Not many people would fall in love with northern Minnesota in the winter time."

Both Gib and Josh were surprised to hear Addison giving history lessons on the Kearny family and speculating over the best way to find the stones. The conversation directly contradicted the pessimism she showed last night. At that moment, Gib realized just how guarded Addison was. There were two distinct sides to her behavior; the openness she showed to only the closest of friends and the icy front she put on for everyone else. Part of him desperately wanted to jump in on their conversation and share their enthusiasm, but he decided it might be better to listen and hear what Addison really thought about their quest.

"He lived up here, though." Ben protested. "I've heard that he loved it up here in the winter time and anyone that really knew him would be aware of that. Family would know that."

"Good point," She admitted. "but Kearny's book focused on family and the experiences that strengthened their ties. Some members of the Kearny family, especially his father, weren't very fond of winters in Minnesota. I believe he would want the search to take place during a time that everyone could enjoy."

"Yeah, but from what I've read of him, Gerald was also a bit of a prankster. He used to sneak into his brother's house when he was gone and move little things around on him to make him think he was being haunted; did it off and on for more than two years before he got caught. Really had him going, too. I don't think you can count on any kind of conventional thought where Gerald is concerned."

Addison considered this thought for a few seconds because there really was some logic to it. Even though she didn't agree, she deferred the argument out of respect for Ben. "You might be right. If things don't work out this time, maybe we'll try a winter trip."

She then turned to give Gib a telling smile that revealed just how lightly she was taking the conversation.

At the other end of the lake, Ben stopped only long enough to let his passengers off and wish them good luck. There was no need to show Addison where the canoes were; she'd guided for him many times in the past. Before leaving, he made Addison promise to show him the stones, if they were lucky enough to find them. They both knew he was only keeping up a hopeful pretense for the benefit of her patrons.

'Rocky.' Josh thought. 'Or maybe hilly.'

He was trying to find the best way to describe the landscape to his friends back home. The ice age had sculpted out a terrain of sharp rocky hills and gently flowing knolls. It was as if the glaciers had scraped away the skin of the earth and left its spine exposed to the elements. Its bones were now covered in orange and green lichens. There were deep run-off trenches and rock wall cliffs with steep drops. Gigantic boulders had been dropped in the most unusual places and often sat at peculiar angles that seemed to defy gravity.

Of course there were trees, but Josh never knew how hearty a pine tree could be until he saw them here. They grew out from under the boulders, their trunks bending and curving around until they found nourishment from the light above. Some grew on the tops of rocks and others sprouted up out of narrow crevices. Nothing seemed to be too extreme for them; they made the best of what was available.

"Continue." He ordered his phone and it resumed recording the message he'd already started. He ended his description with one word, "Rugged."

Addison walked past Josh carrying a green fiberglass canoe on her shoulders. "Do it while you can, Josh. By the end of the day you won't be able to get a signal. And unless you don't mind it getting wet or smashed, you better let me pack it away."

Gib followed behind her with a set of paddles and three lifejackets.

"O.K." She said with a single deep breath. "I know Gib has some experience in a canoe. How 'bout you Josh?"

He had been in one at least once before, maybe even twice, he thought, though it was a long time ago. The last thing he wanted was to show Addison one more flaw in his camping abilities. He quickly responded with the best evasive answer he could come up with. "Oh I've been around boats all my life. You don't have to worry about me."

"I didn't ask about boats." Addison corrected. "I asked about canoes. There's a big difference. You can step right down into a boat with no problem, but if you try it with a canoe, you'll probably end up in the water. It's all about balance."

"If it floats, it's a boat." He said. "I'll manage."

Addison slid the canoe out into the water and straddled the very end of the back still resting on shore. "Alright then. Get in front." She invited with an overly pleasant tone.

It sounded polite enough, but Josh understood she was daring him. He was not about to back down. He defiantly stepped into the "boat" and carelessly began making his way along the narrow fiberglass body. As he did so, Addison used her legs and arms to counter his haphazard steps to keep the canoe balanced. She was about to show him the difference between a boat and a canoe, but she waited to do it until she was sure he wouldn't fall in the water or get hurt.

The boat swayed a little as he walked, but it was no different than any other watercraft. With his last step before getting to the front seat, Addison stood up, let go of the sides and watched as the canoe tilted sharply to the left. Josh tipped with it and his arms flailed wildly while his upper body rocked from side to side. Addison immediately resumed her stabilizing position again and

Josh managed to drop forward onto the seat before falling into the water.

"Lesson number one:" Addison said confidently. "Always walk in the middle of the canoe and go as slow as you need to keep it balanced."

"Point taken." Josh answered from his precarious position bent over the seat.

"Alright, come on out of there." She ordered. "You're not ready for the front yet."

This time Josh was careful to step correctly and he actually did it quite well. When she had used this teaching method in the past, her students usually crawled back out with their hands holding tightly onto the sides for support. Josh, on the other hand, stood almost upright as he came back and didn't even slow his stride. She noted that he was a quick learner with natural athletic ability and thought how helpful that could be for the long trip ahead.

"Gib, you'll take the front seat first so we can teach the rookie how it's done." She said. "Hand me that orange pack, Josh."

Josh did as he was told and watched as she situated the pack in the middle of the canoe. She continued doling out orders until the canoe was completely full. She waited for Gib to get in then directed Josh to sit in the middle where a cozy hole had been made between the packs.

Their first stretch was a short paddle across the eastern end of the lake. Addison held them to a leisurely pace so she could explain the art of canoeing to Josh and assess Gib's stamina before really pushing him. As they slowly went along, the two shorelines drew closer together and the lake narrowed into the Bear Island River.

The short portages were her favorite part of the lesson and the best indicator of her passengers' true abilities. When the water became too rocky to navigate, they would pull over to a path leading through the woods. Here she showed them how to wedge the paddles into the canoe's frame then roll it up onto their shoulders. Gib had experience with the right way to carry a canoe and he handled himself well. Josh, on the other hand, struggled to master the fine art of twisting his body and lifting at the same time. She also noted his very vocal dissatisfaction of the pain in his shoulders while carrying the weight. He never said he needed to stop and she took his complaining as just another of Josh's "city boy" traits.

These little tests were a typical beginning of her trips so she could get a better idea of what to expect. That was her job. Her father had always taught her that a good guide knows how to make effective use of a camper's skills and she remembered that lesson well. After lunch it was Josh's turn to paddle in the front. It took him just an hour to pick up a rhythmical stroke, but no matter how many times she barked at him he never would stop trying to steer them from the front.

By the time they arrived at the campsite on One Pine Lake, she was already well aware of their strengths. Gib was strong at paddling and could probably go at it all day while Josh showed an almost uncanny ability for knowing their location. He constantly quizzed her about the direction they were heading and where "true" north was in relation to their position. He even surprised her a few times by correctly identifying merging rivers that lead to other lakes and by knowing the right names of those lakes. With dozens of bodies of water in the immediate area, and almost as many rivers and streams, not many people could easily recall which was which after looking at a map only one time.

As early evening approached and they prepared to set up camp, she felt confident that she didn't need to dote over either of them. They were capable of keeping up with the swift pace she preferred, but she wasn't about to tell them that.

CHAPTER 6

Archer gazed triumphantly upon the stones. Their intricate lines twisted and curved across the glassy green surface; shining gold upon shimmering, translucent emerald. They would carry him wherever his heart desired; above the mountains or across the seas or to distant lands not yet seen. The options of a deity, Archer thought, but such kingly desires no longer enticed him. Prosperity and joy were far less elusive than he once believed.

Harris sat rereading Kearny's book - the fifth time now, since Temple's sight had turned to the stones. This time, he was reading the chapters backwards in a vain hope to find some new insight. Next he might try reading it up side down, if it came to that. He hoped it wouldn't.

They'd arrived at their campsite on the northern shore of White Iron Lake early and he was thankful to be sitting in a collapsible nylon chair instead of on the hard bottom of the canoe.

Every now and then he stopped reading and stared blankly across the sprawling water while he considered possible clues. The rhythmic swaying of the waves and the light lapping of water against the shore helped him concentrate. He needed that. The pressure was on him to provide solid leads. No matter how many hundreds of people had failed before him, success was the only outcome is boss would allow.

Beside his comfortable seat was a three foot square table that had conveniently folded out from a small box - a little bulky for real campers to consider bringing, but Temple insisted that it was necessary. He wasn't the one lugging the equipment.

On the other side of the table, Temple sat clicking away at the keys of a laptop computer connected to a small portable satellite dish. Positioning the satellite correctly had been difficult, but after an hour of patiently scanning the sky he was able to find a signal even in this remote place.

"How are you coming along, Harris?" He asked as he continued typing.

Harris laid the book face down on the table and rubbed his weary eyes. "Well, I have definite ideas on where to look, but I can't promise they've never been tried before. I doubt I've uncovered anything earth shattering yet."

"The first eight chapters are the key." Temple said. "Everywhere they went after that is merely a result of finding the path - a succession of events. You must look at it differently than everyone else. The answer is most likely in the themes and the wording, not just the obvious narrative."

'Yes sir, thank you for that supremely astute observation.' Harris thought silently and bitterly. His boss' contribution was nothing he hadn't already thought of.

Temple abruptly let out a loud annoyed sigh. The screen on his computer suddenly went black. "Great." He mumbled in disgust. He looked over to one of the men tending the fire and shouted, "Meyers! Bring me a new battery."

Meyers, the leader of Temple's personal militia, was the tallest and thickest of them all. He was also the ugliest and most intimidating. His face showed the deep pitted scars of an adolescence plagued with terrible acne. There was a bluish-green tattoo on the right side of his face that peaked on his forehead, arched around his left eye and drew back to a point again on his cheek bone. It resembled a crescent moon and, like the source of its inspiration, this one too was full of craters.

While he waited for his order to be carried out, Temple flipped over the lap top and removed the infused alkaline battery; the very latest development in portable power. "I thought you said this was supposed to last for a year?" He asked, holding the battery out to show Harris exactly what he was talking about.

Harris looked up with a dread feeling of guilt. He was the one that recommended this battery and the fact that it didn't work cast a dark shadow on his judgment.

"Mine have been working very well." He replied and looked closer at the battery Temple held. From one of the seams, he saw thick yellow foam oozing out. "It looks like it's cracked. Be careful not to let that stuff touch your skin, sir. It's acidic."

"Piece of junk." Temple huffed and he casually tossed it into the lake.

It landed with a plop just a few feet off the shore. Harris watched this transgression against nature and he tried to hide his appalled reaction to his boss' blatant disregard for its delicate balance. He didn't cover it enough. His eyes widened slightly and Temple immediately noticed it.

"Something troubling you, Harris?" Temple asked.

"No…no. Um, well, it's just that those have to be disposed of in a certain way." He fumbled nervously. "The chemicals are bad for the environment."

He rarely challenged his boss, but on the few occasions when he did, he sounded like a timid child questioning the authority of his parent. It was awkward and without confidence and Temple found it revolting to see a grown man acting so spineless and fearful.

"There are millions of gallons of water in this lake, Harris. One little battery isn't going to destroy the ecosystem. You have more important things to worry about than the welfare of the fish. I suggest you focus on that if you want to remain useful."

With the final word, and the distinct threat to Harris' job, Temple left the table and went to see what was taking Meyers so long to find a simple battery. Harris sat watching the chemicals from the sunken battery as they floated up and spread across the surface of the water. In the setting sun's reflection, they created brilliant iridescent shades of blue, green and red. It could almost be considered beautiful, had it not been so completely foreign to the natural environment.

'It's not right.' He thought.

This latest harsh lesson in obedience sparked thoughts of finding new employment as soon as this project was over. He already had a mental list of companies that would appreciate a man of his skill. He always updated it after such exchanges.

'This time would be different.' He told himself, vowing not to give in to his complacency just as he had every time before.

A single distant howl pierced the calm blue twilight. Another followed right after, then another. Within moments the air was filled with the echoing cries. Addison had given Gib and Josh a list of tasks and they were all busy preparing to turn in for the night.

Josh was kneeling over a brown pack by the fire when the commotion started. He finished packing the dinner ware and looked around for the source. He judged them to be just across the lake and One Pine Lake wasn't that big at all. "Are those wolves?"

Addison was standing off to his side tying one end of a long rope around a rock. She wasn't affected at all by the noise. "No, this is wild dog territory. Sound travels a good distance out here. They sound close, but they're not."

She stood up and threw the rock over a thick branch jutting out from a tall red pine. The rope followed up and over the branch and fell back to the ground a few feet from her.

"Wild dogs?" He scoffed. "Where are the bears and moose I've heard so much about? Wild dogs are kind of a let down."

"Don't worry, you'll see them soon enough." She assured. "We're still in the outer edge. Once we get closer to Old Ely and the inner waters they tend to be less careful about hiding. Not many people venture that far into the forest."

Gib finished rolling out the sleeping bags in the tent he'd be sharing with Josh and came out to join Josh by the fire. "Are wild dogs a big problem up here? I've never heard much about them."

"That's not surprising." Addison answered. "Dogs aren't as glamorous as bears or wolves."

She took the pack Josh had filled, buckled its straps, and carried it over to the branch with the rope. Josh watched her with a curious look as she tied the rope to the pack.

"Rumor has it they've been around since the expansion." She continued. "This whole area used to have rural country homes. The airport was just a couple miles east of here. Several of the people that lived out here were dog-sledders. Kearny's brother was one of them for awhile. He had a house just a mile or so south of here. Some of the yards held over fifty dogs. I heard one guy just turned his dogs loose and moved to Florida after the government bought out his land."

She walked over to the free end of the rope dangling from the tree branch and began pulling it down. Josh still couldn't understand her reasoning and he looked on as the pack levitated higher and higher into the air.

"What are you doing?" He finally asked.

Addison realized his ignorance and responded with a hint of annoyed arrogance. "We're probably going to have animals roaming around our camp throughout the night. Do you want to lose all our food to a bunch of dogs?"

He didn't respond to her mildly condescending reply. Instead, he imagined a scene of wild dogs ripping into the tents to get at their food – the dogs that she said weren't that close. Back in Illinois, on his other camping trips, their food had always been safely stored away in the camper.

"Did you know Steve was a dog-sledder, Gib?" Addison asked as she tied off the rope around the tree trunk.

Something in her tone told Gib that her question wasn't about educating him. She was challenging him. Since their first meeting, and every conversation after that, he had a growing suspicion that there might be some subtle resentment of all the detailed facts he readily threw around about their family. She hadn't pushed him on the issue before, but out here she was the leader. Gib was beginning to think she didn't like having another "expert" around.

He had no interest in a power struggle over family history and he humbly conceded the point. "Interesting. I didn't know that."

Addison picked up one of the cooking pots, went down to the lake, and filled it with water. She wasn't done with the conversation, she was just taking her time. She came back up and dumped the water onto the camp fire. A huge billowing cloud of steamy smoke rushed up from the coals. Gib stepped back to avoid it.

"Yeah. He did pretty well in the races." She continued then went back for another pot of water. "I always thought that if Kearny really did make the stones, he would have needed Steve's help in hiding them. He knew the area much better."

"Possibly." Gib admitted, still trying to avoid the argument.

But Addison wouldn't let go and after she doused the fire again, she confronted him with the conclusion she was leading to. "In fact, Steve always maintained that the stones were nothing more than a fairy tale. I always took that as proof that they probably don't exist."

"Well, all of the siblings were skeptical." Gib countered calmly. "Steve was just more vocal about it. He knew half the town of Ely. Do you really think Gerald would tell him and risk it getting out when he was so careful not to reveal the secret? Also, Gerald did many trips into the boundary waters without his family and he played a key role in the reforestation when the town was moved. He had plenty of opportunity."

Addison returned from the lake again with yet another pot of water and after further soaking the smoldering logs, she addressed the main point of contention between them. "What makes you so certain? Is it because you found some chest that would have been a perfect place to keep them? Kearny did a lot of things to enhance the mystery of their existence. That is just another ploy of his to keep people guessing. It's a gimmick."

"He tells us they're real in his own words." Gib rebutted a little more strongly now. "He told us in the book."

"Oh, Gib." Addison exclaimed. "Please don't tell me this whole trip is based on the thought that the book is actually speaking to you. I thought you were smarter than that. That is what tricked everyone in the first place. It was Kearny's great big joke."

Gib gave a frustrated laugh. "Everyone believed it because it's an obvious conclusion."

Though Josh thought it was best to just stay out of the conversation, he hesitantly offered his own opinion, even at the risk of contradicting their guide. "Well Addison, you have to admit that some paragraphs of certain chapters do seem like they are speaking specifically to the reader."

Addison squatted down and picked up a thick stick. She used it to stir the coals of the dying fire then she handed the pot out to Josh and motioned for him to get more water.

"Look." She said. "I'm not saying that it wasn't an exciting plot device. I loved the book and I loved the fact that it was a book about a book. It drew me in too - when I was a kid. I'm just saying that it was nothing more than entertainment. If you look at it objectively, you can tell it wasn't meant to be taken so seriously."

When Josh returned with the water, Addison pointed where to dump it while she continued stirring the soupy ashes. Gib waited until the sloshing sound of falling water had finished before countering her again.

"I've listened to or watched every interview Gerald ever gave. I've read every transcript. The clues are there. If you're going to look objectively then you have to look at everything."

Addison stood up and stepped back from the fire grate, pausing before bringing out her last, best argument. "He wrote it to encourage future generations of his family to come up here, Gib. To share in what he felt added so much to his family. If the stones were real and if they were found, the mystery would be gone. So what would inspire future generations to come after?"

Gib was stunned into silence. It was an argument he'd never heard before and there was no quick answer ready to roll off his tongue.

"Well, that's it." She said and headed for her own tent. "I'm going to get some sleep. We've got a lot of water to cross tomorrow. G'night guys."

Josh was left feeling awkward over her sudden departure. Gib was still stinging from the lost debate. They turned in as well, but Gib couldn't let himself sleep until he'd reasoned out Addison's point. Her logic was undeniable. Worse than that, it was very much in line with the mischievous nature of their uncle.

The answer never did come. But as he lay on his stomach staring out at the moon's reflection on the dark lake, he realized it didn't matter. There was an answer. It was hidden in the pages of Gerald's book. He just couldn't see it. Five minutes later, his low snoring blended in with the noises of the night time forest creatures.

CHAPTER 7

Josh woke to the smell of frying bacon and the sound of a log occasionally crackling in the fire. Everything else was quiet. As lingering images of peaceful dreams left his mind, he slowly became acutely aware of the odd lack of noise. Back home, in his downtown apartment, he usually woke to a blaring radio alarm and the sound of commuter traffic outside his window. Here, there was nothing. The log popped again from the heat and, in the absence of anything else, it seemed as loud as a clap of thunder.

His first instinct was to go back to sleep. It was much earlier than he normally woke up. But as he lay there enjoying the stillness of the morning, he realized that he wasn't really tired and he was actually eager to get the day going. Through the mesh tent flap he looked out and saw Addison tending to breakfast with Gib sitting on a log beside her. He wasn't sure if they were purposely being quiet to keep from waking him or if they just didn't feel like betraying nature's peaceful silence.

Beyond them was the lake, utterly still and covered in a light mist floating just above its glassy surface. The sun had just broke over the trees in the east and the clear sky held the promise of a warm, beautiful day - but not yet. The forest was still in its process of coming alive and it was in no hurry to do so. Josh was mesmerized by the scene and he watched the lake's fog slowly dancing into the air for another ten minutes before Addison started plating breakfast.

He thought the meal was one of the best he'd ever had and he ate slowly as he also eased himself into the day. Along with the bacon, Addison had made eggs and hash browns. Cooking over a fire really did add something extra to the taste, Josh realized, and he now understood why she preferred the old wood stove in her cabin.

The pace turned much quicker after breakfast, not only for the campers, but for the forest as well. Birds began chirping and chipmunks scurried around the campground attending to their daily chores. Gib and Josh packed up the tents and sleeping bags while Addison loaded up the canoe. By nine a.m., they had already paddled the rest of One Pine Lake and half way down the river that would take them to White Iron Lake.

Josh was given the front seat of the canoe to practice his paddling on the calmer water. The rivers, he concluded, were much more exciting to travel. Their twists and turns held the mystery of some new, natural scene around every bend. A mother deer and her fawn enjoying a drink at the river side was his first sighting of real wildlife. He had seen many deer before, but it was thrilling to see them in this raw wild. He quit paddling and held perfectly still in hopes of getting close enough for a really good look at them. The gentle swoosh of Addison's paddle kept steady and the two animals didn't stay long once they spotted the intruders.

Further ahead, a giant barrier of earth crossed the river's course. At first he thought it blocked its flow, but as they glided closer he saw that it actually disappeared into its base.

"Is that natural?" He asked.

"No." Addison answered as she steered over to a break in the trees lining the shore. "It's old Highway one; the road that once to connected Old Ely to the north shore of Lake Superior. They left it so that people didn't try to keep paddling down the river. It's too shallow."

Beside the mounded earth, Josh saw the telltale path that meant it was time to carry the canoe again. "Is that the portage?"

"Yep, all two hundred and seventy rods of it." Addison answered.

"And how long were the ones we did yesterday?" He asked, hoping that the hardest ones were already behind them.

"The longest one was eighty."

"Great." He mumbled softly, his heart sinking as he remembered the pain in his shoulders from yesterday's much shorter portages. "Great."

Addison heard him. "Don't worry, Josh. It's by far the longest one we'll do and we'll split it up between us so it's not so bad." She was trying to present it in the most positive light then she decided to motivate him by once again challenging his outdoorsman qualities. "Now remember Josh, be careful getting out. You wouldn't want to mess up those pretty hiking boots."

When the canoe slid onto the sandy shore, Josh purposely planted his first step in the water, even though he could have easily avoided getting wet. His second foot also went in and he stood defiantly ankle deep.

The right side of Addison's mouth curled up in a slight smile and she slowly shook her head back and forth. "Get out of the water you bonehead." She ordered playfully.

"Way to make a point, Josh." Gib said as he carefully walked up the middle of the canoe and got out on dry land.

"A real man doesn't care if his feet are wet." Josh stated, still wading around in the water. "Give me that canoe. I'm ready to go."

Addison's little manipulation worked even better than she expected and that was good since she was about to show him how portaging is really done. "Are you ready to do it with a pack on your back?" She asked as she pulled the canoe out of the water.

Josh stayed quiet for several long seconds, watching her and waiting for some sign that showed she was joking. She was all business. "You're kidding, right?"

"Sorry, bud. We're not sending one person all the way back across a three hundred rod portage just for one pack. Come on. It's not so bad - I'll show you."

Even with the extra weight on her back, Addison was still able to roll the canoe onto her shoulders in one fluid motion and she took off down the trail at an even quicker pace than she'd kept yesterday. Josh carried it for the last third of the trail. It took two tries and a little help from Addison before he finally managed to get the canoe into position. Gib hadn't faired much better when it was his turn and that made it significantly less embarrassing.

Just like the day before, his hike started out with no problem. The heavy load didn't feel all that bad for the first fifty yards. After that, the pain in his shoulders flared up again and the heavy pack strained his back as well.

The pain he could ignore. The mosquitoes he could not. They were particularly relentless on this portage. Even through the thick coating of bug spray, some still dared to attack and Josh was helpless to do anything about those that were out of arms reach. His exposed legs received the worst damage. Gib and Addison had zipped on the legs to their shorts before starting out on this trail. Josh wished one of them had shared that little convenience with him before this trip began.

"Well, thank good Lord's graces!" Josh huffed, finally catching a glimpse of open water through the trees. He was almost there and he picked up his pace for the promise of relief.

Addison met him at the water's edge. "Here, let me help you with that."

"I got it." He insisted. The dismount wasn't nearly as graceful as Addison's, but he successfully unloaded the canoe from his shoulders without dropping it or falling over.

"That kinda sucked." He said, bending over to scratch at the bites on his legs. "Although I did notice that my shoulders became kind of numb to the pain after awhile. Any chance we can have something to eat now?"

"Not yet." Addison replied. She was already loading the packs back into the canoe. "We'll do a quick jaunt up to that point for lunch. There's a good breeze so we won't be bothered with the bugs. Then you and Gib will switch seats for the paddle across White Iron."

"I can keep going." He protested.

"You're doing just fine, but there's a hard wind today and the waves can kick up pretty high on this lake. Besides, Gib's had it too easy today. He needs a little exercise."

Gib understood what she was saying, even though she hadn't really said it at all. Josh wasn't ready for the rough water yet. He enjoyed the vote of confidence from her and the boost to his ego stayed with him through the short paddle to the point. When they arrived at their next stop, he decided to take it upon himself to reinstruct Josh on the canoeing lessons Addison had given yesterday.

It wasn't a sandy beach they pulled up to this time, but a shelf of long black rocks that gave no secure place to land. As Josh carefully stood up and prepared to climb onto shore, Gib shifted his weight to the side in one sudden motion. Josh's arms flailed and his body rocked back and forth as he tried to keep from falling in the water. He dropped back into his seat before tumbling over the side.

Gib's low, devious chuckle let him know it was no accident that nearly caused him to take a swim. "Quit kiddin' around! I almost fell in."

"Just testing you to see if you learned Addison's lesson on balance." Gib responded between laughs. "You're a graceful little dancer."

On his second attempt, Josh quickly stepped onto the rock and turned to hold the canoe still. As he steadied it for the others to get out, Addison could see the brewing thoughts of retaliation in his eyes that she knew might lead to a serious injury if she didn't put a stop to it.

"That's enough!" She said more forcefully than she really meant to. "No playing around in the canoe."

She wasn't trying to sound so commanding, but she did and Gib immediately regretted the childish behavior he'd started. "Sorry." He apologized knowing it wasn't the safest or smartest thing for him to do. He tried to down play his poor judgment by changing the subject. "Is my camera in the food pack?"

"I think so." She replied and now her tone was noticeably lighter as she tried to atone for her snapping. She even thought about apologizing, but she was never good at saying sorry so she left it as a serious point that needed to be made.

On shore, Josh headed directly into the woods to take care of some personal business while Addison pulled out the food. When she was finished, Gib quietly brushed past her on his way to dig out the camera.

Josh reemerged from the woods and saw Gib bent over the pack. Now that they were out of the canoe, Josh took this opportunity to exact his revenge. As he walked past, he gave a sly sideways kick to Gib's rear end.

Gib didn't flinch at all. In fact, he had expected it. "I knew you were going to do that." He said flatly, as if his clairvoyance somehow detracted from Josh's attempt at retaliation.

"Oh yeah?" Josh replied and without missing a step he spun around on his heel to send a second, harder kick to the same place. "Did you know I was going to do it twice?"

Addison's let out a hearty burst of laughter; not necessarily for the panned kick, but for Josh's quick wit in his second response. Finally there was a crack in her stoic and reserved demeanor. Gib and Josh joined in and though neither of them realized it, it was the first unrestrained laugh she shared with them.

Once again in the bottom of the canoe, Harris was squeezed into a tight space with his legs drawn close to his chest and his shoulders hunched forward. With all the gear they carried, he was only allowed a two-foot square area while traveling across the water. His arms rested uncomfortably on his boney knees as he continued to read.

> *Archer clung tightly to the cliff wall, his legs quivering as they strained under such precarious footing and his finger tips raw from the rocky climb. Still he would not look down. The opening was thirty feet higher up. Slowly, with the burning pain of each new grip and with the tedious task of finding secure footing, he forced himself higher. The promise of what could be numbed his pain and fear.*

"Up there." Temple ordered pointing to a section of the shore that looked exactly the same as the seven other sites they had already checked out on Garden Lake. "It looks like there's a break beyond the trees."

Meyers signaled to the other canoes and turned his toward shore. Harris didn't even bother to look up this time - at least not until they were closer. Their whole morning had been spent playing out this same scenario over and over.

The canoe hadn't even landed when Temple suddenly stepped over the side and into the water. He pushed through the sparse trees concealing the open area and stepped into a long rectangular field of tall grass sloping up a moderately steep hill. Even after a century of growth, the site was still relatively clear. The slowing of foot traffic from curious visitors had allowed a few scattered trees to take root in what used to be the Kearny's yard, but its outline could still be seen for now. In a couple more decades it might be just another part of forest.

Half way up, the slope became less dramatic and Temple could still see the depression where the Kearny cabin used to stand. "This is it." He stated loudly and emphatically.

Harris stumbled out of his canoe and scurried up the hill after him. As he trotted along, he took specific notice of the trees lining the small field. There were tall red and white pines, tamaracks, maples, cedars, balsams and spruce. All of them stood in a nearly perfect row against the surrounding forest.

"I believe you are correct, Sir. The variety of different trees and their placement suggests planned landscaping."

Temple looked back and shot Harris a glare that clearly showed his utter annoyance at the pointless comment. "Thank you for verifying my conclusion,

Harris." He grumbled. "Now why don't you scour the area for something useful?"

Temple called for Meyers and the two of them began discussing the set up for the camp. Harris headed off with his head hanging down as he stewed over the scolding from his boss. He believed his observation was rather astute. His sulking consumed him until the sound of trickling water caught his attention.

'Nature.' He thought, refocusing on his task and reminding himself of another major theme in the book. Among the trees lining the southern border of the property he found a small creek. Flocks of yellow marsh marigolds sprung up in different areas along its course. They were the same spring-blooming flower that defined the illusive "beaten path" in Kearny's book. Certainly they had been inspected by every other person that came before and certainly that would have been too easy to have not been discovered already.

'How many people wasted their time looking for a pattern in this wild foliage?' Harris wondered silently. And, 'Will I have to resort to that as well if I can't find anything else?'

The possibilities were overwhelming. They were surrounded by nature, the clues could be anywhere. He calmed himself and started tackling the problem one step at a time. He knew it had to be a combination of the other themes as well. Just being here, at this specific place that was so important to Kearny, met the condition of his theme for heritage. Strength of character was the other, though Harris didn't see how that held any significance.

After rounding one last peninsula, Addison steered them into the largest section of open water on White Iron. Finally she felt she was back. This first big lake on their journey was also one of her favorites. The water was deeper here and soon they'd be far away from the safety of land. For her, it was that first separation from security that meant they had really left civilization and entered the wild.

Gib was also inspired, though not for the same reason. He'd lost his feeling of security the moment they entered the Bear Island River. His excitement came from the recognition of a place that he had only seen in photos.

To his left, the northern shore of the watery expanse heaved up in a giant ridge that dominated the remaining landscape. To his right and just ahead, there was a tiny island of bare rock. Their destination was directly ahead. Though neither intended for it, both Gib and Addison quickened their strokes. Each one pushed even harder when the other had matched their pace.

The wind countered them, blowing from the south east and sending rhythmic waves crashing into the side of the canoe. Addison's long hair flowed freely and wildly to her side. Sudden shifts in the wind would whip it back across her face, but she never lost her stride with the paddle. She couldn't afford to in this wind. It gusted often, nearly taking Josh's hat with it, and sometimes created waves large enough to break over the canoe. He wouldn't say it, but Josh was nervous and thankful that Gib was in the front instead of him. It took a strong, steady paddle to beat this wind.

Their competitive strides didn't break until almost an hour later when Gib caught sight of something oddly reminiscent of a photo from the Kearny's keepsake box. Closer to shore now and sheltered from the worst of the wind, he relaxed enough to notice a break in the ridge of the northern shore where the waters of White Iron flowed through to the next lake. His viewpoint was from the exact angle as he'd seen before, but in the older version there was a long white bridge that provided safe passage over the narrows known as the Silver Rapids. No rocks broke the water's surface, but he could see the telling swirls of fast moving water.

Before them, a long row of boulders sat along the shore to protect the land from being washed away during heavy storms. Gib recognized these as well, but there used to be a dock near by and a raft for the beach area. There was no mistaking the place where the Kearny's first came to explore and enjoy the northland; the place they couldn't wait to come back to year after year. Before Addison had even laid out their route for this trip, he insisted that they camp here one night. He had to see the place that inspired the Kearnys and their descendants to keep coming back.

He gave no more help to Addison as she coasted them up to the sandy beach next to the first large rock. In his fascination, he also forgot to steady the canoe for Josh and Addison once they landed - until she reminded him.

Josh climbed out of the canoe and leaned over the first boulder to stretch his back. "Man, you guys were really moving on that last stretch. I could have water skied in your wake." As he bent forward to really pull out the muscles, he noticed that the boulder was not free standing. It was joined to the next in the row with a crude cement mortar. Each one after was the same. "What did this place use to be?"

"It was a resort." Gib answered, interrupting his own surveying of the grounds. "The Kearnys vacationed here for sixteen years before they bought their own cabin. Gerald spoke of this place often. There used to be cabins all around here. This was the beach and the kids used to hop along those very rocks."

Josh stepped up on the first boulder, looked out across the lake and thought how exciting this place must have been for a child. The waterways lead anywhere their young imaginations could take them and the dense forest held intriguing and dangerous mysteries. This was why the trip was such a thrill for Gib. It was about exploring their history and the Kearny parents had provided a wondrous place to do so.

"Com'on, guys. Let's get camp set up." Addison suggested strongly.

"Oh, sorry." Gib apologized realizing they had left her to unload all the gear by herself.

Josh stayed in his distant thought for just a moment longer. He pictured four young children in old fashioned swimsuits jumping from rock to rock, their hair wet and matted and carrying big bright beach towels. By the time he went to help the others, the only thing left was the food pack. Apparently Gib and Addison intended to keep up their fast pace even on land. In less than a half hour they had the entire camp set up and Addison had already found two armfuls of firewood.

She carefully arranged the logs and tinder under the fire grate so it would be ready when they came back. "Alright, who's ready to do some fishing?" She asked eagerly.

Gib had another plan in mind, but he was glad Addison made the offer. With both of them gone, he'd have a chance to walk around by himself. "Why don't you guys go on ahead? I'd like to look around a little on my own if you don't mind."

Addison didn't mind at all, but Josh was now more interested in checking out the area too. Had Gib not made it so obvious that he wanted to be alone Josh would have joined him, though he was not at all upset about being forced to do some fishing.

Addison took them far up the northern shore until she found just the right spot. "You ready to kill some fish, Josh?" She asked, though it was really more of a statement than a question. She set her fishing pole then grabbed her paddle down close to the blade and began a slow back paddle to troll them along the shoreline.

Josh dropped his lure in the water and watched the line sink down. "I'm ready. How deep is it here?"

"About twelve feet." She answered. "So, Gib tells me you're going to be a police officer. What made you decide on that?"

Josh let his lure drop to the bottom of the lake then reeled back up two turns. He cranked his head around to look at her and tilted his hat further down his forehead to keep the early evening sun out of his eyes. "My dad, I guess, and my granddad."

"Ah, they pushed you into it." She assumed. That made sense because she couldn't quite see the fit otherwise. He seemed a little too jovial and a little too insecure for such a serious and dangerous profession.

"No, not really." He answered. "The hope was there for sure, but not really the expectation. They never told me to. I believe in it. It's important. But I guess I do like the sense of tradition, the idea of carrying on the family vocation. My dad just about jumped out of pants when I made the choice."

She didn't respond and stayed silent long enough for Josh to think the conversation was over. Then she started again. "So what do you really think about Gib's little goose chase?"

He knew this would be coming at some point, it was their first time alone together, but he didn't think she'd bring it up so soon or so abruptly. He twisted the upper half of his body sideways in his seat and thought carefully before answering. This question called for a more direct response. The entire conversation would, most likely. "I'm not sure it really matters what I think. He obviously believes in it and I'm just happy to be invited along."

"Yeah, well, he's not the first believer." She said back.

"He's certainly got the enthusiasm. If there are stones to find, I think he's the one that can do it."

"Maybe, I don't know. I've seen others with a lot more passion than him."

"I think that's a good thing. He's level about it, you know – not too crazy or over the top. Rational."

"Rational is understanding the meaning of symbolism." She said a little cynically.

"Now be nice, Addison." Josh playfully retorted. "It's not like he's asking us to follow the devil. There are worse things we could be doing with our time than chasing ghosts."

"Ghosts?" She reiterated, her tone a little less condescending this time. "So you do think it's a wild goose chase?"

"I didn't say that. I just don't see any harm in going along with it."

"I suppose." She admitted. "It's all just a little sappy for me."

"Yeah, but it's still a good message." There was more he wanted to add to his thought, but just then he felt a strong tap on his line and the tip of his pole quivered lightly. He waited, quietly, and a second later came another.

"You have any brothers or sisters?" Addison asked.

"…two brothers." He answered, distracted and focused. Suddenly the tip of his rod bent down toward the water and the line from his reel zinged out. He jerked back the pole to set the hook and felt the wiggling fight of a heavy fish below. "Fish on!" He hooted.

As soon as the initial resistance slowed, he reeled a couple slow turns. The fish pulled back and this time it took the drag for a good five seconds.

Addison reeled up her line to avoid a tangle. From what she could tell it looked like a decent fish. "Don't force it." She said, though she really didn't think she needed to. The city boy was doing everything right so far.

She grabbed the fishing net from the bottom of the canoe and got ready to hand it to him.

The fish stopped running and Josh started again with a slow reel. He regained about six feet of line before it ran again. Ten feet out from the canoe, its tail broke and slapped the water's surface. Josh whooped out a low, excited call.

The fish dove and burrowed its head with frantic shakes as it swam for the bottom. Josh kept his line tight and waited it out some more. Only a little line came out on this attempt then the fish tried a different tactic. It turned and darted underneath them. Josh let the top of his rod dip into the water as he carefully directed his pole around the front of the canoe, always keeping the line taut and always keeping just the right gentle pressure to let the fish wear itself out.

Its struggle slowed to shorter and shorter bursts of energy as Josh continued to wait and reel over and over. He'd broken it and as he brought it to the surface he caught his first sight of a long white underbelly. "Wow." Josh muttered. "Look at the size of that, Addison."

Addison looked over the side of the canoe at the fish floating next to them. "Not bad. Looks about four pounds or so. We'll keep it." She stretched forward to hand him the net. "Here…"

Josh waved her off and reached his hand down to the water. At the same time he tilted his pole skyward to raise the fish's head from the water.

It took Addison a second to realize what he was thinking and even then she didn't really believe he was thinking that. She had never seen anyone do it before. "What are you doing?" She asked incredulously.

Josh stopped to answer. "I'm just going to lip it in. Why?" Then he continued reaching down and tilting his pole higher.

"That's a northern pike." She gawked. "It's got about fifty razor-sharp teeth that will shred your fingers to hamburger."

He had just brushed the head when her warning registered. Fortunately the northern reacted before he got any closer to its mouth. It flipped and arched its body, slammed hard against the side of the canoe, and dove one more time for safety. The line ran out again and Josh reacted with a quick tug of his pole. His line snapped right after. His first Minnesota fish had been a good one and now it was lost – disappointing, but definitely better than losing his fingers.

The line from the end of his pole gently flowed away in the breeze and Addison realized he'd lost it. She still couldn't believe what she'd just seen. "I thought you said you've done a lot of fishing?"

Josh cranked his head around and gave her a defensive grimace. "Yeah, for bass and channel cat - not some monster fish that can take your hand off."

"Well did that look like a bass or a channel cat?" She asked back.

He didn't know what it looked like because he was too excited with the thrill of the catch to really take a good look at it. He didn't answer.

"From now on you use the net to bring any fish in the boat." She said. "I'm not paddling you all the way back to the Ely hospital."

He had plenty more chances to do just that. Over the next hour he caught four walleyes and got to know that species of pike rather well; more sharp teeth to avoid, but excellent eating from what Addison said. After that she found a school of crappies for them to tangle with. These Josh already knew, but these were much bigger than the quarter to half-pounders he was used to catching down south. Two hours later they were still pulling them in fairly consistently and Addison had to convince Josh it was time to stop for dinner.

Gib walked around studying the grounds and mentally fitting in scenes from the old photographs he remembered. He knew that the area along the boulder-lined shore used to be a drive and he even thought he could discern its route. The first ten feet of the shoreline was mostly filled by bushes and untamed weeds. Further back there was the line of the older and darker green pine forest. It looked as if it was being held at bay by some unseen border. Once the people had gone, the more prolific ground cover reclaimed the packed dirt road before the firs had a chance to spread.

Farther down there was a second break in the line of rocks that allowed for another beach. That's where the ghost road turned deeper into the forest. It climbed up a steep hill where the non-lakeside, and less popular, cabins used to stand. The Kearnys sometimes stayed in these and Gerald said nothing about their vacation experience being lessened by not being right on the water. The adults would spend hours fishing the remote parts of the chain of lakes and if the children didn't go with them they would spend their days on the beach or running through the woods or playing games in their cabin on rainy days.

After passing the hill's crest, he had circled around to where the main lodge once sat. Again he saw the evidence of strategic rock placement and he looked around for some evidence of the lodge's existence. There was not even a trace of the building nor was there any sign of its old foundation.

He did find a flat, slate-colored rock set into the ground at the very edge where the hill fell off in a steep slope back down toward the lake. It seemed out of place among the smoother and rounder boulders. As he looked closer, he could see another such rock set into the ground below the first. There was another below it and more going down. It was a staircase that once led to the cabins at the bottom.

Its purpose seemed pointless now, but he still found the mystery of its remains exciting. He made his way down, kicking off the plants that tried to conceal each successive step as he went. At the bottom, two upright stones standing almost three feet high marked the entrance to the staircase from that end. He went up and down four times, giving closer inspection on each pass. Finally, at the bottom, he made his way through the thick brush toward the shore, coming out only fifteen yards from the place they had set up camp.

When Addison and Josh returned two hours later, Gib didn't tell them what he'd found. That could wait until after dinner. It had been six hours since they'd eaten and he was famished. Addison served up five walleye and two northern with fresh green beans and fried potatoes.

Gib ate quickly and once he was full his excitement about the stairs returned. He got up and started collecting dishes even though it was Josh's turn to wash. Addison and Josh talked about the restoration of the forest.

"If everything was supposed to go back to natural habitat, why were these boulders left alone?" Josh asked. Gib pulled away Josh's dish just as he grabbed his last bite of fish.

"They were *supposed* to restore everything." Addison answered. "The government only allotted a certain amount of money to the project. When the funds started getting low, they made a list of things that weren't considered 'great offenses to nature'. Those things could be left behind. In Old Ely proper they just started leveling everything to the ground. Anything below, like basements and sewers, were left to be filled in by the forest."

"Have you ever been there?" Josh asked.

"I've gone through the outskirts twice in the winter. There are a couple of old dog sled trails that go there from this lake, but we won't be going anywhere near there."

"Why not?" Josh asked. He was fascinated by the thought of an abandoned town and of the different old artifacts certain to be found there.

At the lakeside, Gib scrubbed out the pans as quickly as he could, but he did listen carefully for her reply. Old Ely had a vague history he wanted to learn more about, but for some reason there wasn't a lot of information to be found. When he was younger, he had tried asking a clerk at the bait store about it. "Not much to tell." Was the only answer he got and it was said rudely enough for Gib to understand that people didn't want to talk about it.

"Well, first, it's basically a ghost town without the buildings and that's just plain creepy. Also, most locals make it a point to avoid the town out of respect."

"Respect for what?" Josh asked.

"Most locals?" Gib bellowed at almost the exact same time, forgetting about the dishes for a moment and even forgetting about the staircase he was waiting to show them.

Addison searched for the best way to explain the unwritten pact among the new Ely natives, but explaining the psychology of a small town was no easy task and she struggled to find an accurate description. "The land belonged to their forefathers and it was taken away. It's like they see it as some kind of sacred place and they take it seriously."

"I say *most* locals, Gib," She said louder. "because there definitely has been activity there since the relocation. Right after the move, somebody decided to go back and erect a giant stick person made out of logs to mark the place where their house used to be."

"A stick person?" Josh scoffed, unable to see any significant purpose in doing something so pointless.

"Yeah, I think it was meant to be like a totem or something. And it was made to last. Whoever did it covered it in black tar to keep the logs from rotting. Now, either they told somebody about it or somebody saw it for themselves because more and more kept popping up in the years after. I think the last guy that went there counted just under two hundred of 'em."

"Two hundred!?" Josh choked. "Who builds them? Previous landowners? Their kids?"

"No one knows. Nobody has ever admitted doing it. Personally, I think that's just another part of the Old Ely secret the locals are careful to keep. Not knowing who built them adds to the mysticism. The residents were forced out. I think the totems were built to scare people away from what was rightfully theirs. And their construction still goes on. Twenty years ago the DNR and a local news station went in there to do a story on them and to get an official count. At that time, there were only a hundred and eighty-three so somebody's added another ten or fifteen. There are always people in Ely who will carry on the old traditions and preserve what once was."

Her last comment reminded Josh of his interest in the resort that once sat here and he shifted the conversation from Old Ely. "Hey Gib, did you find anything interesting around here?"

With that opening, Gib was unable to hold his secret any longer. He abandoned the rest of the dishes to hurry back up to the fire.

"Come on. I'll show you." He said, barely able to contain his excitement.

Like Gib, Josh was also thrilled by the abandoned staircase that led nowhere. This evidence of an area once thriving with people increased the connection he was beginning to feel with his ancestors. The stairs twisted their way to the top and Josh ran up to see where they came out. There was nothing remarkable to see, but it was the hint of what was once there that started his mind pulling together images of what the place might have looked like in its day.

"Look over here." Addison called out from the bottom. Her announcement was significantly less enthusiastic than the excitement the others showed. She stared into a tangle of weeds and wild ivy to her right. "This looks like it was once a terrace. You can still see the stone retaining wall."

Josh and Gib joined her back at the bottom of the hill. It did look like a terrace, though it seemed too small for any specific use. Two tiered walls of well placed stones had been cut into the hillside without any apparent reason.

"Do you think Kearny would have hidden a clue around here?" Josh asked.

Gib looked around as if searching for anything to indicate that their uncle had done as such, but he really didn't hold any hope for it. "I doubt it. Gerald said they never returned to the grounds after their parents bought their own cabin."

Addison gave him a bewildered look. Most of the treasure hunters she guided only wanted to go to the places they thought would shed some light on the location of the stones. She assumed that was why Gib insisted they camp at this specific site.

"Then why are we here?" She asked in a distinctly accusing tone.

Gib realized that the historical significance of this place was lost on her. "Don't you want to see what life was like for our great grandparents? Don't you think it's interesting to walk in the same steps they used to walk over a hundred years ago?"

"It's a staircase, Gib." She responded. Her words were sarcastic and biting. "Hundreds of people used it – maybe thousands. Are we really gonna go through every step the Kearnys might have taken? 'Cuz that could really torque my nerves after a while."

Gib recoiled from her brusqueness. "No, I don't want to retrace every step, but this is a look at where we came from - how we came to be and how we came to be here."

"Gib, do you know how many other people have contributed to my existence?" She snapped back. "The Kearnys aren't the only reason I'm here."

Her voice was getting louder and again he stepped back. "I know, but how many of your other ancestors have left behind as much information about their lives and their passions. I think it's amazing that we are here now, the offspring of Kearny's siblings, reliving his family history because of the simple little story he created. This was the place that started that. The place they came to be together; to reconnect with each other far away from the things that pulled them apart. It's the place that helped bind them together as a family. You don't see any value in that?"

Addison's normally emotionless front suddenly, and violently, cracked. Her eyes drew narrow and her face flushed red with anger. "Why would I, Gib? I'm an only child. I have no idea what it would be like to have nephews and nieces following my footsteps. That means nothing to me...and it doesn't mean I'm any less of a person for it."

The response summarized her feelings for this adventure perfectly. It wasn't about her or for her. Kearny's story and the mysteries it held were about some other family, some romanticized version of a family that she just happened to share blood with. It wasn't written with her situation in mind.

Gib felt no animosity for her outburst. Instead, he looked away shamefully. He knew she was an only child. He had found that in his research of Steve's line. And hadn't Alise said something about her parents being deceased? Her grandparents were gone too, if he remembered correctly. His constant droning over "family" must have seemed heartless to her. The fierce independence she wore so proudly and so prominently was, at least partly, just a cover for her utter isolation.

"I'm sorry." He offered humbly. "I didn't mean to..."

Addison cut him off before he could finish his apology. "Sorry? Gib, it's not a bad thing to be an only child. It's not like a disability or some life-threatening illness. You don't have to apologize for it. I get along just fine."

"I wasn't apologizing for that." He countered softly. "I'm apologizing because I just assumed you knew what it was like for me; because I didn't realize..."

"Fine, whatever." She said curtly then she headed back to camp to begin packing up for the night.

Josh gave Gib an empathetic look of understanding, but didn't say anything. There was really nothing to say. It was an unfortunate circumstance that the two of them would just have to work out.

Addison scurried around the campsite roughly throwing everything into packs, even the last few unwashed dishes. Once the food was safely hung from the tree, she retired to her tent without a word to either of them. Josh and Gib put out the fire and went to their own tent soon after.

CHAPTER 8

The sound of constant drops hitting heavy on the tent walls pulled Josh from his sleep. Outside he saw the sun brightening the tree covered hills on the northern ridge. "Hunh." He uttered, wondering how there could be rain on such a beautiful and clear morning.

Gib's eyes cracked open too. "What are you doing up already?" He mumbled.

"The rain woke me. It's sunny though - must be passing us by."

Gib rolled onto his stomach and looked at the lake. There were no droplets disturbing the water nor was there any sign of water on the ground. He looked up to the top of the tent and saw that it was covered with dark shadows. Each one was about an inch in length and they were all moving slowly across the green nylon fabric.

"That's not rain - it's the caterpillars dropping onto our tent." He said. Suddenly, he popped up, threw back his sleeping back, and began searching for his clothes.

"What?" Josh gaped as he looked up at the shadowy spots on the peaked roof. "Unreal. I thought we were done with those things."

"Nope. They've been around the whole time. They just get thicker in different areas at different times. Check out the ground outside the tent."

Josh rubbed the blurry sleep from his eyes and focused beyond the mesh opening. The ground looked like a swaying blanket of blue and black. Closer to him he could see hundreds, thousands even, of the furry black and blue caterpillars.

He never really minded bugs before, but this was ridiculous. From the tent next to theirs, he heard Addison unzipping the fly and he watched her get out. With each step she took there was a light crunching of loose gravel and also a faint popping sound. It reminded him of the sound of a sheet of bubble-wrap being twisted, though much softer. It was the bodies of caterpillars exploding under the weight of her steps.

"Yeah, that's great." He said and slowly began sorting through the pile of clothes he was using as a pillow. He found his hat first and flipped it on even before he'd decided on a shirt.

Gib was already dressed. "Let's go." He said with a stinging slap on Josh's back. "We've got a big day today."

Throughout breakfast, Gib and Addison spoke only short, guarded phrases to each other. Gib wasn't sure what to say without offending her again and Addison felt that she might have been a little unreasonable last night. She had spent half the night reliving the confrontation and debating whether or not she should apologize. She decided she would, if an opening came up. It never did.

As they were packing up, Josh had to use a towel to brush the caterpillars off the two tents. He found that their little bodies were really quite fragile. The bigger ones popped at the slightest pressure, splattering their yellow guts all over the sides of the tents. He thought again of the happy lumberjack getting drunk on their innards.

No matter how often he cleared them away, there were always at least ten more falling from above. They dangled from tiny threads in the trees as they searched for their next meal. Even for all his effort, he was certain that there were probably a couple dozen that would be going with them to the next campsite.

Once Addison and Josh settled into the canoe, Gib shoved them off from shore before jumping into the front. As they slowly backed away, he gave one final look at the old resort site and thought how fortunate he was to have seen the place, even if it had caused a rift between Addison and himself.

This day's journey started off quickly as the swift current of the Silver Rapids sped them down the chute that lead to the next lake; Farm Lake, Josh confirmed with Addison. He was doing his best to ignore the unbearable tension between the others.

He kept talking until he found a mutually interesting topic that would help her and Gib over their awkward hump. "Are these the inner waters, Addison? The original boundary waters?"

"No. We won't enter them this way." She answered soberly. "We're taking that left just ahead. If we went to the right we could connect with them at the river."

"Oh. So then the inner waters don't start until the mouth of the Kawishaswishee River."

"Ka-wish-a-we." She corrected nicely, and without even a hint of sarcasm. The frequent butchering of the river's name was normally cause for a good laugh, but she was too impressed that he had figured out the route she referenced to really care about the humor in it. "The border of the old boundary waters is a bit of a tricky thing. After years of fighting between private landowners and the government, the original border was drawn to accommodate some of the community development that already existed at the time."

Gib wasn't aware that the expanding of the boundary waters was a case of history repeating itself. He finally jumped in their conversation. "People lived in the original boundary waters at one time?"

"Yeah, parts of it. The people of this area have made more sacrifices for the land than just the last restructuring."

"Who was most affected by it?" He asked.

While Addison gave the history lesson, Gib continued asking questions. Within ten minutes, Josh was totally bored with the discussion of land owners, the Section 30 iron ore mine, and the township of Fall Lake, but he was glad that his plan to get them talking had worked. The two of them kept at it until they had traveled more than half way across Garden Lake. They would have kept going, if Josh hadn't interrupted them.

"How will we know for sure that we found the old cabin site?" He asked.

"Not a problem, Josh." Addison assured him. "I've been there dozens of times."

"Yeah, but does anyone know for sure that it is the right spot? I mean, did one of the Kearny's take someone there to verify it?"

"Well, I don't know about that, but where we're going is accepted as the right location. Steve Kearny even drew a map for my grandmother once."

"Plus," Gib chimed in. "there is a little spring creek flowing into the lake that marks its location. A small part of the Kearny's land was wetland. Gerald dug out a small river course to help it drain into the lake."

Finally Gib produced a fact that Addison didn't already know, but still found interesting. She was very familiar with the creek. As a child, when her parents would take her there, she would always play by the creek. It fascinated her.

In her youthful imagination she had many adventures while following along its snaking path. She would throw in a thick stick and follow it down the hill to the lake, pretending the stick was a canoe and she was the navigator. It was these childhood fantasies that fueled her passion for the Boundary Waters and now she had to admit that her distant uncle was at least partly responsible for nurturing her love of the outdoors.

By the edge of the small creek, up on the flat of the hill, Harris stood staring at the tract of running water as it curved and twisted around trees and rocks. This was the Kearny's back yard. This was where the journey should begin, if he could figure it out.

His attention had been captured by a fork in the stream's path. The two arms joined back together just five feet after leaving a tiny little island inside. Its edge was bordered with a row of flat, jagged red rocks that Harris thought looked out of place with their surroundings.

"You've been at this for the better part of a day." Temple's deep voice thundered from behind. Harris was too caught up in the mystery of the strange rocks to hear him coming and the sudden break in his silent thoughts caused him to jump. Temple continued, "Please tell me you have something to go on."

"Well, I…um. I think I may have narrowed it down a little." Harris fumbled as he motioned Temple to follow him. The only conclusions he'd drawn were simple and obvious and he nervously searched for a way to present his finds as valuable insights. "I think we can rule out anything within the area where the cabin once stood. Many people have dug up the ground thinking that something might have been buried there. Obviously, nothing has ever been found."

Temple sighed impatiently. He had been Harris' employer long enough to recognize when he was trying to double talk him and he immediately saw through it this time. Harris always fell into unfocused rambling when he lacked information. "That has been an accepted conclusion for the last two decades. I hope you've got more than that."

"Yes, yes, of course." Harris replied and stopped at an area next to the old foundation. "This, however, this used to be a screened-in patio - probably where the family would often come together for meals or maybe for entertainment. I thought, maybe, it might be a good place to start."

Temple couldn't recall if he'd ever heard this bit of conjecture before, but Harris' babbling was even less coherent now and Temple was suspicious of its worth. He was about to chastise him for his ignorance when Meyers came trotting up the hill to join them. In his arms he cradled an old fashioned rifle.

A cold shiver crawled across Harris' skin as he watched Meyers approach. He couldn't stand the sight of the barbaric firearm. First, it was loud and its cracking rapport always caused him to shudder. Second, it was illegal to use gun powder fire arms anymore and the fact that he was associated with people that still used them was a harsh reminder of how deep he'd fallen in to the world of "questionable practices". The last reason he hated the shotgun, the most unnerving one, was the finality of it. There were no second chances for whatever target was unfortunate enough to earn its wrath. There was no opportunity for the recipient to justify their actions or plead their case for life. One shot – BANG! – and it was over forever. He often thought that was why the police now used taser guns as their standard weapon. In an age of reason, there was always a reason for a second chance.

"Sir, someone is coming across the lake." Meyers reported. "Two men and a woman in a single canoe. What would you like us to do?"

Though he couldn't see anything beyond the trees, Temple looked to the direction of the water just the same as he carefully considered his options. "They're probably just tourists, but I'd prefer our presence go unnoticed. Break camp and try to conceal our tracks as much as possible. We'll take cover at the top of the northern hill until they pass."

"What if they decide to set up camp here?" Meyers asked.

This time Temple responded without hesitation. "Then you will kill them, sink the bodies in the lake and hide the canoe and gear in the woods."

Harris winced at the cold, detached manner in which Temple spoke. It was no auspicious occasion for his boss to have someone murdered.

Meyers hurried back down the hill. Temple sensed Harris' unease. "This isn't a competition." He said. He leveled a heavy, piercing stare into Harris' eyes until his underling turned away from its weight.

As they drew closer to their destination, Josh heard the faint sound of trickling water. He couldn't see its source, but it grew louder with each forward thrust of the canoe. It wasn't until they were within ten yards that he spotted the tell-tale swirling of the water, and still its mouth was buried beneath a patch of tall ferns.

They landed to the right of the creek and Addison stayed completely quiet. There were no orders to unload the packs nor any push to move them faster. Despite her familiarity with the grounds, she allowed Gib to take the lead.

He didn't go far. He walked just a few feet from the canoe, stopped, and looked back across the lake. He then looked back up the hill, and then to the lake again. Whatever he was he was trying to see, he wasn't at the right angle. He moved over a step and repeated the same routine. He did so three more times until he had placed the location of the old dock he remembered from the Kearny's pictures. Omitting certain young trees from the scene, he could visualize it perfectly.

The modest wooden dock once stretched twenty-five feet into the lake. Three generations of Kearny's walked its length and for a brief moment Gib felt as if he was right there with them, watching the adults fishing off the end or the grandchildren jumping out into the water.

With one landmark in place, he turned around to look up the hill where he knew the cabin once stood. Even without the indentation in the ground, he would have known its position exactly. Sided in camel brown vinyl, it wasn't his ideal version of a log cabin, but it was cozy and still modest. A large window had dominated the front of the structure affording a generous view of the lake. Gerald's mother Mary often sat there to enjoy the sunrise while she ate breakfast.

There was a large deck attached to the left side of the house and to the right there once sat a swing with a single white bench. Its iron frame had been twisted out of shape when Norm Kearny accidentally left his truck in neutral, and unattended. That swing was the only thing that kept the truck from ending up in the lake. He never replaced it no matter how many times his kids begged him to or offered to buy a new one. "It gave the place character." Norm Kearny had said.

It was all there in front of him. The handed down pictures and the stories from Gerald's interviews had brought it to life. Further along the shore was a small wall of stones stacked in a circle. Inside it was a fire pit; the very same pit the Kearny's had used so long ago. These days, people probably assumed it was created by the forest preserve as an official fire grate, but Gib knew it wasn't. He wanted to point it out to the others, but he wasn't ready to risk offending Addison again.

"Somebody's been here recently." Josh stated. "Look at the paths of crushed grass."

Addison looked around the grounds. "That's not unusual. This place still gets used sometimes in the summer."

Gib snapped back to the present. "I didn't think anyone searched for the stones anymore."

"There are still some here and there, but people who make it this far in usually stop at the site. Some have ideas of stumbling across something that hundreds of other people missed. Mostly, people just like to say they've been here. It's also a really nice campsite. Ben brings people here all the time."

"So what now?" She asked. "Where's the path?" Her words were still a little sarcastic though she really didn't mean to sound that way.

"I have some ideas." Gib said slyly. He went back to the canoe and pulled out the orange pack. "But there's something we need to do first."

Josh and Addison followed behind as he methodically scoured the grounds on the southern edge of the property. He checked out everything close to the creek, Addison noted. She assumed he was simply comparing things to how they once were. Josh thought differently. Gib was looking for something specific and Josh found himself looking as well, as if somehow he too would know the sign if he came across it.

Gib stopped once they reached the top of the hill and the small island in the creek circled with flat red rocks. After a long, careful inspection he said, "It must be here." From the pack, he pulled out three collapsible shovels and handed one out to Josh.

"What must be here?" Josh asked. "What are we looking for?"

"A time capsule." Gib replied as he gave Addison her shovel. "I've read that they were a pretty popular thing in the late nineteen hundreds. Given Gerald's emphasis on preserving ancestry, it would make sense that they buried one."

Addison didn't accept the shovel as readily as Josh. She had seen people go the route of digging before. She didn't help any of them then and she had no desire to do so now. "And this is a hunch you think we should spend time on?" She asked doubtfully.

"Well," Gib started. "if they did bury one, Gerald would make sure that its location would be easily identifiable for anyone that knew to look for it. See those red rocks circling that little island in the middle?"

"Yeah." Addison answered dryly. "They're iron ore rocks. Pretty common for an area known as the iron range."

"Sure, but there's no iron mine sitting around here. They had to be brought here. They are the only things that are out of place. Sometimes, it's O that marks the spot."

Addison finally took the shovel, mostly just to be polite. She discreetly passed it along her side and laid it on the ground as she knelt down. There wasn't much chance to use it anyway. The little patch of ground was barely big enough to accommodate two people.

The shovels, or "little pieces of crap" as she thought of them, made the process painfully slow. Kneeling close by, she assisted by pulling away the loose clumps of dirt that weren't scooped away by the annoyingly small blades of the shovels. After a half hour they had dug a hole only two feet deep. She again started thinking that this time could be better spent fishing and her assistance with clearing the hole slowed as the deeper dirt turned into damp mud.

She was keeping up the pretense of interest as best she could only for Gib's sake, but then, with another pass of Josh's shovel, there came a loud "clang". It was too tinny for a strike against rock and it sounded hollow. "No way." She whispered.

She reached in for another, bigger scoop of mud just as Gib was about to send his shovel down again. He held up in time to miss her hand, but had he been a second slower he could have taken off some fingers.

Addison didn't notice her good fortune. She moved closer to the hole, now straddling the creek as she began pulling away more loose chunks. When those were gone, she started clawing away what hadn't been loosened up yet.

Josh pulled off his sweat soaked hat, drove the shovel's blade into the ground beside him and leaned heavily on its handle. "Is that it?" He asked between deep breaths.

"Must be." Gib answered as he also stopped to rest.

Addison scraped away at the mud until she had uncovered a long rectangular top. In her tenacity and focus, she didn't care that her hands and most of her arms were getting covered in mucky slime. She wriggled her fingers down the sides of the box to try pulling it out, but it was still too firmly packed into the ground. Josh, standing right beside her and still resting against the shovel, stumbled sideways when Addison pulled it right out from under him. She began widening the hole with hard thrusts around the sides.

Josh and Gib exchanged a quiet smile for her new found enthusiasm and stood back watching, and stepping out of the way of the clumps of earth she carelessly tossed aside. Strands of her fine hair pulled loose from her tight pony tail and swung freely around her face. Sweat beaded on her forehead. She stopped long enough to wipe her brow with the back of her hand then, with a hard-driving heave she wedged the shovel deeper down one of the sides.

The pass over her forehead left a long brown smudge just above her eye brows. Josh found the sight of her too funny to not comment. "Who would have thought we'd ever find something here?" He mocked.

She was too busy carefully leveraging her weight against the handle to pay attention to him. A sloshy squish and a watery plop and it finally came loose. "Got it." She cried out.

The metal box was no wider than a briefcase, but it was twice as deep. As she held it up to find the latch, she saw Gib patiently standing in the back ground. It was his find, she suddenly remembered, and she handed it over for him to open.

She didn't have to. He was just as happy to see her excitement. He took it knowing that it was a gesture of respect, and he set the box on the ground so they could all see what they'd found.

There was no lock nor was there any trick to opening it; only a simple clasp and a rubber seal around the seam to protect its contents from the wet earth. When first cracked, the lid released a strong scent of stale and oddly sweet air. Gib flipped the top over and the contents, which may have appeared simple and unimpressive to any other, held all three of them awe.

A bundled stack of photographs grabbed Addison's attention, but when she reached for them she got her fist real look at the mess she had made of herself. The pictures would have to wait. She reached over to the shallow creek to let the cool water flow over hands as she scrubbed away the dirt.

Josh picked up a collection of colorful fishing lures enclosed in a clear plastic case. Jigheads, spinners, and flicks; they were all variations on what was still used today. Some were brand new, but others looked like they'd been used many times. He couldn't believe Addison didn't go for these first.

Gib didn't reach for anything right away. He simply took stock of what was there. They were ordinary objects that most likely revealed something personal about each family member. He only recognized two things that he knew were of importance to the Kearny family. The first was a small package of red licorice, a Kearny family staple during fishing trips and the reason for the hint of sweetness in the smell. It hadn't been opened, but that didn't stop time for drying it out and discoloring it to a dusty pink. The other was a deck of cards that he knew was one of the family's favorite past times. The significance of everything else was probably shown in the pictures and he could wait until Addison had a chance to look at them.

Only one other thing caught his immediate interest, mostly because of its apparent lack of function. It was a milky white quartz rock shaped as a pyramid with soft rounded edges. It was large with a polished finish, but what really caught his eye was the three inch long cylinder that extended out from its base. It was still part of the rock, but obviously it had been carved. At the end of the cylinder, a little round node jutted out. A future step, he thought, a key to something later on, if he would know the lock.

"This stuff is all great," Josh blurted out as he placed the vintage lures back into the box. "but is there anything that points us in the next direction?"

Gib stuffed the key into the pack and motioned for Josh to follow him. Addison was now drying her hands against her shirt. She didn't hear Josh's question as she picked up the pile of photographs.

"No." Gib answered, leading Josh to the tree line at the back of the lot. "I already know what we're looking for."

He looked up at the tree tops searching for the answer he'd already come up with long ago and began explaining his conclusion to Josh. "In the book, the path is created by the short-lived flowers growing on the forest floor. Considering the creative and tricky nature of our uncle, the ground is the last place he would have hidden the path. We're looking for something completely different…there." He said with a confident smile. He was pointing to a group of trees - specifically their tops.

Josh followed the line of his finger, but he saw nothing. There was only a mass of tree tops covered in army worms. Now, with the blue sky background, he saw thousands and thousands of the little caterpillars hanging from branches by their silk webs. "What are you talking about? There's just a bunch of worms."

"Yes, but look at the tree tops, there." Gib said, pointing them out once again.

First he thought Gib was teasing him, but as he kept looking an unusual pattern began to form. All of the deciduous trees had been stripped bare of their leaves while all of the conifers were left untouched. The stripped trees were the only leafing trees in the area. They cut a distinct path between the pines, balsams and spruces. They were evenly spaced in two rows and they flowed along side each other in almost perfect unison.

It had to be some odd occurrence of nature, he thought, but as he looked around the rest of the landscape he saw that everything else was much more random. There was no other symmetry like this. When he looked back to the path, it practically jumped out at him and he wondered how he ever missed it in the first place. Now that he'd seen it, he couldn't *not* see it. It was a clear strip of brown trunks in the predominantly green landscape before him.

"Whoa. Addison's never going to believe this." He muttered softly then he yelled over to her. "Come here, Addison."

Addison ignored his call as she continued slowly sifting through the stack of pictures. She stopped to study one in particular that showed all four of the Kearny children together at the cabin. They were sitting at a picnic table in a screened in porch and they were caught up in a fit of laughter. Even now, well over a century later, the captured moment was so infectious that Addison found herself smiling at its sincerity.

Gib and Josh realized her fascination and went back to where she was still kneeling on the ground. "Addison, you've got to see this." Josh said.

"Huh, oh." She mumbled, coming out of her trance. "I was just looking at this picture. I've never seen pictures of the family before, even when you sent them to my grandmother, Gib. I didn't really care to look at them. I figured they were just like any other family, tolerating each other just because they were related. But it wasn't just about blood. They really seemed to like each other. Look, you can see it."

Josh took the picture and studied it. He couldn't keep from smiling either. "Is this one Kelly?" He asked, pointing to a woman with long dark brown hair sitting at the table. Her left hand was pressed against her forehead and her eyes were squinted tight. It was as if her laughter had become so uncontrollable that she feared her head was about to balloon up and explode.

"Yeah, and this one is Chris." Gib said. The view of his distant grandmother was harder to see. She was doubled over from laughter and her blond/brown hair partially obscured her face.

"The men look so much alike. How do you know which one is Steve?" Addison asked.

Gib showed her which one he was and went on to explain how Steve had significantly more hair than his brother. Steve had his shoulders shrugged and his hands thrown up in the air as if feigning ignorance to some unknown accusation, or perhaps, playing the innocent to some secret joke. It was obvious that something he said had caused the others to laugh so heartily.

Addison flipped back to the top of the pile and began sorting through the pictures again. They meant much more now that she knew who was who. Josh pulled her up by the arm and dragged her toward the back tree line. "Come on, Addison. You won't believe it."

She stumbled along with them still not completely taking her attention from the photos until they stopped at the edge of the woods. She was not impressed when she looked up.

"They're trees." She said sarcastically and to better illustrate her lighthearted teasing she pointed out the other trees around them. "Oh look, there's another one over there. And there. There too." Then she shouted, "Hey everyone, come look. We found real live trees in a forest!"

Gib's semi-scornful stare suggested that he didn't find any humor in her behavior. He forcefully grabbed her shoulders to turn her around. "Look again – at the trees *without* leaves."

Addison continued to mock him by squinting her eyes in an exaggerated manner while scanning the tree line. "Nope, still just a bunch of trees."

"Okay. Now close your eyes." He instructed patiently. "When you open them, look at the big picture and the sky behind it. Don't focus on any one thing."

Addison opened her eyes and did as she was told. Still she saw nothing and again she squinted her eyes jokingly. Now she did see something. There was something there. Through the blurred vision of her slitted eyes, lines and shapes became less discernible. There was a mass of green with a distinct slash of brown trailing off in the distance. In her disbelief, her eyes popped back open wide thinking she had somehow tricked herself into seeing something that she never believed in. Even with her clearer vision she could still see it.

"Oh my, God." She uttered beneath her breath. "That's it, isn't it? That's really it."

"Yes it is." Gib replied triumphantly. "This is the use our uncle found for the annoying army worms."

"I wonder if it leads to the old Fernberg trail." Addison said blankly. Her face was a vacant stare as her mind adjusted to the reality of the path's existence and the stirring of her growing excitement.

"You know about the Fernberg trail?" Gib asked, even though he knew this shouldn't have surprised him at all.

"Yeah. It used to be the end of the road. Highway 169 used to run right through the middle of Ely, then past Winton and on up to Lake One where it ended. Once you got past Winton, it was called the Fernberg. It was the most popular way for people to start their trips into the inner waters. Why? What do you know about it?"

"When the order came down to move the towns and reforest the area, Gerald volunteered to lead a group of people in reforesting the area. He started with the Fernberg Trail. He planted those trees. That and one of his interviews about the army worms are what made me think to look for this."

All three of them stood, marveling at the phenomenon until Josh finally interjected. "So, let's get going."

Gib smiled back at him. "There's plenty of day left for a hike in the woods."

"Wait." Addison said. Considering Gib's fascination with the old resort, she just assumed he would want to camp here at least one night. She planned on it. "Don't you want to stay here tonight?"

Gib looked around. "We'll be back. Next year maybe, when we can spend more time."

A sudden thought occurred to Josh regarding the path. In his rush to share the revelation he blurted it out abruptly and loudly. "Oh, I get it. Beaten - been eaten."

Though Gib doubted the validity of his conclusion, it was logically sound and he didn't have the heart to contradict Josh's creative thinking. And, it really didn't matter anyway. His theory had been confirmed and his satisfaction was matched only by the thrill of knowing that the adventure was just beginning.

———

Kneeling among the underbrush from their strategic hilltop perch, Temple watched the intruders as they brought their gear up from the lake. These were no simple tourists just passing by. The taller of the two boys knew exactly what he was doing and had already uncovered more than anyone before. Now, something in the woods had shown their way.

Harris was crouched beside him, also watching the group below. They hadn't found the stones, but he delighted in the fact that they did find something within the ring of red rocks. He knew they held some possible significance and he had been proven right. He could have found the box, if his boss hadn't been pressuring him so.

"What do we do now, sir?" Harris asked quietly.

Temple reached up to a small black radio curled around his ear and pushed the talk button. "Meyers, join us at this position." He whispered.

Harris looked down to the group again. His skin turned cold and clammy and his eyes darkened with helpless fear. He knew why Meyers was being called.

A desperate solution suddenly flashed in his head and he quickly began pointing out the logic in keeping the three kids alive. "Sir, it's obvious that these people know more about what they are doing than we do - what I do. Maybe we should follow them for a while and see what else they find. It could prove beneficial."

The suggestion, Temple knew, was born merely of Harris' cowardice, however it was not without merit. Again he touched his radio and amended his order to Meyers. "Bring the camera with the telescoping lens."

Harris let out a low, secret sigh of relief.

"Okay Harris, we'll wait to see what they do next." Temple said coolly.

Meyers responded to his order remarkably fast. He startled Harris when he slithered up next to them and almost caused him to let out a revealing cry of surprise.

"As soon as that group leaves, I want you and Walsh to follow them." Temple said. He took the camera from Meyers' hand and passed it over to Harris. "Stay out of sight and update me regularly on their progress and your position. We'll keep this area as base camp."

"Do you want me to go with them in case they find something?" Harris asked, thinking that was why he was given the camera.

"No. I want you to get pictures of all three, download their photos into the computer and search the driver's bureau for their identities. Find out everything you can about them." Temple motioned for Meyers to get moving and lifted his binoculars again to study his new adversaries. "You don't have the stomach for what may happen if they do find the stones."

CHAPTER 9

"We're never going to see water again." Josh thought out loud bitterly. With the canoe on his shoulders, he had no idea how far ahead of him the others were. He didn't care. He wasn't expecting a response. Then, snidely rebutting Addison's claim from the day before, "two hundred and seventy rods is by far the longest portage we'll do."

It wasn't the pain in his shoulders bothering him now – well, it wasn't just the pain in his shoulders.

He had no idea how many "rods" they had walked so far, but two-seventy would have been a garden stroll compared to this. They hadn't seen a sign of water in more than two hours and that was just the crossing of the river leading out of Garden Lake. They probably could have swum it in less time than it took to load and unload the canoe.

He missed the water. He needed it. It was easier to navigate and he always had a good idea of where they were. The forest was different. There were no distinct shorelines to use as a reference in determining their direction. There was only the sun in the middle of the sky, and under the canoe he couldn't even see that.

He kept looking from side to side to make sure they were still between the path of "been eaten" trees. He couldn't see their tops, but he knew their trunks. He'd committed that to his memory right away. 'That's the way back.' He thought. 'If this goes nowhere, that's how we get back to the water.'

He'd made a subtle comment about that to Addison earlier when Gib was carrying the canoe. She told him they would follow the trees until they ended and if it got too dark they'd just camp in the forest and pick up again in the morning. It didn't seem like a problem to her, but that's when his mind really started working. That's when it started doing double-time against him.

Now, roaming through the woods with only the monotonous view of an upside down canoe and forest floor, his mind had time to pull up his most vulnerable memories. 'I was only a kid then. It's different now. I know better.' He thought dismissively.

'But was I eight or ten?' He wondered. He couldn't remember and it really didn't matter. It was a time when he was too young for reason and when the unknown was more readily explained by the superstitious.

There was a forest, different than this one with a more open floor under a canopy of leafy elms, walnuts, and oaks. There had been a path when he started walking, but it had faded and in the busy daydreaming of his childhood fantasies he didn't notice when it completely disappeared. He didn't realize it until the trees in front of him had become too crowded to let him go any farther.

"I think I was eight." He mumbled.

He remembered turning in quickening circles as he looked for some sign of familiarity. Every tree he thought he knew, every rock or clump of bushes, they were all the same as any other in the forest, or at least the same enough for him to be unsure. There was no way to tell and no path to show him. His sense of security had faded too and everything began to move in suspicious and unnatural ways. Tree branches swayed against the direction of the wind. Brush wavered for no apparent reason and twigs snapped as if being stepped on. Something was out there and it was watching him.

After that he couldn't remember things clearly. There was a lot of running and the running only took him deeper into the woods, past more similar looking trees and the not-quite familiar rocks. He ran until he couldn't run any more then he fell to the ground and started to cry. After that, he started screaming. Only then was he found, when another camper heard the screams of a terrified little boy.

'I wasn't paying attention then.' He thought. 'I panicked.' But in his secluded thoughts, underneath the canoe, doubt was eating away at the maturity of reason. Was there something in the forest that day?

"Not much further, Josh." Addison yelled back, breaking him free of his building anxiety without even knowing it. It was almost her turn to carry the canoe again.

Trailing just behind her, Gib asked, "Do you have any idea where we're heading?"

"My guess is the old Fall Lake campground. We turned north a while ago and that would lead us there. We should be coming up on it pretty soon." At least she hoped so anyway. She wasn't exactly sure. She wouldn't let the others know that, but she trusted that they would eventually run into some body of water she would recognize.

"This is good, Gib." She said when they came upon a relatively open area in the path of eaten trees. They both dropped their packs and found a place to sit while they waited for Josh to catch up.

For Addison, their last moment alone was quiet and awkward. Ever since they'd left the Kearny site she'd been wrestling with her pride. She'd been particularly tough on Gib, tougher than she'd ever been with anyone else searching for the stones, and she was wrong. Now, before Josh caught up to them, she had to somehow admit it. "I've got to tell you, Gib, I'm pretty impressed. You never doubted yourself. It's admirable."

Gib shrugged off the compliment. "It's a little early for congratulations, I think. We still haven't found the stones."

"I'm not talking about the stones…the way you never give up no matter how stubbornly people argue with you."

She was apologizing, he realized, or at least she was doing her best. "Well, I could have just as easily been wrong." He said coyly.

"But you knew you weren't. Like I said, I admire it."

"Thanks." Gib said, ending the conversation. Josh was almost to them and he was sure she wouldn't want to continue this conversation when he was around.

Josh tilted the canoe back on his shoulders until it hit the ground then he dropped it off to his side and let it land with a thud. He unbuckled the pack on his back and headed straight for the one Addison had been carrying – the one with the food. He didn't bother to find a rock or log to sit on; he just plopped onto the ground and began digging for a snack. "Will we be coming up on a lake soon?" He asked as he stuffed a mix of raisins, nuts and chocolate chips into his mouth.

"Pretty soon." Addison assured him. "There's a small jug of water in the food pack." She pulled out the map from her back pocket and walked around to find some kind of distinctive landmark.

Gib followed her. "Not getting nervous, are you?" He asked.

"Wha…oh, no." She answered distractedly. "I'm just getting tired of this endless portage."

"Meh thoo." Josh yelled through a mouthful of food.

Gib looked down at the map and this time he talked softer. "Do you know where we are?"

She circled out the small area that was her best guess, passed the map over to Gib and walked a couple steps further along the path to look around. "That small stream we passed a while ago should empty into Fall Lake. If that's right, we've probably got about another quarter mile or so."

Gib looked closer to the area she had pointed out. Her reference to the stream didn't help him at all. There was no way of knowing exactly where they had crossed it. "How can you tell?"

She didn't answer so Gib clarified his question. "The place where we saw the stream could be anywhere along its course. How do we know for sure?"

Again, she didn't answer.

"I think we went at least a mile northeast from the cabin site before turning." He continued.

"Hold on." She whispered back.

Gib looked over to her. She was perfectly still and staring deep into the woods. He followed her gaze and he suddenly forgot about figuring out their position as well.

"Put the food away, Josh." Addison commanded softly.

"Hey - all I got for lunch was salami and cheese." He protested loudly. "I'm not going to make it ten more minutes…"

"Shhhh!" Gib hissed back at him. "Put it away."

Josh looked over to them, fully intending to argue his point, but stopped when he saw that something in the woods had taken their attention. "What are you guys…" He started then his words trailed off once he saw what they were looking at.

Standing at the base of an old birch tree, a large black bear was greedily licking at its trunk. It was not more than thirty yards away. As Josh looked on he realized that the bear's interest in the tree was not for the bark, but for the hordes of army worms clinging to it.

The hungry bear hadn't noticed their presence, or maybe it just didn't care. At over five hundred pounds, there were few things it had to worry about in the forest. But Josh saw something different in this bear than those he'd seen before; a wildness totally unlike the playful and endearing ones he'd visited at zoos. Patches of fur were missing from its black coat and what hair was left was mangy and matted. It was gorging itself as if unable to get the tasty little worms down fast enough. The same worms, Josh realized, that were on their clothes and whose guts were splattered all over their shoes.

As if somehow hearing and somehow understanding Josh's thought, the bear looked over at them. Now Gib and Addison saw something different about him as well. Trails of creamy, blood-streaked drool streamed from its mouth and its eyes glared with a wild and vacant stare.

Josh rolled up the bag of trail mix to eliminate at least one of the scents that might have caught its attention. It didn't help nor did it matter. This bear, half out of its mind from whatever disease ravaged its body, was now only concerned with defending its territory.

In a burst of furious speed, it charged after the intruders, cutting half the distance between it and them before rearing up on its back legs and belting out an enraged growl.

Addison winced from the loud, bellowing roar. She, several steps in front of Gib and closest to the bear, was the target of its rage. For all her experience, there was no immediate answer for this. There was no secret north woods insight to save them. An act of submission was her only plan. She took a step back and turned her head to the side to show that she wasn't a threat.

The bear belted out another, deeper growl and she stopped. All of them held still, watching, but mostly waiting, certain that the attack would come and knowing it would be brutal. They could see it in the angry eyes.

Blood Stones

Once again the laptop went blank. The connection was lost. Harris stretched back in his chair and rubbed his eyes. His progress on the research project was painfully slow. Just when he would start getting somewhere, the satellite signal would become too weak and he was forced to wait. Not even Temple's satellite cell phone was strong enough to receive signals this deep in this wild.

He was glad for the break. He'd been sent off to complete his assignment as soon as the kids left and he still hadn't seen the answer in the trees that had shown them their way. With his work now on hold, he walked up to the tree line to see for himself. Temple was there, at the spot where they first entered the forest, staring at it again.

"Have you figured out what they saw?" Harris asked quietly, being exceedingly careful not to surprise his boss as he approached.

He had figured it out - hours ago, right after his competition left and he had a chance to see for himself. The three of them staring up at the trees made it quite obvious where to look. He was there now admiring its creativeness once again while he considered his next course of action. He could have them killed and follow the path himself, but if there were more Kearny riddles to be solved it most likely couldn't be done by him - and Harris was proving less and less useful. "I see it." He confirmed arrogantly.

At the risk of giving his boss even more ammunition to assault his intelligence, Harris needed to know. "What is it?"

"A door is not a door." Temple replied.

Harris looked up to the trees for any possible connection to the strange answer. "Excuse me, sir?"

"It's an old riddle, Harris, designed to jar the mind into thinking differently. A door is not a door when it is ajar." He explained, cryptic still and reveling in his superior intellect. Then he pointed to the tree tops. "And, a path doesn't always have to be on the ground. Look at the bare trees."

With the secret shown to him, Harris was able to pick it out quite easily. It was obvious, but brilliantly disguised. No doubt, hundreds of people had looked right at it. He quickly recalled the passage from Kearny's book that most likely provided the insight:

The world looked different now; its absolutes had dissolved into mind-bending abstractions. The once clear sky now rained upon him countless dark drops, the solid earth beneath his feet held untold chambers with unimagined dangers, and the ever flowing river now swirled and eddied as if to question its proper direction. These were the same as ever, of course. The change was within him and he could afford no such doubts now. The riddler would have his answer or the people would perish. Indecision was now Archer's enemy and he felt ill-equipped for such a battle.

A flash of distant memories filled Haris with the wondrous aspirations and limitless imaginations of adolescent excitement. When he was younger he had dreamed of being a great explorer. It was he who was the finder of the fabled path and it was he who Kearny was speaking to. His dreams were given strength when he used to read Kearny's book so many years ago when he was carefree and without the cumbersome responsibilities he now carried.

"You have something for me." Temple said, snapping Harris from his youthful escape.

"Huh. Oh, no, not yet. I lost the net connection."

"…and you thought wandering around aimlessly would somehow get it back?"

"No. No, of course not. Deek has figured out the timing of the satellites available to catch our signal out here. There won't be another clean signal for at least six hours."

"Sir, we've got a problem." Meyers' voice broke in over Temple's radio. Harris was spared Temple's lecture on the merits of efficiency and expediency under the constraints of limited resources.

Temple walked off, shooing Harris away before answering. "What is it?"

"The group has come across a very angry bear. It looks like it's about to attack. Should I kill it?"

His answer was swift and decisive. Such pressured decisions were easy for him. All he had to do was remove muddling side issues like sympathy or kindness or, most importantly, morality. The group wouldn't lead them to the stones if they knew they were being followed, but they couldn't lead them to the stones if they were dead.

"Do not do anything to reveal your position unless the taller of the two men is in danger. Do you understand? He is the key to finding the stones. The other two are dispensable. If anyone gets hurt, move in and report back to me."

Meyers begrudgingly acknowledged his understanding of the orders with a deflated "yes, sir." His disappointment was not from concern for Gib or the others, but because he really wanted a chance to kill the federally protected bear. The head would have been a nice souvenir to hang on his bedroom wall.

"I'm going to try backing away really slow." Addison said, her head still turned, but slyly watching the bear from the corner of her eye. "If he charges, we'll split up. I'll head west, you guys go east."

"No Addison." Josh countered. He had discreetly slid the trail mix back into the pack, but his arm was still buried deep in the pack pushing around pans and boxes of dried food as he searched for the only thing he knew could help them.

"I know what I'm doing." Addison insisted. Her careful backward retreat only angered the bear further. It charged again and this time it didn't stop.

She ran off to the right, waving her arms and making certain that the bear's attention stayed on her. She didn't have to. Its focus was singular, it was furious, and it was only for her. She darted into the woods with the bear following close behind.

Gib took off to the left, as instructed, but it didn't take him more than ten steps to realize Josh wasn't behind him. "Josh!" He snapped. "Come on!"

"We're not splitting up." Josh yelled back and his hand emerged from the pack with a flat wooden case. Inside, a sleek black gun about twice the size of a pistol rested on a foam pillow. Beside it was a power cord and battery pack. It was a Taser gun given to him by his father as a graduation present. Josh picked it up, switched on the power and turned the voltage dial to the highest level.

"You can't go after it with that." Gib yelled as soon as he understood his intention. "It's meant to knock out *people* not bears."

It was too late. Josh was already off and running and Gib was forced to follow after.

She bounced through the woods like a deer fleeing a predator, hurdling boulders and fallen trees while weaving her way through the branches and bushes that crowded the forest floor. Her movement was amazingly swift and graceful, but it could never be fast enough to keep the bear from gaining on her. No matter how many obstacles she tried to put between them, the bear chased faster. Its determination became more and more obvious as it grunted out deeper and deeper snorts and low, guttural growls. The closer he got, the louder they became and Addison could actually feel the hot, panting breath beating down on her.

She was about to be tackled. She was certain of it. It was ridiculous of her to ever think she could out run a bear. It was a chance she took thinking that maybe she would come across something in the woods that would help her or something to deter the attacking bear.

The muscles in her legs burned and her lungs could no longer suck in enough air to sustain her pace. She was losing. Stomach-turning images of the berserk bear ripping her apart flashed before her eyes. Ahead she saw one last chance to gain some distance and one last chance for safety. The river they had passed earlier cut a ravine in the ground easily four feet deep and seven feet across. It was a leap she hoped she could make that the bear could not.

She hit the edge and launched her body into the air, sailing across the gully with her forward leg stretched out to its fullest length and her arms pulling large circles of air to drive her farther. She landed on the other side with only inches to spare and with her pace unbroken.

The bear didn't try the jump. Its progress was going just fine. It ran down one side of the ravine and kicked up sprays of water from the river bed. The slight detour only aggravated it even more. Emerging on the other side, it saw its prey escaping and it screamed out a bone-shattering growl before redoubling its efforts.

She looked back. She had to. She needed to know how much she'd gained. She shouldn't have and it proved a costly mistake. Her foot caught on a knotted root. She stumbled and slammed hard onto the forest floor. Her momentum skidded her fifteen feet along the ground where small rocks and twigs tore away thin layers of skin on her hands and arms then she crashed head first into a rotting old tree stump that crumbled under the collision.

Her only hope now was the slimmest. She pulled out a small utility knife from her pocket and flipped the blade open. If she was lucky, she might get a jab in an eye socket or maybe the throat; anything that could inflict enough damage to stop it.

With both hands before her, trembling as she prepared to strike with short, thrusting jabs, she watched and waited. Her slim hope quickly disappeared. The bounding and hulking bear shook violently and uncontrollably as it closed in. It was sick beyond the point of sanity and certainly beyond any pain she could possibly inflict.

Once Josh felt he was close enough, he stopped at the edge of the river and took aim. His first shot hit its mark as the bear climbed up the embankment, but the tiny electrically charged dart only brought a shrieking growl. Two more shots and each time the bear reacted with a mere quivering shudder of its massive body. It kept on, getting dangerously close to where Addison had fallen. This time Josh opened fire until he emptied the twelve remaining darts into the bear's hide. With one final, quaking shudder, it fell to the ground in a fit of convulsions.

Addison lay in stunned disbelief. Something had saved her, though she couldn't imagine what. The bear was only two arm lengths away from her, its body still heaving for air and its muscles still twitching. She slowly got to her feet and brushed the embedded debris from her arms and chunks of the tree stump from her face and hair. She saw the reason for her good fortune when Josh came running toward her with his weapon in hand.

"You went after a bear with a taser gun?!" She scolded loudly. "Are you out of your mind?"

"I just saved your life." He replied just as loudly. "You should be thanking me."

"Oh Yes, thank you. Thank you for almost getting yourself killed. Those things aren't meant to stop bears, you idiot. What if it didn't work? He would have come after you."

"This thing was at full power." Josh said, holding out his gun to show her the setting of the voltage. "At that level, one dart can knock out a three hundred pound man for twelve hours. I was pretty confident it would work."

"Really, and how many darts did it take?"

"It stopped him didn't it?" Josh protested, and avoiding her question.

When Gib caught up to them, he was relieved to see the bear on the ground while his friends remained standing. He was even more relieved when he heard the way they were bickering with each other. It reminded him of his younger sisters. The danger was over. This was simply a release of the anxious energy from their close encounter.

Gib walked over to where the bear lay. He'd never been so close to one. Part of him wanted to touch it. He wouldn't because he couldn't risk waking it, but more than that he was in awe of being so close to it. It was majestic and peaceful, for now. Beside him, Josh and Addison were still arguing.

"You guys about finished?" He interrupted. "Cause I'd really like to get as far as we can before nightfall."

"Huh." Josh said, jovial almost and no longer defending. "Oh, yeah, I think were done now."

"Hold on." Addison paused. "The bear's still breathing. We have to kill it."

Gib looked back down at the bear. He felt sorry for it. It wasn't the bear's fault they invaded its territory. "Do you think it will come after us when it wakes up?"

"Well, that's a possibility I guess." Addison answered. "But it's sick. Look at the blood running out of its nose and mouth. And who knows what effect Josh's little toy gun will have on it. We should put it out of its misery."

"So how do we do it?" Josh asked. He didn't want to kill it either, but he was unable to deny Addison's logic.

Addison held up her utility tool, the knife with a deep toothed serrated edge was still ready. Josh and Gib watched as she cut into the fur of the bear's neck, but both turned away as soon as the blood began spilling onto the ground.

Addison's thought on their destination was correct and the path of eaten trees led them right to the shores of Fall Lake. Far enough for this day, Gib decided, and they set up camp on a wide sandy beach. Once again Addison insisted they fish for dinner and once again she knew exactly where to find them.

Gib joined them this time and though he was thrilled with the six pound walleye he pulled in, he was just as happy to be lazily enjoying his seat in the middle after their eventful day. The sun still shone brightly in the western sky. Its rays tipped the peaks of rippling waves creating twinkles of white across the water that sparkled like a field of diamonds spread out before them.

"I don't see any other rows of stripped trees." Josh said as he retied a new lure to his line. He thought about asking Gib if he could use one from the time capsule, but decided against it. He'd already lost a dozen or so of his own to the lake and the Kearny antiques deserved a better fate than that. "Where are we going from here?"

Gib was already aware that the path didn't continue past the shore of the lake. He had noticed it as soon as they got there. It was part of the reason he decided to fish with them. He expected the trail to pick up again somewhere further down the lake. "I'm not sure. Maybe there is something in the pictures that will give us an idea."

Addison already had an idea of where they were going, or at least where she hoped they were going. As she slowly sculled the canoe across a reef, she offered her opinion. "I think we're heading for Basswood. Most of the pictures in the time capsule were of fishing trips and the most logical lake from here is Basswood."

"That makes sense." Gib added. "Gerald's father loved fishing that lake."

"Everybody loved fishing that lake." Addison said. "The question is which way do we go? There are two ways to get there from here: two short portages into Pipestone bay or the 4-mile portage up to Hoist Bay."

"Four miles!" Josh blurted out, thinking how difficult another long hike might be for him to endure. "I vote for the easier way."

Addison lifted her paddle up and slapped the blade across the surface of the water. A sprinkle of heavy drops jumped up over the side of the canoe and soaked Josh's back. "We aren't going to choose one just because it's shorter, 'ya big dope."

"Hey!" Josh yelled out, jerking forward from the unexpected cold dousing. "If it's just a matter of picking one or the other, then I say we go with the shorter one."

He pulled out his own paddle and returned the favor with a splash of his own. His inexperience in wielding a paddle showed as most of his water flew well wide of its target.

"Nice shot, Sally." She goaded. "What if we take the shorter way and find nothing? Then we'll just end up doing the 4-mile anyway. Besides, it's more likely that Kearny wanted us to explore more of the woods before finding the stones."

Just as her last words came from her mouth, Josh sent another shot of water and this time it was right on target. Trickles of water streamed down her face, but she ignored that. Instead, she responded with another splash, and he did again. Within seconds, it became a war of who could strike their paddle the fastest with little care for accuracy. Both of them screamed out with each shower of water that drenched them.

Gib was accidentally included in their battle as stray sprays of water hit him in the head, chest and back, depending on who took the shot. "Alright." He said in a calm, adult manner.

Addison stopped, placed her paddle across her legs and began wiping water from her eyes. Josh did too - until he turned to see that Addison was still much drier than he was. Gib had given him the perfect opportunity and he capitalized on it with a giant, arching swing that soaked her in a huge wave. The war started again.

"Alright…" Gib tried to interrupt. Now he was getting hit even more often with even bigger splashes. They didn't listen. "Alright!…ALRIGHT!" He finally yelled. This time it ended for good.

"If you guys would just hold on a minute, I think I've got it figured out."

Addison stopped, but remained wary of Josh's crafty tactics. She held her paddle up in the air just in case he decided to take advantage again.

"Okay." Gib started. "Most of the pictures I saw showed a big boat - not a canoe. And it had a motor on the back. If Basswood was part of the boundary waters, then they shouldn't have been heading there with a motor."

"Well, not really." Addison interrupted as she slid her fist down her long pony tail to wring off the excess water. "A couple of lakes on the border did allow for boats with motors of twenty-five horsepower or less. Basswood was one of them. People would but their boats on portage wheels and roll it over the trails."

Gib thought for a moment, piecing together the information. "The Kearny's did mostly day trips into Basswood. A boat with a heavy motor seems a little big to be pushing four miles for just a day. I think the shorter one is the best bet."

"Ya know, Gib," Addison said, "it's sick that you know so much about this family. It's helpful, but it really is kinda sick."

She let her paddle fall flat against the water next to him, sending up one final splash just to be sure Gib didn't escape with any dry clothing either.

The next morning, Gib was awake before either of his friends and even before the sun broke over the trees. His sleep was interrupted throughout the night by dreams of the stones. They floated above his head and just out of arms reach, swooping down closer when he wasn't on guard and ready to catch them. They taunted him. Only one time did he come close to getting them, but then he woke to find himself reaching into the darkness. At the first crack of light, he'd had enough of the subconscious torment.

He sat sipping coffee on a large rock partially submerged in the water, debating whether or not to wake the others. As he surveyed the woodland scene around him, he noticed something different about this area; different than the other places they had camped. The trees seemed bigger and broader and the wildlife was much more visible.

Two pairs of loons occupied this part of the lake. Regal looking in their black and white colors, they would call out every now and again with their soulful, echoing cries. One of the birds came surprisingly close to where Gib sat and he was able to see a fledgling chick riding on its mother's back. Her red eyes regarded him cautiously when he lifted his cup for another sip, but she didn't panic and kept steadily on her course.

His gaze drifted up the shoreline until he spotted two enormous dark brown animals standing amidst a patch of wild rice in the shallow water. It was a mother moose and her calf and they were close enough for Gib to see the features of their faces. The younger one started tromping through the water playfully, trying to entice its mother to have some fun. Her feeding couldn't be interrupted for long, but every once and again she would respond with a soft head-butt or gentle nudge with her long snout.

Behind him, Addison began wrestling around in her tent. The strong scent of fresh coffee had pulled her out of her sleep and she poured herself a cup before joining Gib on the rock.

"Can you feel it?" She asked as she carefully lowered herself beside him.

"Feel what?" He asked back distantly, still enjoying the antics of the moose.

"Everything - the trees welcoming you and the animals accepting you as just another creature of the forest. We're in deeper than most people ever go. Those that come this far understand the value of nature and make a conscious effort not to disturb it. These animals haven't been conditioned to fear us."

He could feel it. Thinking back to yesterday, he had felt it as soon as they got there. It was a difference he couldn't quite place. It wasn't the same forest he had always known. "Is this the inner waters?" He asked.

Addison pointed across the lake, to the direction they would be going after breaking camp. "We're right on the cusp. The old border was just over there. Part of this lake was in the old boundary waters."

Gib sat silently thinking as he continued taking in this new world around him. The green of the trees was more vibrant than he'd ever seen. They were radiant and glowing and their feathery arms really did seem to be reaching out for him. And despite their utter solitude, he did not feel at all alone or isolated with the presence of such majestic animals near by. Even the rocks seemed different. Each one was unique with its various chips and dents and each mark hinted at incredible stories of their existence and how they came to rest in their place.

This new awareness, he realized, wasn't just from their location; it was the length of their absence from civilization that had brought it on. Without the distraction of life's daily hassles, he was able to see so much clearer and so much more. Everything outside of this moment was vague and unimportant. Even his search could wait and he left Josh to wake up on his own.

CHAPTER 10

"What lake are we in now?" Gib asked as he looked out across the new stretch of water. They had left Fall Lake behind with their first portage and were about to set off in the canoe again. Narrower than any of the other lakes they'd been on, this one looked more like a big river.

"This is Newton." Addison answered. "It'll take us to Pipestone falls at the other end."

Josh was again in the middle and he shifted the packs around him until one was set to support his back while the others were pushed to the side so he could stretch is legs.

"Don't bother getting too comfortable, Josh." Addison said. "We won't be in here too long."

He knew what her idea of "too long" was. It didn't quite match his own so he continued moving around the packs until they were just right. "Should we be looking for anything special, Gib?" He asked. He thought Gib might still be holding some secret knowledge like he had with the been-eaten trees.

There was no secret nor did Gib have any idea what their uncle had in store for them. This lack of any specific direction didn't bother him. He was confident that he would know the sign when it came. "I'm not sure. We'll just have to keep our eyes open."

Something was different about him, Josh thought. He wasn't the same as when they first started out. His anticipation was gone. There was no drive to reach their next goal. There was no expectation of where they were going or what he thought they might find. He really didn't know what was next and, it seemed, he didn't really care.

Josh did just as Gib said. He kept his eyes open as they went along and he listened. First he noticed the Chickadees whistling their calls: deeee-dee-d-d-deeee-d-d-deeee-d-d-deee. He'd been hearing that tune ever since they arrived even at Addison's cabin. It was like the first bars of some catchy little ditty that the chickadee was waiting for someone else to finish. Every once in a while there was a reply and he imagined the two meeting up on a tree branch now that they'd found each other.

Next he listened specifically to the light trickling of water off the paddles as Gib and Addison reached forward for each new stroke. That was suddenly interrupted by an agitated squirrel letting out a long chittering warning to something that was bothering him in the woods.

There was also the whoosh of a constant breeze rustling the leaves of the trees and streaming around their branches. Its sound continued to grow as they pushed on until finally it was too loud for a simple wind; too loud when the trees weren't swaying and the lake was still.

Josh realized it was the roar of rushing water and he shifted from side to side to see around Gib for a preview of what lie ahead. After twenty minutes of thinking they were almost to it, the end of the lake disappeared behind a point of land to their right. From the course Addison steered it was obvious they would land well before the falls.

"Will we get to see the waterfall?" Josh asked hopefully.

"It's not a waterfall really, more like a really steep rapids." Addison said as they coasted to the landing. "But there are a couple places to stop along the portage."

The entrance to this trail was wide, much wider than the others they'd crossed. Gib could see how a full-sized boat could be pushed over, though he couldn't image what a chore it must have been. He was glad they wouldn't be attempting the same. His restless sleep from last night had left a stiff pain in his neck that was steadily growing more and more annoying.

As the others unloaded the canoe, Gib stood on the shore with his head tilted back while he gently massaged the kink in his neck. The warm sun beating down on his face was soothing and relaxing. There was no need to rush anymore, no need to push. He only had to be open to what was around him and open to the possibilities.

"Hey, princess." Josh hounded him. "How bout grabbin' a pack?"

Gib didn't stir. He was too busy taking it all in, enjoying the sun and the sound of falling water. When he opened his eyes, he noticed more of the stripped trees. They were scarce though, and only dotting the forest. There wasn't any pattern. There was, however, a clump of four bare birches huddled closely together off to his left - the same number as siblings in the Kearny family, he thought offhandedly. He looked back up to the sun and rubbed his neck some more. That coincidence nagged at his sensibility until he couldn't take it anymore.

Josh called after him as he watched Gib walking toward the clump of trees and away from the trail. "Where 'ya going?"

"Hold up a sec." Gib answered.

The thick trunks jutting up from the ground were spaced evenly apart. In the center, was a large smoothly textured boulder that looked oddly plain in its appearance. There wasn't a single chip or dent on it. The perfect surface was out of place, as was the perfectly consistent dull gray color. This rock showed little age. It suggested no history.

It wasn't a natural stone, Gib realized, but made to look as such, and why would someone leave such a well crafted replica of what nature had already amply provided?

He pulled away the weeds that crowded it and brushed off piles of decaying debris. It was shaped with three distinct sides that ended abruptly at a flat top. There, in the center, the exact center, was an almost perfectly round hole. It was only almost perfect because the circle was broken by a small notch.

"Heron's rock." He breathed softly. Then he shouted for the others, "This is it! Bring me the orange pack."

Josh already had the orange pack on his back and he jogged over. He was excited to see what Gib had found, until he actually saw the find. "Hey Addison, come quick. Gib found a rock."

"It's a fake rock." Gib corrected. "It's Heron's rock, from the book. It's made of cement." He spun Josh around and unbuckled the pack to get the quartz stone he found in the time capsule.

Addison begrudgingly put the canoe back down and went to join them. She knew Gib would only point it out if it was significant, but she couldn't help joining Josh in his mockery as she trotted over. "A rock, oh boy! I hope it's a real big one."

When she saw it, she noticed its peculiar shape too, but it looked unfinished. The top was missing. Gib now stood next to her holding a white rock that was triangular in shape. Its size would be a perfect compliment to complete the peak of the pyramid.

"Does that go on top?" She asked more seriously.

Gib smiled back at her. "Let's see."

He bent down and lined up the pole of the key with the hole in the rock. It fit, but only when he twisted it to align the bump on the end of the pole with the notch that accommodated it. They all watched, breathlessly waiting as he slid it all the way down.

Nothing happened, but the white cap didn't quite finish it correctly. The edges of the top didn't match those of the bottom, until he turned it. A click vibrated through the cement as the little node moved into place and released a lock.

Still nothing, though none of them knew what was supposed to happen. "In the book, didn't the rock crumble or something?" Addison asked.

Gib stared at the rock quizzically, thinking maybe they needed to do something else. "It fell apart into separate puzzle pieces."

"What's that?" Josh asked, pointing to a break in the water fifty feet out.

Gib and Addison looked over just in time to see a giant ball, at least four times the size of a basketball, bursting through the water's surface. Its long trip from the lake's bed caused it to take a short hop into the air and bobble up and down a few times before settling. Years of green algae covered some parts, but its original color was royal blue. A second broke free just after it then another and, finally the last. Four blue/green marbles swirled around on the lake's surface with the current quickly pulling them to the falls.

Addison took off running along the shore first with Gib and Josh right behind her. They pushed through the trees, careless of their footing and tripping over fallen branches in their excitement, until they came out on one of the rocky crags lining the Pipestone Falls.

The first ball freed was the first to go over. For a moment, it seemed to hang suspended on the very edge where the flat, calm water dropped into the foamy rage below. Then it was off, swept up in the powerful currents that tossed it from one converging torrent to the next. It traveled back and forth across the wide, cascading rapids on its way down to Basswood Lake far below. One after another the next three fell over and each one was thrown into a different course.

Josh backtracked to the trail. "Come on, guys." He called. Only Gib followed.

Addison hopped from ledge to ledge to keep pace with them all. The first one was already almost finished with its trip, but she wanted to watch each one on its journey down.

One of the balls caught up in a swirling eddy and Addison was mesmerized by its frantic circular dance. The water, pounding and dizzying in its flow, yielded to obstacles only when necessary, still moving forward, but making its voyage infinitely more interesting. It had direction and purpose. It had life.

A few more circles and the ball broke free, dipping into the low troughs and jumping over the high breaking peaks. She never took her eyes off it as it went down, farther and farther on toward the calm bay below – the bay where she saw Josh already walking out into the water to retrieve the first ball.

"Josh stop!" She screamed, but her voice couldn't compete with the deafening noise beside her.

Gib watched him as he waded out. He knew what Addison would say about this and though he didn't want to sound as forthright as she, he still needed to express the obvious concern. "I don't think that's such a good idea."

Josh ignored the sensible advice and went further out. They were well beyond the base of the falls and he was certain the danger was minimal, despite the strong current pushing against his legs and waist.

The water inched higher up to his stomach, but the ball was just out of arms reach. One more step and he'd have it. He found that step on a flat stone. It felt safe enough to him, but he didn't know it was covered in slick moss. His foot slipped out as he moved forward, his balance shifted and he was left vulnerable to the powerful undertow. One quick gulp of air was all he got before going under.

"Josh!" Gib yelled.

Suddenly Addison was there too, running out into the water to help, though only a few cautious steps into the water.

"Oh no." Gib gasped. "The current could have taken him anywhere. How do we find him?"

"I don't know." She said blankly.

But she did know. She just couldn't bring herself to say it out loud. She couldn't admit that they were helpless and that there was nothing to do but wait until his body resurfaced. Only then could they act and she wasn't ready. The canoe was still at the other end of the portage.

"What have they found?" Temple asked then he released the radio button to wait for Meyers' response.

"Four large balls of some kind came up from the lake. They went over a waterfall and the group is on their way to retrieve them."

"Are you still able to see them?"

"No. They left their gear on this side of the trail. We have to wait for them to clear out or we'll risk being spotted."

"Risk it." Temple ordered. "Don't let their find out of your sight. And get someone to bring me to your location."

"Yes, sir. I'll have Deek escort you."

Thirty seconds later a man with cropped orange hair sauntered up to Temple with confident swaggering strides. His face, foul looking and harsh, was covered in a rash of freckles darkened by these long days in the sun. "The group is on Pipestone Bay of Basswood Lake." He grunted. "There's a quicker route to Fall Lake from here so we won't be following the path. I can get you there inside six hours."

Temple nodded his approval and motioned for Deek to lead the way.

"Sir!" Harris shouted, as he came running up the hill. "Sir!"

"Not now, Harris."

"But I found the information you asked for."

In his hands was small stack of papers. On his face was a triumphant smile. His assignment was finished and he was impatient to show Temple his thoroughness.

"It's about time, Harris. What have you discovered?"

"The two men are from Illinois and the woman is from Cloquet, just south of here."

Temple took the neatly ordered report and carelessly flipped through it. "Gib Larkin - A history major from Illinois State. Addison Gethold is studying nursing in Duluth. And Josh Bertram – political science. They're just a bunch of kids."

Harris fidgeted anxiously as Temple quickly scanned his report. He barely read it at all and completely skimmed over the most interesting part. "They are all descendents of Gerald Kearny." He pointed out excitedly. "distant grandchildren of his siblings."

Temple ignored this fact, unsure why Harris thought it would interest him in the least, but there were several other significant points that caught his eye. "Mr. Bertram will be attending the police academy in the fall and Ms. Gethold was employed for several years by our backwoods friend, Ben Jurick."

"The girl's great grandmother is the granddaughter of Steve Kearny. She's still alive. She could be of some help to us if we…"

"Later, Harris." Temple cut in, his normally stoic face broken with a deviously gleeful smirk. "It's time to see what little trinkets we've found."

Josh didn't realize the danger at first. The sudden dunk was only a little cold and only somewhat disorienting. It wasn't until he tried to kick to the surface that he understood the seriousness of his situation. He was stuck in the undertow and the brief gulp of air was holding thin.

The current swept his body over the lake bed, twisting and turning him as it sped along. He kicked harder to free himself, but only succeeded in cracking his knee against a boulder. On his next attempt the flow caught one of his outstretched legs and sent him cart-wheeling end over end. In the spinning madness he couldn't tell which way was up and in the spinning madness he couldn't know how long this ride might last.

The jet stream rounded a massive boulder and slammed Josh sideways against it. A muffled and muted "unhh" escaped from his lungs along with the precious last of his air. Around to another big rock, turning him over again, and this time he collided head first.

His chest began to heave in its desperate need for air, but even through the pain he found the clarity to purse his lips tighter to keep from sucking water into his lungs. That, he knew, would be his end. His sight dimmed and his consciousness faded and the dark deep grew darker still.

He reached out hoping he would find the lake bottom in front of him. It wasn't there. He felt behind him and found nothing there either. Finally, to his side he felt it and he clawed at the lake bed debris as he raced past. His fingers pulled up small rocks and slipped off greasy boulders. He curled his fingers tighter and dug in harder. His nails bent back and some ripped beyond the quick until finally he caught the sharp ledge of a giant slab.

No longer tumbling along, up, he now reasoned, was the opposite of where he was now. His fingers trembled against the force of flowing water and threatened to give, but with all his desperate strength, he pulled his knees tight to his chest. He posted his feet against the slab then exploded up from his balled position to break free of the killing current. Through his foggy thoughts, as he kicked frantically for the surface, he feared that the light from above was still too far away.

Gib stood half in the water, his head sweeping from side to side as he methodically scanned its surface. Each second passed as long minutes that counted away Josh's fate. He felt helpless and he felt guilty for not having been more like Addison when he tried to warn him.

At last there was a break with a dramatic splash three hundred yards out. It was closer than he expected, after the endless wait he'd just gone through.

"Josh!" He yelled, but the only answer was the echoes of raspy, coughing gasps. He ran further up the shore, away from the falls and the current until he was sure enough that he could safely swim out to him. "Hold on, Josh!"

Awake but dazed, Josh didn't hear the distant voice. He was perfectly content to float on his back, recover, and assess the damage. A dull ache pulsed through his knee, but he was able to move it. Then he touched the stinging lump on his forehead and found blood on his fingers when he withdrew his hand. A couple of his finger tips were burning and he had lost his hat.

"You alright?" Gib called as he came upon him.

Josh looked over to him. "I lost my hat." He complained.

Gib let out a tired, breathy laugh, thankful that Josh's perspective was comparatively trivial to whatever happened below. "You can have mine. You're bleeding. Can you swim?"

"I got a little banged up, but I think I'm alright."

"Yeah, well, at least until Addison gets a hold of you."

Josh took one last deep breath then rolled onto his stomach for the swim back. "Maybe I was safer at the bottom of the lake."

They swam with leisurely kicking strides. Addison was back with the canoe. She had one leg standing in it with a paddle in hand. She was prepared to come out at the slightest sign of trouble.

Josh didn't think she looked too upset, but the closer they got the more sour her face turned. The safer he was, the more her concern eased and the angrier she became. He had escaped the wrath of the water, but there was no escaping the wrath of Addison.

"Get over here!" She commanded as soon as he started walking the rest of the way in. She connected her angry eyes with his a couple times to let him know how upset she was, but mostly she focused on the watery blood running down his face.

He hadn't even gotten all the way to shore when she came to meet him. She roughly grabbed his head and began jerking it from side to side to inspect the gash just below his hair line.

"Gib, there's a small black box attached to the bottom of my canoe seat. Get out the bandages so I can fix up the genius. Tell me Josh, just how have you managed to survive twenty-three years of such crippling stupidity?"

"Okay, that *was* pretty dumb." He conceded. "But I still think I did the right thing with the bear."

Addison pulled a bandana from one of her pockets and started drying off his face. There was nothing gentle in her attention. Her fingers pressed firmly into his skull to steady his head and her dabs at the wound were hard and stabbing. A knot had already raised under the cut and he winced each time she hit it.

She hit it often; more than necessary, Josh thought. He kept pulling away, fidgeting and looking back across the water. All of the balls had cleared the falls and were drifting far out into the bay.

"Hold still." She ordered and pushed extra hard on the bump.

"Owww." He yelped.

"Then quit moving around and let me put this bandage on."

"I'm alright, Addison. We have to go get the balls before they float too far away."

"Why are you worried about it – you're not going out to get them. I had to run across a rutted, downhill portage carrying a canoe on my back and Gib had to swim all the way out there to get you. That, my friend, earns you the fun task of catching us up. *You* will go back and get the gear from Newton and *you* will carry it all down that foot path over there to the campsite up the shore."

He looked up the shoreline to the only area open enough to be a site. It was an awful long way to carry everything. He wanted to argue, but she flashed her serious eyes to him again. She wasn't going to budge and he did deserve it, really.

"You will blah, blah, blah." Josh mocked even though there was no one around to hear him. "And you will nya, nya, nya."

He was on his third and final trip back from Newton with the last pack and the fishing poles. His head throbbed horribly as did his knee. It was probably bleeding too, but he decided not to tell Addison that. He didn't think he could endure any more of her sadistic bedside manner.

The portage widened he came back down to the Basswood side. As he turned onto the smaller path, he spotted a dense group of young balsams settling back from a frenzied quiver. He stopped and stared intently into the trees.

'It's nothing.' He thought.

In all the excitement he'd almost forgotten about the hidden things in the forest. It hit him now, all at once, and his senses flared. Something had to make the trees move in such a way, but he couldn't quite see. There was only darkness behind the outer branches and that darkness could conceal anything.

'It's just an animal.' He tried to convince himself.

Up the shore he saw the canoe was already at the campsite; Gib and Addison were at the campsite. That was comforting. Only this last trek and he'd be back there - back with his friends who were less inclined to fall victim to such silliness.

He resolved himself to move on and not let his wild imaginations get the best of him. His paranoia was resolved as well. He walked slowly past the suspicious trees, fully expecting them to move again and watching them from the corner of his eye. They stayed still, but his doubt remained even after he passed and now the other trees took on a sinister look as well. He picked up his pace to quick loping strides at first then to a brisk trot. Only when he was close to camp did he begin to feel relieved and only when the others were in sight did he forget about his concerns with fictional monsters.

Gib and Addison were listlessly ambling around the campsite, inefficient in their tasks and completely disinterested in getting things set up. Gib kicked at the edges of a tent to spread it out while Addison was retying a sloppy knot for the clothes line she was stringing up. The four balls were neatly lined up against a fallen tree that had been placed as a bench in front of the fire grate.

"It's about time." Addison said when she saw Josh. She forgot about the rope and hopped over to the bench.

Gib perked up too. "Here." He said as he tossed his hat over to Josh.

Josh wasn't ready just yet. His clothes were still soaked. His first priority was to change into something dry. When Addison saw him heading for the tent, she realized they were going to have to wait even longer and she gave him a long, aggravated sigh. It only motivated him to move slower.

He pulled out four shirts before picking one and the specific shorts he wanted were buried at the very bottom of the pack. Finding the right socks proved just as complicated. The tan hat Gib gave him was much stiffer than his lost one so he spent a few minutes rolling the bill around with his hands.

"Josh!" Addison snapped.

Only then he did he come out of the tent. Only after he knew he'd gotten Addison a little riled up did he join them over at the fire.

Gib rolled over one of the balls. One of the lighter ones, Addison noted. She knew which one was likely to hold the stones. It was the one that had sat lowest in the water, the last ball that popped up from the bottom of Newton, and the one that didn't bounce through the falls quite so freely as the others. That was the only one with enough weight to hold two heavy stones. They all knew, so why was he waiting?

'He's *that* kinda guy.' She thought with a smirk. He was the kid at his birthday party who saved the biggest present for last even though he knew exactly what was in it and even though it was the one present he wanted most. The anticipation and the suspense was every bit as important, and as valuable, as the prize. She resigned herself to the fact that the one ball that mattered most would certainly be the last one opened. Though, if she judged correctly, his first choice was the second heaviest.

Gib rolled around the moss covered ball inspecting it for an easy opening that he really didn't expect to find. It had been securely sealed to protect it from its wait at the bottom of the lake. What he couldn't figure out was how it had been sealed and how his uncle had placed whatever treasure it held inside. That little mystery was perhaps even more intriguing than what was waiting to be revealed. Addison didn't let him spend too much time unraveling it.

"Gib." She said nudging him with her hand, quieter than she had been when prodding Josh and now with a hushed reverence as she passed him her knife.

He pierced the rubber shell and a stream of air hissed out. The ball crumpled and deflated until its shape was held only by what was inside. Gib slipped two of his fingers into the slit and gently pulled apart the skin. Tightly packed wads of wrinkled brown paper fell away to reveal a colorful glass replica of a north woods cabin.

"It's stained glass." Addison said. "Was it made by Gerald?"

"Yes." Gib answered immediately.

She wondered how he could be so certain, but she was far too captivated with the piece to really care. The pitched roof was done with swirling green glass and there was even a red brick chimney attached. The walls were of smoky brown and its framed windows of the palest yellow. Each seam was held together with lines of silvery lead and black paint had been used to detail the shake siding. The feel of it suggested warmth and simplicity, but it wasn't exactly the traditional style cabin she knew. The front was dominated by windows with an unusual column of rounded windows running straight up the middle. It was like nothing she'd ever seen before.

On the back, was a small black switch and though she doubted any batteries left inside would still have life, she just couldn't resist. It brightened, but the light was barely noticeable against the day. A few seconds later the batteries' charge faded. Now, she wished she had waited until nightfall to try it. Without asking the others, she picked it up to look for the battery case.

Gib allowed her to take it as he moved on to the next ball. More brown paper hid a wood carving of a leafless oak tree. Elegant in its plainness, the smooth wood glowed in a rich caramel brown. Four arms split off from a thick trunk and more arms split off of those further along, growing up and out to a round top of crisscrossing branches. The trunk and lower branches held the names of the original Kearny family. The parents were written on the trunk and the children on each of the four main arms. Spouses and children were labeled as well and even a great-grandchild in one case. The rest was bare and waiting to be filled in.

It was beautiful and simple, but Josh found something more interesting about it. The four tiered base the tree sat on had a line of tiny knobs, each one attached to a different level. "What are those for?" He asked.

Gib grabbed the top knob with his finger tips and pulled. A disk of the wood pulled away from the base until it came completely free. On it, on both sides of it, was writing that showed the names of more people. Aunts, uncles, and cousins, grandparents and great-grandparents; all of them were relatives of the Kearny family and they were listed in tight, little lettering.

Gib's eyes got wide as he pulled out the next disc. "I can't believe it." He gasped.

Addison leaned over to look. "They look like genealogy records."

"They are." Gib answered. "They're Norm Kearny's records. Late in his life he got really deep into his family history. He traveled all across the country to do his research. Christine had a copy of *some* of his stuff, but no one knows where the rest went. This is it - the names and birth dates of everyone he found."

"*All* of them?" Josh said disbelievingly.

Gib looked at the last disc and searched for the earliest date. "As far back as the seventeen hundreds."

Gib's own research only went back to the early twentieth century; to the records recent enough to be transferred into computer databases. Anything before that could only be found in old record rooms filled with endless rows of boxes. That's where he stopped. He could study these discs for hours, matching these names to those that he already knew. He would, but he would wait until he got them home to compare them with what he had.

The next ball, the lightest, held a number of colorful figurines that were intricately blown in delicate glass. Each one represented a season. First was a cheerful scarecrow nailed to a post among a field of eared cornstalks. The two black crows perched on his left arm were obviously not intimidated by his jovial presence.

The next one was a young boy in baggy denim overalls standing on a grassy shore. His face was strained with his tongue stuck out the side of his mouth as he pulled up on a heavily arched cane fishing pole. Beside him sat a flop-eared dog with its black, white and tan face anxiously waiting to see the catch. Spring was shown through an elderly woman in a wide brimmed hat and gloved hands sitting in a garden of vibrant purple and red tulips.

All were incredibly detailed in their painting, but the simplest one pleased Josh the most. A glittering, chubby black bear clung to a brown tree stump partially covered with snow. Tangled in a rope of colored lights, its coppery face smiled mischievously. This was the true nature of bears, Josh thought, unlike their recent experience. In this wild north where bears rule the forest with their imposing presence, he thought this a perfect winter ornament to adorn a Christmas tree.

Finally they were to the last ball and Gib rolled it toward him. It lurched forward along the ground as something heavier inside rolled too. There was no packaging in this one. This one was not so delicate. Josh and Addison put down the lesser treasures and watched as Gib picked up the ball and slowly peeled apart the skin.

A round, clear stone fell out, hit the dirt with a dull thud and rolled a little way along the uneven ground before coming to rest between them. It was five inches round and polished just as expected, but it wasn't the same as described in Kearny's book. It was a crystal with a milky white core; a quartz like the top of the pyramid that released it, but more pristine and refined. The grooves were there with deep flows of gold lines twisting around its transparent surface.

Captivated by the reality of it, none of them spoke. None of them could find words exciting enough to describe the moment or magnificent enough to describe the stone. After a hundred years of searching by thousands of people, they were the ones to succeed.

Gib took it and held it up to the sky to allow the sun light to filter through. The core fascinated him most. Slivers of white spikes shot outward from its center like an explosion caught in time - a spectacle of nature's complex design forever held within its center. He turned it and the sun refracted the brilliant colors of a prism through the geometry inside. They gave the stone depth and life.

Josh, his disbelief fading and his speech returning, whispered softly, "It's not green."

"It wouldn't be." Gib answered, his voice soft, but steady and with absolute certainty. He never expected them to be emerald. Even on his first reading of the book, when he was just a young boy, he couldn't picture the stones in emerald green. He didn't know why, but it just didn't seem to fit. In the years following, as he learned more of his uncle, he became even more certain of this conclusion. In the midst of all his riddles, Gerald wouldn't leave the biggest of them to something so obvious.

Gib realized he was being selfish and he held the stone out for the others to inspect. Addison got it before Josh could. It was heavy, much heavier than she expected and she cupped it with both hands as if afraid to drop it.

"Where's the other one?" She gasped.

Gib's eyes twinkled as he watched her studying the surface of the stone. He said nothing until she finally took her eyes off it. He wanted her full attention for the cryptic clue he was about to give.

"Gib?" She pushed.

His eyes beamed with an almost smug delight then he pointed at the stained glass house. "It's there."

She looked at the replica of the cabin then back at Gib. She cocked her head to the side and raised one eyebrow.

She wasn't about to play this little guessing game. The irritated smirk she gave him demanded a clearer answer.

Gib gave in immediately. "Or, it's somewhere around there. That is modeled after Gerald's cabin on the north shore."

"Really?!" Josh gawked, forgetting about the stone and turning his attention back to the house.

Addison wasn't so startled, or at least she didn't show it. She stayed still and unaffected with her thumbs rubbing across the smooth surface of the stone. She thought that his answer came too easily and too quickly. "You already knew that, didn't you? You knew it even before we started this trip. You didn't tell us."

"Not for sure," Gib lied. "Not until I saw the cabin. But it makes the most sense. The Kearny's lives went on even after this place was taken away and Gerald would want to show that. Just like Archer's family in the book, the Kearny's went on to develop new traditions and new memories. They adapted in the face of adversity. Their lives were as full and rich, just in different ways."

Gib paused for a breath then spoke more slowly. "That is why I already have the cabin rented for two weeks."

"No way!" Josh croaked excitedly. "Really, we're going to his cabin?"

Addison was excited too, but she wasn't ready to show it. Instead she teasingly challenged him on his highly confident foresight. "And yet you didn't know for sure until you saw that little cabin?"

Gib smiled back.

He had manipulated them, she thought. It was with good intentions, but it was a manipulation just the same. She wasn't angry about it, but she wasn't about to let him get away with it so easily either. "So why'd you wait to spring this on us?"

"I wanted it to be a surprise. Besides, what would you have said if I had told you earlier?"

She wanted to believe she would have said something gently discouraging. More likely it would have been sarcastically disparaging. She had never shown an interest in Gerald's cabin before. Her friends had suggested a visit on several occasions, but she always feigned arrogant disinterest. In doing so, she somehow felt above this little mystery of Gerald's that didn't really apply to her. Now she was excited though, and the surprise of it was a nice touch.

On the western ridge of Pipestone bay, Meyers knelt among the bushes waiting for Deek to arrive with Temple. He knew they were getting close, he had heard them. Sloppy, he thought with distinct annoyance. Not only on Temple's part, who wasn't trained in the art of covert surveillance, but also from Deek who certainly did know better. He would have to remind him about the importance of being diligent in his movements, though he wouldn't be too harsh with his reminder. He had almost been caught himself when he was in the trees watching the shorter kid on the portage.

Standing beside him, a short man with his face painted green and brown was camouflaged perfectly among the foliage. He was keeping a watchful eye on the kids across the bay through a set of high-powered binoculars. Stunted and brawny, he stayed unmoving even from the commotion of their new arrivals. If their position was revealed through carelessness, it would not be by Walsh.

"Report." Temple whispered.

Meyers handed his binoculars over to Temple. "The four balls contained different things, but only one stone. At least, I think it was the stone. It has the same gold lines, but it's clear instead of emerald. It looks to be about the right size."

"Gemstone?" Temple asked, curiously hopeful.

"I couldn't tell, sir. Certainly too big for a diamond."

"Only one, though?"

"Yes, sir."

Temple sighed, long and exasperated. He'd been brought out here for nothing.

In the story the stones were found together and through them the main character was reunited with his lost family. "*Two from one and each of the other, finding their way back together.*" Temple mumbled, quoting a line from the book. The symbolism had been reversed and that was not at all surprising, though he did think Harris should have caught it before this. He should have prepared him.

"What, sir?" Meyers asked.

"Nothing. What about the other balls? Was there anything valuable inside them?"

"Nothing special as far as I can tell. Some sort of wood carving, a house made of colored glass, and four small statues of some kind. I suppose they could have some possible value."

Perhaps, but Temple thought that was getting ahead of themselves. The stones were his goal. They were the prize, and the second was most certainly hidden just as cleverly. "Alright. They've set up camp for the night. Alert me if anything unusual happens. In the morning you will stick close to them and give me regular updates. Have your men ready to move the base camp in case they come back through. Stay only close enough to keep them in sight. If they take notice of you, hold back and pretend to be fishing."

Meyers nodded his understanding. "Walsh will take you back. Deek, you'll stay with me."

Walsh slipped away between the trees, quietly and without disruption to the branches. The right way, Meyers noted.

"What if they catch onto us?" Deek asked before Temple left.

Meyers rolled his eyes in frustration. Deek's question was a plan for failure and not the sort of question Temple would entertain, even if it was only a back-up plan.

"Do whatever is necessary to stay with them." Temple answered, surprisingly not angrily.

"What about the one with the taser gun." Meyers asked.

"When the time comes, I want him killed immediately."

"It's only a tazer gun." Deek said arrogantly and foolishly, and a little too loud. "It's not a problem."

Temple's stern, angry eyes pierced through him and suddenly Deek's cocky attitude melted away. "I said I want him killed. We don't need some rookie playing the hero and causing problems. The taller one must not be hurt…and keep the girl alive for leverage."

As soon as Temple was gone, Meyers gave Deek a firm whack on the back of his neck and snarled at him. With a silent hand gesture he motioned for him to set up the tent.

CHAPTER 11

"It's Basswood." Addison whined, emphasizing the lake's name as if its mere mention would invoke some deep reverence in them. "You don't come to Basswood and not fish it."

She'd been pleading her case since they first woke up and all through breakfast. Gib hemmed and hawed whenever she brought it up, but he had already secretly decided there was plenty of time for a little fishing. Putting her off was only a bit of harmless torture. Josh knew he was having some fun at her expense and each time Gib avoided her question Josh cracked a private little smile at him.

"Just for the morning, I promise." She said. Then, cleverly, "Gerald would want us to fish it."

Her last desperate comment was too much. "Alright." Gib relented with a long, drawn sigh. "I guess we can for the morning."

Josh snorted back a chuckle then quickly dropped his head to hide his silent laughter. She caught him just before he covered himself and she understood what he found so funny. One pancake was left on her plate. She carefully picked it up and called Gib's name as she whipped the last of her breakfast at his head.

Her timing couldn't have been better. He turned and was smacked directly in the face with the soggy, syrupy mess. This time Josh's laughter came out booming and unrestrained.

She kept them on the bay the entire morning, circling the base of the falls and hitting every spot likely to hold fish. Their luck was only fair on this warm sunny day, but Addison stubbornly kept at it. At one o'clock, they lunched back at the campsite where she informed them that as an additional atonement for their earlier game, part of their afternoon would be spent fishing the length of Newton as well. Her grudge stayed strong even through Fall Lake.

From his cushy spot in the middle of the canoe, Josh grew more and more restless as the day went on. First, he sat with his arm over the side, twirling small circles in the water with his fingers and watching the ripples as they fanned out across the water. On several occasions Addison had to point out to him that his fishing lure was only a few feet below the surface.

After that, he started shifting around more and more frequently in his seat. Sometimes he would twist all the way around when he wanted to talk to her, instead of remaining forward and just talking like he usually did. Other times he would tilt his head all the way back until he was looking at her upside down. He also kept switching lures throughout the day even though he didn't need to and each time he had to turn around for the tackle box between her feet.

Now, Addison watched as he turned around again and began rummaging through the pack he was using for a back rest. She didn't know what he was looking for and he apparently wasn't able to find it. Until today, she hadn't seen him so fidgety.

"Your butt starting to hurt, Josh?" She asked, though there was not even a hint of sincerity to her question. Her full concentration was on the tip of her fishing pole. His constant movement was distracting.

"No."

"You getting bored?" She asked again, just as callously.

"No."

"Then be a good boy and sit still or I'll tie you to the yolk."

Gib laughed. Josh only rolled his eyes. He had his reasons for moving around so much. He was just waiting for the right opportunity to tell them. He waited a few moments then decided it was time. "I'm checking on the guys that have been following us for the last four hours."

"What?" Addison scoffed as she twisted around to see behind her. "What are you talking about?"

"Don't look at 'em!" He snapped back softly. "They just went behind that second island back there. There are two men in a canoe. They've been behind us since Newton. They disappear every once in a while into some bay, but they always show up again. It's like they're trying to stay just close enough to keep us in sight."

"Maybe they're from the forest service or something." Gib offered.

"No." Addison countered. "They wouldn't bother with us for so long. They're probably just campers, Josh. Let it go."

Probably, but Gib couldn't help thinking it a little strange as well. "Do you think they could be drug runners?"

Josh had been thinking that since he first noticed them. He thought about the possible danger in stumbling across a drug transaction and he thought about how easy it would be to get away with murder in this remote area. The bodies could be dumped anywhere and no one would ever find them. It would be simple, he thought, but he kept that to himself.

"Maybe." Josh replied. "Basswood shares the border with Canada. It would be the perfect place to make a drop."

"Knock it off, guys." Addison ordered, now frustrated with their nagging suspicions. "We're not the only campers in the forest."

"You said not many people come in this far." Josh argued.

That was true, she thought. Not many people did make it this far, but some did and on a pretty regular basis.

"They also have only one pack." He added. "How can you come in this far with only one pack?"

Addison huffed out a frustrated sigh at his persistence. "They've probably got a base camp on Basswood and just came here for the day. People do it all the time; pack a lunch and go exploring the other lakes. You guys are just being paranoid."

"And they just happen to be fishing the same path we are?" Josh continued. "For four hours?"

She ignored his last comment, but his efforts were not without effect. She discreetly turned the canoe in a slow trolling circle and kept a sly watch as she waited for a clear line of sight.

The canoe was there, but only briefly before steering further behind the island. There was only one pack, just as Josh had pointed out, but she already had a good explanation for that. The man in back did not have a fishing pole, at least not one she could see, and that did seem odd - explainable, but odd nonetheless. The strangest thing, the thing she knew from her vast experience with this lake, was the spot they had chosen to fish. It was only about three feet deep.

"They might just be part of a scouting troop or something." She said out loud, more to herself than the others. Her words weren't so certain this time and now she too was getting sucked in to Josh's suspicion.

"What should we do?" Gib asked.

Addison thought for a moment. "We keep fishing and we keep in mind that they probably have no interest in us whatsoever. We'll head down to the other end of the lake. There's an easier portage to get back to Garden. Maybe we'll camp there instead."

"If they're really just campers, couldn't they also be heading down to Garden?" Josh asked. "Maybe we could go a different way and see if they still follow us?"

"One step at a time, Josh. If they're still with us at the other end, we'll decide what to do next. We can take the river that connects Fall with Shagawa, if we have to. Hardly anyone uses that passage. After that, we'll start worrying."

She kept their pace casual, or as casual as she could without wasting too much more of the day. Her plan was to bounce from reef to reef, just as she would if they were really fishing, but she often found herself steering a straight course to the other end. They passed the inlet that led to the Garden Lake portage and were now approaching the mouth of Shagawa River.

Blood Stones

"This is our last chance to look for a while, Josh. Are they still with us?"

Josh raised his arms up with a deep, stretching yawn and twisted his upper torso as if trying to loosen his back. "Still there and they've passed the portage for Garden. What now?"

"Relax." Addison answered. "We still don't know if they're after us. Shagawa is a popular lake with a lot of big fish. For all we know, they came up here from Shagawa and are just making their way back."

"And if they're not?" He asked suggestively, even more certain that this was no coincidence.

"We've got options from there if they are still following us." She answered. "But just in case, you might want to get that taser gun ready."

"Ohhh, so now my little toy gun is your friend." He said.

"Just get it out."

"Sorry. It's useless. I needed the entire charge to save your butt from the bear."

She vaguely remembered asking about that after the bear incident. After some quiet thought, she distinctly remembered him dodging the question.

Temple's angry voice boomed through the receiver in Meyers' ear. "What's happening?"

First Meyers had radioed his men at base camp and told them to be ready for the kids to come their way. Then he radioed again and said to wait, then another time to tell them to forget the order. Temple heard it all. The contradictions were a sign of chaos and poor judgment and that simply was not acceptable.

"I thought they were headed back to Garden," Meyers answered. "but they passed the portage and are going to the end of the lake."

"They know you're following them." Temple assumed coldly.

"Sir, they've shown no interest in us all day. We've been very careful and we've..."

"Where are they now?" Temple interrupted impatiently as he stomped over to the table where Harris was rereading the book. To him, he mouthed the words "the map".

"They just entered a small river at the south end." Meyers came back. "It leads to a lake called Shagawa."

Harris unrolled the map and waited. He wasn't equipped with one of the high-tech radio sets like all the others. He wasn't important enough to be plugged in to their conversation and, truth be told, that was just fine with him.

"Hold your position." Temple ordered. He slid his finger along the map until he located the river Meyers spoke of. He tapped it twice to show Harris.

Harris understood his question immediately. "They could be heading out by way of Burntside Lake." He offered, tracing a route of loosely connected waterways that lead over to the town of Tower.

"Perhaps." Temple admitted, though he thought it a slim possibility. "Or they're trying to throw us off. Could the other stone be somewhere along that route?"

In the pressure of the moment Harris answered quickly, spitting out a rationale strangely confident compared to his normal waver. "Unlikely. Kearny had some friends on a couple lakes around there, but no family – nothing to tie him there."

"How about the old town site?"

"No." Harris said emphatically. "The themes of his story support family and tradition. He most certainly would have viewed the moving of Old Ely as challenges to both of those. It could possibly be there as a reference to revisiting ones roots, but that would be a rather obscure form of symbolism for Kearny. The old town is likely the last place he'd hide the second stone."

Temple watched him closely as he spoke. This is when he truly valued Harris' opinion; when he was completely engrossed in a mystery and unaffected by anything outside. This is when he knew Harris was on the right track. Another possibility crossed Temple's mind and he looked closer at the map. "Could they be heading out the way we came? White Iron?"

Harris studied the map for a moment, but couldn't find any connection that would take them back to the route that had brought them in. "The closest point between Shagawa and White Iron looks to be at least two miles and the map doesn't show any trails between them."

Temple hated not knowing their intentions, but he also believed time was on his side. "Whatever the case, they haven't got much more than a couple hours before nightfall. They will have to set camp on Shagawa."

"Or hike through the woods in the dark." Harris added.

"Fall back, Meyers." Temple ordered. "Don't meet them on the river. Give them time to get out then verify their position on Shagawa discreetly. And keep me updated."

This river, with its twists and turns, wasn't as exciting for Josh anymore. It was daunting now and dangerous. Walls of tall green reeds lined both shores. It was a perfect place for someone to hide and follow. The river's course wound wildly and nearly looped back over itself in several places. Its constant curves made it impossible for him to know how far ahead they were. Their suspicious guests could be there, holding back just before the last bend and close enough to strike.

He didn't think the others fully appreciated that. There was anxiety in their idle chatter, heartier laughs at comments that weren't really that funny and neither allowed any uncomfortable silence to last for long. But there was also playfulness and levity. For now that was fine, but Josh knew this river between Fall and Shagawa was short and they were almost out.

Their current topic, minnows versus leeches for the best fishing, had been going on for twenty minutes. Addison began to wind down her tedious explanation about the shape and movement of leeches in the water, enough for Josh to solemnly bring them back to the more urgent matter. "What will we do when we get to Shagawa?"

Addison was still unwilling to completely abandon her optimism. "We still don't know if they even came this way. Maybe they were just heading down to fish the river mouth. Or they could still be coming back to a campsite here."

"How will we know?" Gib interrupted. "It's getting late. If they do come this way, we won't have much time to paddle on to the next lake."

Despite all her rationalizing and downplaying, she did have an answer. There was thought given to it. "We'll head over to Miners Lake, right behind Shagawa. It's a dead lake so no one would have any reason to go there."

Josh cranked his neck around to look at her, also past her. "What do you mean a dead lake?"

"It's a mine pit from when they used to dig for iron ore up here. There are a couple of them around the area, but that one's the largest and deepest. They've been filled with water since the mid-twentieth century. They're dead because they don't have any fish in them any more."

"Any more?" Josh asked.

"They did once, but when the town was ordered to move, the state allowed Miners Lake and the other pits to be used as dumps. Anything that wouldn't pollute the environment was bulldozed in - mostly torn up pieces of roads, houses and frames of buildings."

"They just pushed everything in there?" Gib gawked.

"Pretty much. The lake used to be over a hundred feet deep. I've heard that now there are some places where the debris is just a few feet below the surface."

"Have you ever been there?" Gib asked again.

"Only in the winter, when it was iced over. There's a trail that the dog-sledders use that cuts across from White Iron to Shagawa."

Josh didn't remember seeing any lake behind Shagawa when he looked earlier and he reached again for the map. Addison knew just what he was thinking. "You won't find it, Josh. The lake is a hazard and the DNR doesn't want anyone going in there. It's not on any maps."

Gib, now completely fascinated, "So nobody really knows about it."

"Locals do." She answered. "I know a guy who used to travel it in the summer when he wanted to fish Shagawa without paddling all the way around the White Iron chain. He said the water is crystal clear and always flat, even on windy days. He called it a window into the tortured past of Ely."

"Is there a portage to it?" Gib asked.

"From Shagawa, not really. Just a small break in the trees no one would notice. There are a couple trails you can pick up just past the lake that go to White Iron; pretty good ones really, but the DNR doesn't list any of the trails around Old Ely. I thought it was spooky in the winter. My friend said it was just plain creepy in the summer."

Josh huffed cynically, "You make it sound like its haunted or something."

"Well…" Addison hinted. "There are stories about an eight year old boy drowning in the lake during the restructuring."

Josh didn't ask for clarification. He didn't want it and they certainly didn't need it in their current situation. Gib, however, couldn't resist. "How?"

"They say he was trapped in one of the trailer homes when it was dumped into the lake. The guy that was operating the bull dozer saw him in a window just as it sank away into the deep."

Josh sighed and rolled his eyes, already spotting the implausibility of an urban legend. "I don't suppose there was an obituary or something to confirm this?"

"I'm not sure." Addison admitted candidly. "But just about every one in Ely says they know the family it happened to."

Josh countered her again. "And of course the boy's parents just happened to be so stupid as to leave him alone when all the houses were being dragged to a dump."

She had an answer for that too. "As the story goes, theirs was the first house to go in that neighborhood. And the parents had gone to Tower to try to get a court order to stop them."

Even more implausibility, Josh thought, but he let the inconsistencies of that explanation go and turned to the next most obvious question. "And the poor kid just couldn't figure out how to get out of the house during that whole time they were pushing it over to the lake?"

"Well, I always heard that he had some type of developmental disability." Addison explained. "Anyway, when the bulldozer operator saw the boy in the window, he was so distraught with grief that he dove into the lake, swimming farther and farther down to save the little boy in the window. He never came back up."

"Well, yes." Josh scoffed. "Otherwise it wouldn't be a good story. And somehow there's probably no written account of his great heroic efforts either."

They were quiet then, as they headed out into the new lake. Josh was especially so as he continued analyzing and tearing apart the silly tale. But his sensibility wasn't so confident in his brooding thoughts and soon each disjointed fact had at least a hint of plausibility.

The story was creeping up on him as his imagination created images to match the details – trying to make it fit no matter how hard he argued against it. He pictured a white trailer home with a brown roof drifting down to the bottom of the lake and a gritty man in faded jeans and white t-shirt following after it. He even put a pale face to the boy in the window. He pictured him with stringy blond hair and wide, horrified eyes staring up to a sky he would never see again.

The outlet of the river opened into a bay and Josh peeked around Addison once more. A flash of sun reflected off something shiny in the brush, beyond the last turn of the river and too high up for the evening sun to be bouncing off the water line. His eyes widened for only a split second – just long enough for Addison to see and to understand what it meant.

"They're coming out?" She asked.

"No." He answered solemnly. "They're back behind the reeds."

"Stopped?" She asked doubtfully.

Josh discreetly looked again. "Yep, just sitting there."

There was no rationale to easily explain that away. There was no good reason for them to be waiting other than the obvious one she still refused to admit. The option they were left with, the only reasonable one was the one Addison really hoped to avoid. Her skin turned cold at the thought of passing through Old Ely.

Gib rested his paddle over his lap as the canoe coasted into the southern shore. The "break in the trees" Addison had referenced earlier was a very generous assessment. They were no farther apart than any of the other random forest growth. There was a clear line into the woods, but any existing foot trail was completely hidden by a thick cover of fanning ferns.

"Where are they, Josh?" Addison asked.

Josh stole another look back. "They're out of the river mouth now, into the bay."

"Fishing?" She added hopefully.

"No. Both paddling, and at a pretty good clip – not right at us, but this general direction. What's the plan?"

She barely heard his question. She had purposely slowed their pace on the last crossing to give the men one last chance to come out and pass them; to prove that their interest was in some place further down the lake. Obviously they didn't want to pass.

"Addison?" Josh prodded again.

Her answer was sudden and blunt. "We'll go over and camp on White Iron, just to be safe."

It didn't sound like much of a plan to Josh, just extending what he thought was inevitable. "And just hope they don't catch up to us?"

"There are two trails we can pick up after Miners. Gib and I will take the canoe over the shorter one. You will take the bulk of the gear down the longer one."

"No way!" Gib suddenly snapped as he pulled the canoe higher on shore. "We're not splitting up."

"We'll move faster, Gib." Josh answered calmly and firmly. "We have to. They're traveling lighter than us. Hopefully they won't know we've split up and they'll have to carry their canoe down the longer trail after me. I should be able to outrun them easily."

Gib plopped down hard on the front of the canoe and waited for them to come out. "Hopefully." He echoed sourly. "And if they don't?"

Josh grabbed two packs and walked out of the canoe. "I'll make sure they do." He answered suggestively.

Addison then stepped out of the canoe with the map in hand. "Okay. Miner's is a real thin lake so it won't take us long to cross. We'll do a hard paddle across to give Gib and I more time with the canoe."

"And I'll hang back and wait until they come out." Josh added. "Then I'll make sure they see me going on one trail."

"Yes." She said quietly, glad that he had the same thought and glad that he offered it before she did.

She pointed out the two routes before going on, each one covered large spans of land. "Both trails meet up with White Iron. The shorter one comes out at this small creek, here. The longer one goes through part of the old town and lets out in this bay, here."

Gib tried to follow, but got stuck as soon as he saw how far they would be traveling. "Can we make that before nightfall?"

"I think so." Addison answered. "We'll really have to hoof it, though. Josh, we'll pick you up somewhere around here. I'm not exactly sure where the trail comes out."

"We should lighten the packs if we can." Josh suggested.

"After we've crossed Miners, I'll hide any gear we don't need in the woods. We'll drop one of the tents, the fishing poles, a sleeping bag and any food we don't need. That should get us down to just two packs. Gib and I will take one and you'll take the other."

Gib took up a pack and the fishing poles and quietly started up the path. He didn't wait for the others to finish their plans. Their solution wasn't his choice, but this game of cat and mouse didn't suit him. It blurred his focus and jumbled his thoughts. In the face of danger, he wasn't so sure of himself. In the face of danger, he felt safer relying on the others.

The forest was different here. It was uncomfortable and tight. Everything felt closer and more crowded and the air around him was thick and humid. The tree branches that once reached out to him now seemed more intent on blocking his way. The short, firm needles of the smaller jack pines scratched at his face and tugged at his clothes. He wasn't welcome any longer.

The new lake was unlike any he'd seen before, beautiful really, but severe and unnatural. A treacherous shoreline of dramatic red cliffs dropped straight down into brilliant icy green water. The lake bed didn't gently slope to a deeper middle. The men of old Ely had carved it straight down. Looking across, there was only one place level enough for them to climb out on the other side, still steep, but probably passable enough even with a canoe.

Josh came out of the woods, also quiet and also feeling unsettled. The little boy's face was persistent and would not allow his thoughts to wander too far from his attention. At the shore, he kicked a rock into the water and slowly counted as he watched it sink. Twenty-seven, before he lost sight of it and had it any real size he could have followed it even longer.

Farther out from shore, the deep was darker with a grayish hue. That's where the town was now. That's where the houses had been sunk, if they really had been sunk as Addison said. They were about to cross right over them. She came off the trail with the canoe and in five minutes they were back in the water again.

The keel slicing through the smooth glassy surface barely disrupted it at all and made it too easy to see everything below. To their right, in the distance, Josh saw peaked piles of cement slabs sitting as a scaled down version of a majestic mountain range. Closer, a field of twisted electrical towers and broken telephone poles poked up to the surface, threatening to tear a hole in any craft sitting too low in the water.

It was divided into sections, he realized. The town had been dismantled systematically and dumped in different piles. A pile of broken wooden banisters, some still attached to chunks of stairs, was the last thing he allowed himself to look at. That image was too residential and too close to the one thing he didn't want to see. He turned his sight to the shore and the trail that would lead them out, determined not to see any more of old Ely.

Gib and Addison made it impossible. Their constant wowing and calling of each other's attention to each new spectacle taunted him and dared him to look. "Look at all those old mail boxes." Gib said.

"They were one of the last things to go." Addison said. "The mail kept on going right up to the very last day."

Next they glided over a stack of long metal poles, some with traffic lights attached to the top, others with street lights. It wasn't all of them from the old town, just the ones the demolition crews needed until the end. "Those too." Addison said. "You can almost picture how they would have stood on the streets. This really is like a window to the past."

Josh didn't think so. He saw it as more of a tomb dourly displaying the rotting bones of Old Ely to anyone morbid enough to look. He still refused to do so until Gib pointed out a heap of old gas station signs and pumps just coming under them.

The huge plastic signs, once colorful and eye-catching, were now faded and broken. Josh recognized only a few of the shapes, the symbols of those companies that had successfully adapted to modern energy markets. Outlines of letters could be seen on the others, but cracks and holes made them impossible to name. They were reminders of a time he often dreamed about, when loud cars and motorcycles ruled the road before the more environmentally, and less powerful, vehicles took over.

Next, before he could divert his eyes, came the distinct inverted "v" of a rooftop. The house, with its walls bloated out and skewed cockeyed, were sided in white panels. He wanted to look away, he told himself to look away, but the house was just too much of a mystery to ignore. It sat, precariously tilted on the edge of a cement pile, looking as if it would slide off the downward slope with the slightest touch.

It was someone's life from a time long ago now sitting underwater. It could have been the little boy's life, except his was supposed to be the first house in and should have been on the bottom – if Addison was right. A large living room window revealed dark hints of what its interior once looked like. One shudder hanging only by its top hinge still framed the opening and an empty flower box was still attached to the bottom sill. Just inside, a swath of light colored wallpaper wafted in the slowest motion of a faint current.

Inside, darker, a trick of the light from the setting sun illuminated a blurry white form. More wallpaper maybe, or a reflection of the window's glass, or perhaps, a pale face. Josh jerked back suddenly and unexpectedly. His weight shifted and the canoe dipped down to the far side, tipping it to within an inch of the water's surface.

"Hey!" Addison hollered as she shifted her own weight to counter.

Gib shifted too and now they rolled to the other side, nearly going over that way. Addison jammed her paddle flat against the water and pushed down, saving them and rocking them back the other way again. They wobbled three more times before settling.

"What was that about?" Addison yelled.

Josh didn't answer. He couldn't. First he had to verify what he knew he could not have seen; what he knew was impossible. But they were already over the top of the house, past the window and past any chance for him to disprove his foolish imagination. "I just…um, nothing. I just thought I saw something."

"Well then quit looking." She scolded and gave the side of his head a firm knock with the blade of her paddle. "Or we'll be swimming to the other side of the lake."

Blood Stones

"Sorry." He said absently, looking back again to the house. He kept looking back even after they landed on the far shore, even after he couldn't see the house any longer.

Gib and Addison carried all the gear up to the top of the hill while Josh followed with the canoe. The hard-packed ground was covered in dusty reddish gravel that slid out from under his feet as he made his way up. In two places the incline was so steep that he actually had to put one hand down on the ground to steady himself.

"Hey mom," He said out loud and jokingly. "guess what I did on vacation. I scaled a cliff with a canoe on my back." The others didn't hear him.

At the top, Gib thought this side of the lake was even less inviting than the other. There were barely any real trees at all. The only height of the new landscape came from dense, scraggly brush and tall berried weed-trees. One main path cut through the tangled mess. Another smaller one sprouted off to the east. It was the one Gib and Addison would be using and it was overgrown with grass that would be waste deep even for a taller person. Josh's walked right past it and past Gib and Addison who were there waiting.

"Hold up, Josh." Addison called. "You just passed our trail."

Josh kept on walking, further along the clearer trail as he searched for the right spot. Addison and Gib followed after him calling his name again and again until he stopped.

"What are you doing?" Addison asked.

Josh eased the canoe off his shoulders and gently lowered it to the ground. He still couldn't do it as effortlessly or gracefully as Addison, but he was getting better at it. "You guys can't start back there. They'll see your tracks through the grass. This is all brush around here. You can push through without leaving any sign and meet up with the other path."

Smart thinking, Gib thought, but he could take that logic farther and perhaps keep them all together. "Then why don't we all do that and stay together?"

Josh already had this thought out. "Because it wouldn't take them long to figure out what we did once they weren't able to catch up to us. Or if there's grass further up my trail, they'd be suspicious if there weren't tracks. Trust me, Gib. This is out safest bet."

Gib realized there'd be an answer for every point he could make so he gave up the argument. He wasn't happy about it though, and he made that obvious by turning away from Josh without another word. He hooked his hand under the front seat of the canoe and waited for Addison to grab the back.

"Don't leave me waiting too long over there." Josh joked uneasily. "The bugs might suck me dry and leave you guys with nothing but a pile of skin and bones to carry back."

His levity brought a faint smile to Gib's face. He turned back to Josh, "We'd make better time in the canoe without the extra weight."

Addison chimed in cheerily, "Yeah, but we would have one less person to help us carry on the portages. I'll be back for our pack after I get Gib going."

She picked up her end of the canoe and together she and Gib began pushing it through the entwined branches.

Josh went back to gather the gear they didn't need and hid it deep in the bushes. After that he went back to wait for Addison by the two remaining packs.

The cliff over-looking the lake might have been a beautiful scenic view, had he allowed himself to take it in. Instead, he was studying the map. His stomach turned and knotted as he looked at the large section of yellow land he would be crossing alone.

"Well, Gib's off." Addison said as she came back from the trail. "Did you already hide the extra stuff?"

He knew she was there. He'd heard her coming, but he didn't take his eyes off the map. "How long do you think that is?"

"Do you really want to know?"

He really didn't, but he had to. He needed some idea of how long it would take. If he walked off not knowing how far he had to go, it wouldn't be long before he began convincing himself he was lost. "Just tell me."

"If I had to guess…I'd say somewhere around eight hundred rods."

He thought for a long moment as he calculated the distance then he blurted out his shocked answer. "That's over two miles!"

"Almost three, actually." She smiled and gave him a hearty slap on the shoulder. "At least you won't be carrying the canoe."

She was still light, Josh thought. She still didn't want to see the reality of their situation. In her mind, there was some distant hope that all this was just a precaution. Perhaps that was best, he thought. "And you're sure the path goes all the way to White Iron?"

"It should." She answered. "There are a couple other trails that intersect with it. Just stay on the main one."

Her vagueness sent his stomach turning again, though he did his best not to show it. They were counting on him. He holstered his pack and cinched the straps as tight as they could get. He didn't want it bouncing around and throwing off his balance while he ran.

"Here." Addison offered. She lifted the pack higher up on his back and held it up as he tightened the straps again.

A tinny bang sounded from across the lake, stunning Addison and announcing the arrival of the two men. They were already coming off the portage from Shagawa. The first one, with blondish-orange hair, had roughly dropped the canoe on the rocky shore. The second man came out right after, carrying only paddles, one pack, and one fishing pole.

Now, with the sun hanging just barely above the trees, Addison could no longer deny it. There was no where else the two men could be going; no innocent reason for them to be pushing it this late. Her skin turned cold and clammy. Already the first guy had the canoe back in the water and already he was climbing in. "They really are after us, aren't they?"

"Yes…they are." Josh answered dimly. "Come on."

They walked casually, keeping the illusion that this was simply another portage and that they weren't at all concerned about the men behind them. Addison split off at the bushes where they had forced through the canoe. Josh rustled and fluffed the weedy branches after she passed then he took off running on his own.

CHAPTER 12

Within a quarter mile Josh's trail had widened and the curves in its path had begun to straighten. The thick brush was pushed away at least six feet on either side of him and the ground had suddenly become incredibly flat.

Further along, the trail crossed with another. The angle of their intersection was so exact and so square that Josh couldn't help stopping to figure out its reason. As he looked westward along the new trail, he saw another intersection with the same precision. Beyond that was another. It was part of a giant grid.

"The streets of Old Ely." He gasped.

These traces of the old city remained even now, even out in the middle of this vast wilderness. Years of pounding car traffic and constant road repair were still too much resistance for any trees to reclaim this remnant of civilization. Only ground sprawling weeds now covered what was once tar and cement.

A century ago these city blocks held rows of houses. Josh imagined what the area once looked like. He imagined the town's activities on a beautiful summer day like today; kids running through sprinklers, neighbors calling hello to each other over neatly trimmed hedges, and elderly couples sitting on their porches as they enjoyed the day. None of them had any idea this would be taken away one day. They had gone somewhere else, but it was not by their choice. They hadn't tired of the area or decided it was time to move on. They wanted to stay. For a brief second Josh understood the depth of loss the residents of Old Ely must have felt.

Further up the westward street, the ground began to rise. That's where he saw the first of the immense stickmen Addison had told them about back on White Iron. Two enormous tar-covered logs angled up from the ground to meet at a sharp peak. Another thinner log sprouted straight up from the legs. Midway up its length was a vertical cross piece that formed its arms and the head was a weave of thin branches balled into a large round sphere. Standing at least fifteen feet high, it was the leader.

More followed after, each spaced about a standard city lot size away from the one before it. The line of them continued up over the hill into the late evening sun. They stood like an army of giant log men guarding the memories of homes. They stood as a final word of protest from the people that once lived here. They stood like they were about to go on a march and they were facing him.

A deep croaking voice suddenly echoed through the trees. For a moment Josh actually thought the log men were calling a warning to him. That's not possible, he told himself before realizing the voice was that of the very real danger he was trying to escape. The men were making better time than he expected.

He stumbled first and tripped over his own feet as he scrambled to a sprint. He ran past three more intersecting trails, three more blocks of Old Ely. The last street was the widest one yet. It was the old main street that once pulsed with the steady flow of visitors. On the other side, he passed a large sign of brown painted wood that had been forgotten or dismissed in the town's final days. Its embossed letters were too faded and too worn to make any sense of now and he was running too fast to really look.

With his thumbs hooked under each shoulder strap of the pack, Josh kept his focus forward with few looks back. On such a straight and open trail he felt oddly comfortable. There was no questioning if he was on the right track and he would see the waters of White Iron long before getting there. Then he would have something to look forward to. Then he would have something to chase after instead of being chased.

He was glad for the clear line of sight until he realized it was also a benefit for the men who were after him.

There was nothing to obstruct their view either. He also realized a critical flaw in his and Addison's reasoning. If the men were trying to catch them, not just keep up with them, then they wouldn't need their canoe at all. They could leave it behind and pace the trails just as easily as Josh. That's what they were doing now and that's how they had caught up to him so fast.

The only safe thing he could do was the one thing he wasn't sure he could make himself do. He needed cover and he need to get to White Iron without these men on his heels. He turned to the woods and looked for the widest break in the trees.

"Deek." Meyers radioed then waited for his partner to answer. They had separated at the first crossroads in the trail. Meyers continued south while he sent Deek down the westward trail, toward the odd log formations. "See anything?" He asked gruffly.

Deek touched the transmit button of the radio curled around his ear. "Nothing yet, but there's higher grass further up. I'm gonna check it out for any signs of recent traffic."

"Don't waste too much time." Meyers ordered. "White Iron is their most likely destination. Get the canoe when you're done and catch up with me. The main trail will bring you right to me."

Deek's intentions were not as focused on their task as he had led Meyers to believe. He was much more interested in learning more about the mysterious log creations lining this old street. The first one he came to was almost three times his height and covered in black tar. Even the nest of branches that served as its head was covered in the black goo and long stringy drips of it dangled in the air like sparse strands of hair.

All of them were in a row and that didn't make much sense to him. But behind this first one, deeper in the woods, he saw the top half of another log person growing out of a mass of green. Strangely out of line with the rest, it looked as if it had been abandoned by its brothers. Deek had to know why.

He left the trail and pushed his way through the brush. When he got there he saw that the legs and part of the body were covered in leafing vines. "Why didn't the worms take you guys?" He wondered out loud as he pulled off a leaf from the logman's leg.

In fact, as he looked around, none of the leaves on these vines had been eaten and the vines covered everything. Every bush and every tree had been overtaken by them. They were victims of incorporation robbed of their identities. Directly behind the log man, between two noble maples whose life had been choked out by the vines long ago, was an opening to a corridor between a line of trees. This statue hadn't been abandoned at all,

Deek realized, but placed as a sentry to block this specific entrance.

He should have left. These things were here to scare intruders and he had more important business anyway. But a burst of cool evening air rushed past him and seconds later a chorus of low-pitched whistles sounded from inside the hallway.

If it was meant to be music, Deek certainly couldn't pick out its rhythm. Its melody was hollow and deep and random. The invitation was much too inviting for him to ignore. He stepped around the towering guard and into a long narrow hall of green. The vines, so abundant and so tightly meshed, made it impossible to see through the walls around him.

The hallway ended at a large open room filled with even more of the intricately woven shades of green. Vines crept over every inch of ground, up the walls of trees that enclosed this bigger area and even on the branches that hung over head. The monotonous swirl of leaves distorted his perception to the point where he couldn't tell just how big the room was or exactly where the walls were. It was dizzying and intriguing.

He stepped forward to enter, but his foot found no floor, at least not where he thought it was. The ground was actually three feet lower than he judged and he fell over onto the hard ground.

"Jesus-bleedin'-Christ!" He yelled out and quickly jumped to his feet.

Logic told him that some prankster had painstakingly planned this growth to confuse unwanted visitors, but a superstitious voice, the quieter voice that he had trained himself to ignore long ago, wondered if something supernatural was behind the bizarre occurrence. That quieter voice gnawed tenaciously at his braver ego.

Gib tilted the canoe backward off his shoulders then twisted out from underneath and let it fall. Not gently and not the proper way to put it down, but he just finished tackling a giant hill and he was too tired to care about technique. The canoe crashed against the ground with a dullish thud that was just loud enough to shock the forest animals into quiet. He bent over and planted his hands on his knees to rest and catch is breath.

Sweat soaked his hair and dripped down his face. As always, the mosquitoes were even worse at this time of day and they wouldn't let him rest for too long. A small cloud of the persistent insects swarmed above him seizing every opportunity to dive down and carry out their cruel blood-harvesting mission. Addison, coming up just behind him, was fighting them off as well. All around them the late evening forest started coming back to life after the intrusive sound Gib created. Crickets returned to their chirping and the birds resumed their callings.

It was hard to tell how long they'd been walking. Gib's most hopeful guess was that they'd gone almost a mile and a half. As he stretched and turned to relieve some of the pain in his back, he wished for one of the cooling gusts of wind that had been pushing the canoe around while he was carrying it.

"Please tell me we're at least half way." He said between breaths.

"Okay. We're at least half way." Addison answered dryly. Five days with Josh was rubbing off on her. "At least we're on high ground now. With a good breeze the bugs should lighten up considerably."

Sure, but there was no breeze right now, Gib thought. And if it did come again, it probably wouldn't be consistent enough to give them any long-term relief. He waved his hand through the air to shoo the bugs away as he looked around the forest.

Tall red pines owned this area on the hill top and their fallen needles covered the ground in a blanket of rusty orange. Few bushes grew here and almost no other trees. He appreciated the exposure of the forest like this. It showed all the various dips and humps of the uneven terrain.

Among the thick reddish/gray trunks sprawling out before him, Gib saw a darker one deeper in. It stuck out from the ground at an impossible angle that wouldn't support its weight if it was full sized tree. He took a wide side step and got his first view of an Old Ely log man.

"That's one of them." He said, intending it to be a question, but without the right intonation. He moved a little closer for a better look.

Addison had seen pictures of them and she knew almost everything about them, but this was her first time actually seeing one for herself. This one look was all she needed to satisfy her curiosity. They were a haunting reminder of the past.

"Gib, we don't have time." She said, walking over to get him and pulling at the sleeve of his shirt.

He felt her tugging, but he couldn't leave without learning more about the ominous log totem. "How did they build those things?"

"Building them wasn't hard." She answered, yielding to his stubborn curiosity. "What's really amazing is how they stay up. Since the move, not one of them has ever fallen. Trees fall down by them, but never on them. The strongest winds don't break them. Even vandals leave them alone."

"How's that possible?" Gib asked as he lightly smacked his forehead. In his distraction with the log man, he didn't wipe hard enough and a black smear of the mosquito's guts stayed stuck to his skin.

"I don't know. It's like something protects them. Another of the Old Ely ghost stories talks about how they come alive just after the sun goes down and scour the forest for other fallen trees to build more."

"They protect the land." Gib realized out loud.

"Yeah, from us."

He wanted to go even closer. He wanted to see the log man up close and stand on the sacred land they guarded. But, as Addison said, they didn't have time and he probably shouldn't anyway. They were there for a reason and he would respect their purpose. Then, as if sorrowfully chastising him for even considering it, a melancholy tune sounded a warning. The forest again quieted at the sound and even the mosquitoes stopped biting.

"What is *that*?" He asked.

Addison was taken back to her childhood, to a time when every shadow held the certainty of lurking danger and every frightening campfire tale was real. The stories of Old Ely were coming back to her more clearly now and one of the morals stuck in her mind. In a whisper as soft as a dying breath she spoke, "The ghosts of Old Ely do beckon still and warn to heed its stubborn will."

"Where is it coming from?" Gib asked.

"We don't want to know and we shouldn't be here." She tugged sharply on his shirt sleeve, slightly ripping it along the seam and nearly yanking him backward off his feet.

"I'll just cut off the main trail and meet Gib and Addison as they go by." Josh assured himself. He didn't realize he was speaking out loud and he didn't sound entirely certain of his plan. "If I veer to the left, I'll find the trail they're on. If I go right, I'll hit the trail I just left. Anywhere in the middle and I'm sure to hit water."

The weeds and brush covering the ground in this dense part of the forest seemed to fight against him. The ground growth wrapped over his feet and around his legs whenever he failed to step high enough to avoid them and tree branches poked at him and snagged at his clothes as if trying to stop him. But it was lighter ahead with the promise of a clearing, and he kept on.

He kicked his foot loose from another tangle of particularly stubborn weeds and jerked forward to free himself from a branch that had snaked its way under a strap of his pack. He pulled so hard that he lost his balance and stumbled through the last two trees before the clearing. When he looked upon the open field, his face flushed and his eyes reddened with a glassy glaze. "Oh crap."

The remains of the Old Ely cemetery sat before him, settled into a sprawling hillside. Row after row of head stones stood among sparse trees and tall grass. Some had become part of tree-like bushes sprouting up around them and some were nearly hidden among the overgrowth. Josh wanted to deny what he was seeing, but their shapes were unmistakable.

At the top of the hill, one of the taller monuments, an obelisk, stood clearly above all others and well above the wild grass. It was topped with a thick, block cross of white stone and the setting sun cast a ghostly glow upon it. In the days when the cemetery was still used, it probably looked angelic. Now, with patches of moss and lichens marring its true form, it looked like a beacon of the dead presiding over the souls below; keeping them at bay as long as it was still illuminated, but certain to lose its hold once the last traces of light disappeared from its face.

"Just stay calm." He told himself. "I'll be through in no time."

He stepped carefully around the graves, looking at the head stones as he walked. Among the clumps of grass that covered them, he could just barely make out some dates of each person's life. It was the very beginning of Ely's history. Most of the people in this part of the cemetery had died early in the nineteen hundreds. They were the first settlers in the area and it was their sweat that had built the town. He imagined the rage these older spirits felt knowing that all their work had been for nothing.

Some of the graves were framed by low-rising, rounded cement borders that were obviously meant to show visitors where not to walk. Their purpose, however, had become redundant as the ground within them had sunk noticeably lower than its surroundings. In most cases, it had sunk so low that the heavy stones identifying their inhabitants had slanted over. Some had already fallen and they were already half buried in the ground. Soon they would disappear forever and no one would ever know they were there. It was possible that some had already disappeared and that his care in avoiding them was really pointless. He still continued maneuvering around each grave, or what he thought were graves, because he just couldn't risk that ultimate disrespect.

At the top of the hill, he made sure to steer a wide path around the ghostly cross. The sun was just beginning to dip below the tree line and the shadow that had already overtaken the base of the monument was now creeping slowly up to the top. Three more inches until the shadow started its way up the cross and drained the power it held over the inhabitants below. He still had time.

At the hill's crest, the ground sloped more gently away into the distance and Josh's heart sank. The graveyard was much bigger than he thought. It seemed to go on without end. As he struggled to pull himself together, a rush of wind swept across the field and the blanket of tall gold and green grass swayed back and forth. It looked as if the ground was heaving up and down, pushed up by the bodies beneath as they prepared to break free and come after anyone who dared to pass.

Next to him, he noticed a cherub chiseled into one of the lower sitting head stones. Its youthful face reminded him of the boy in Addison's story. He could be here; not his remains, but certainly his spirit. It wouldn't know anywhere else to go. Round, chubby cheeks tipped the corners of a wry grin and that grin implied a mischievous nature. It dared him to keep going. He could almost hear its child voice taunting him.

'Come on. It'll be fun.' The voice giggled. 'We love to make new friends.'

He stared helplessly as his mind played out its most spiteful scene. The cherub tore itself free of the epitaph it lorded over and began hopping from tombstone to tombstone, snickering and laughing with a sinister smile. Suddenly, he heard a series of low, hollow tones floating through the air around him. Under the influence of his wicked and surreal imagination, it took him a moment to realize that the sounds were actually real.

Deek rubbed the ache in his elbow and flexed his arm back and forth to make sure the damage wasn't too serious. The fall was short, but the ground was hard and ungiving. He kicked away the gnarled vine branches with his boot and saw the cement of an old foundation, a crawlspace under the house that once sat here.

He walked around searching for the source of the music that had called him, determined to destroy it for the fool's trick it played on him. But it was quiet now and there was no reference to distinguish anything among the hues of green.

He focused his gaze on one specific area then he relaxed and took it all in, manipulating his sight over and over to find a pattern to the randomness. Forms began to take shape and images became recognizable. They were strange though, and not as he expected. These were conjured by the imagination behind his quieter voice. Tortured faces became clearer and seemed to silently scream out at him. Demonic monsters with slanted eyes and jagged teeth reached out to claw at his flesh as if wanting to add him to the wall.

"Stupid idea for a joke." He said, shutting away his freakish thoughts.

He turned for the hallway that led him in, or where he thought the hallway was, but in the enveloping green it had disappeared and he let out a nervous "huh."

Another breeze swirled into the room and the somber flute music played again, louder this time and with a bouncing, scornful beat. It was the song of demons, he thought quieter, and they were happy he came.

He looked again for the hallway but was drawn instead to the source of the music. Hidden in the maddeningly redundant green was the outline of a log statue covered behind the snaking vines. The dead log man was fully reborn with new growth and the wind fluttering the leaves gave it movement. As its camouflaged form became more distinct from the back ground, looking as if it was coming out of the wall, Deek realized that it's was not the only voice singing.

He turned again to find the exit and another log man popped out in front of him, so close that Deek jumped and quickly backed away. The haunting melody was also to his right, but he did not look to verify what he knew he would see.

It wasn't funny anymore, this vicious prank. He realized that it was never intended to be. Still retreating, cautiously and alertly, he backed into a wall. A leaf tickled lightly against his ear and he slapped furiously at his head. He spun around with his arm cocked and his fist balled. It was only a branch. In that flash of frenzied energy, in his anticipation of something else, he didn't realize that he had knocked the radio off his ear.

"Screw this." He said and he began pulling at the vines on the tree wall. Their thick, sinewy ropes gave only a little no matter how hard he yanked and refused him the quicker escape he hoped to make.

Another rush of air and the demons sang again, taunting and laughing now that their victim was so shaken. Deek ran from one part of the wall to the next, pulling at the ivy and praying that he would eventually come to the corridor. The music played stronger and deeper and Deek looked again to make sure the log men were not close.

Past them, across the room, was a patch of distant darkening blue sky. Finally, Deek thought, and he sprinted for the exit. His panic and aggravation would soon be over, but from them he had completely forgotten about the drop off at the entry. His knee smashed into the concrete wall and his upper body slammed forward, crashing hard onto the higher ground.

The collision sent waves of pain pulsing through his body, but they were quickly dismissed in his rush to get away from the maniacal log demons. When he reached forward to pull the rest of his body from the pit he was held back by a tugging against his chest. He lunged then, kicking with legs and all his strength to break free. His ribs twisted and something moved deep inside him. The tug wasn't against his chest or his shirt. It was inside him. He had been impaled.

He gasped and his jaw went slack. He planted his hands and slowly pushed himself up. Rigid edges of an old rusted bolt tore from his skin as he rose. It was a sickening sensation he had no choice but to endure. Three inches off the ground and there was still more inside. He looked down to see the bolt pulling his skin outward, visible even beyond the ripped edges of his brown t-shirt. It was an anchor that once secured the house's frame.

He continued to lift, watching with disgusted horror as another three inches came out. When it finally popped out, he fell to his side sucking in air. As he lay there panting with fear and shock, he found that not even his deepest heaves would satisfy him. A lung had been punctured and blood was gushing out of the wound.

The radio, he thought, and reached for his ear. "What...where..." He felt around the ground thinking it had been lost in the fall.

The log men sang their gleeful tune again and Deek looked over to them. They were waiting to claim his body. A terrible image of his tortured face forever trapped in the wall pushed his conscious beyond sanity and darkness took him over.

The music was everywhere around Josh, but nowhere near him. It was in the trees bordering the cemetery and those trees were quickly becoming a foreboding night time forest. There was also the image of the cherub-boy still prancing across the tops of headstones.

"Stop." He told himself quietly, though he was far beyond rationalizations. His head had already gotten away from him. He'd given life to the monster and a face. The image remained and now the cherub-boy was skipping with high-kneed kicks to the music.

He couldn't stay here, but he couldn't get himself to move either. Moving meant the possibility of stepping on an unseen grave and with the cherub-boy watching over him that was unthinkable. Also, he didn't really know where to go. Out of the cemetery and into the woods? Where the music was coming from? Or was it coming from there? In the echo of the open space, it was hard to tell.

He looked over to the border for an easy way out. Behind the base of a tall pine he saw two angled legs.

Further up was one arm and part of the head was peeking out just above it. That's where the music came from and that was the last place he would go.

He forced his foot forward and the cherub-boy sucked in an anxious breath. "Knock it off." He said and stepped lightly down. Each step after came easier, but also with a sickening dread for where each one fell. He pressed on, fully intending to give the singing log man a wide berth before heading back into the woods and away from the haunted cemetery. Ten yards later he looked again to the tree line. Popping up between two spruce tops was the head of another statue.

'Uh, oh.' The cherub-boy warned.

He walked faster, determined to block out the boy who was now hopping the head stones after him and determined to leave this place behind. Again he turned to the trees and again there was another totem. He quickened his pace to a trot, all the while shifting his eyes between the tree border and each next step. Each turn he thought to take was a turn that would bring him uncomfortably close to another statue. Thick sweat slicked his forehead and his breath became shallow as his panic threatened to break.

He was in danger of giving in to the fear and he stopped to try and calm himself. As far as he could see along the tree line, there were more log men waiting for him. "They're everywhere." He muttered under his breath.

'He, he, he.' The cherub-boy giggled as he jumped down onto an old flower planter at the base of a bronze memorial. He planted his balled hands on his hips, turned out his lower lip, and pouted. 'Come play with us.'

"No." Josh's voice quivered as he stepped forward; this time without looking and without care for where he was. The ground he landed on, the burial plot, held a rotting casket far below. The weight of the dirt was already close to caving it in. His extra weight broke its last resistance.

"Aah!" He yelped as the ground gave way below him.

Now the dead *were* coming. The ground was opening up to let them out so they could kill the thoughtless intruder. He knew it. His leg was sucked in with the sinking dirt, past his calf and deeper still. Through his frantic grunts and pants he was certain he felt a bony hand wrapping around his ankle, pulling him down and using him to bring itself up. The cherub boy's giggling turned to raucous cackling laughter.

He dug in with his free leg to break loose, but the surrounding ground was also crumbling and now his other leg was sinking too. "No, no, no, no." He whimpered as the weight of the pack caused him to fall to his butt.

He was young again and terrified, and now he couldn't run. He couldn't scream either. There was no one to hear him this time, except for the men and that threat was not at all imagined. He had to face this and beat it. Gib and Addison were counting on him.

He stopped his attempts at kicking free and he stopped his panicked cries. If the ghosts were coming for him, he would meet them. He closed his eyes for a moment and took in a deep, relaxing breath. In that moment, even with the confusing and fearful thoughts still clouding his head, he was able to separate the real from the not real. The collapse was slowing and he was no longer sinking. His legs were still buried up to his knees, but the bony hand was gone as was the imagined laughter of the cherub boy. Only the scolding groans and whistles of the log men could be heard. They were not his imagination and he would have to brave them too.

He wiggled his legs back and forth, slowly inching them out until they were free. More soil poured into the hole he left and the grave settled to rest once more. He brushed away the dirt from his legs and shoes. His hands were still shaking and his nerves were frayed, but he stood up and with a determined look he headed for the tree line to a spot equally distant between two log men.

"Don't look at them. Just don't look at them."

He did anyway, as he passed between them. Though their songs were softer, they were still menacing and angry. Their thin hair swayed with the wind and their heads seemed to turn as if to watch him go. He imagined the log men being released once the last ray of sun was gone from the old block cross and he imagined them coming after him.

'Then you'll deal with it if it happens.' He answered back silently as he passed into the low lands of the swampy forest.

Between his even strokes with the paddle, Gib's attention was drawn to something moving up ahead on the nearer shore. It was Josh jumping up and down and waving his hands. "There he is." Gib told Addison.

"What?" She croaked as she stopped paddling to scan the shoreline. He was there, but that wasn't where the trail came out. "That's not where he should be. The trail's back in a small bay a little further up."

"Maybe he got lost." Gib offered.

"Or maybe something's wrong." She said nervously.

They paddled harder with a renewed urgency until they got to him. "What's going on?" Gib asked. He looked around Josh, deeper into the woods for any sign of movement behind him. The sun was gone now, but the gray-blue twilight still held enough for a dim view. "Did they catch up to you?"

Josh waded out to meet them, dropped the pack from his shoulders and swung it around into canoe. "Not quite." He answered.

"What happened?" Addison asked. Her voice was getting frantic and she also looked into the woods.

From the knee-deep water, Josh stepped into the canoe from the side - a great big no-no according to Addison, but he wasn't concerned with her. She saw the fear on his face and she didn't say a word about the unconventional boarding.

"Are you alright?" She asked as she shifted her weight far to the opposite side to keep them from swamping.

"Just get us out of here." Josh answered.

Addison and Gib back-paddled until they could turn the canoe around then they pulled long heavy strokes to regain their speed. As they moved out into the lake, Josh looked back to the shoreline. They passed a point of land and around to the small bay where he was supposed to be picked up. He found the trail opening and, suspended among the tall brush, a solemn face staring back at him.

Every muscle in his body tensed in one sudden jerk, not as dramatic as he had on Miners, but enough to get the others attention. Gib and Addison looked back. They both knew what they would see. Being prepared for it didn't make it any less frightening. The head, unnatural in its independence of a darkly clothed body camouflaged among the back ground, didn't stir at all.

Addison, shocked and frozen, held her paddle deep in the water. The drag on their momentum pulled the canoe back around before it slowed to a stop. It was a silent stare-down between them separated by only seventy yards of water.

Josh was certain the floating head's sight was focused only on him. It singled him out more than the others. The face revealed no emotion, but its stillness held an emoting anger just the same. The left eye was darker for some reason, shaded and obscure. A tattoo, Josh realized, boldly displayed as a disregard for societal convention. On such a cold and hard face, this disembodied face, he thought it suggested a certain disregard for morality as well.

Addison was the first to break, understanding that the man was only waiting for his partner to arrive with the canoe. "Go, Gib. Go! Go!" She ordered as she forced several wide swinging strokes in the water to turn them around.

Josh kept the stare on the floating head and even twisted his body around to see past Addison as he watched the face disappear into the night.

Meyers continued watching them move across the lake convincing himself that he'd done the right thing in letting them go. He'd been outsmarted and that never sat well with him. Shooting the one in the middle, the one Temple said was expendable, would have done much to sooth his bruised ego. It also would have been foolish.

They were too far away for him to really do anything and he had no idea where Deek was with the canoe. He touched a button on the radio to report his unfortunate news to Temple. "They got away, sir. It looks like they're heading back to Ely."

Meyers released the radio button and waited for the verbal lashing he'd earned. It never came. Instead, Temple responded coolly and confidently. "Get back to camp first thing in the morning. I have an idea how we can find them."

Meyers trotted back across the long trail, expecting to run into Deek with the canoe. The longer he went without seeing him, the more his anger seethed and the more he cursed Deek for his carelessness in following orders.

Even when he got back to Miners Lake where the canoe still sat, even after finding no trace of Deek, he still refused to believe there was any good excuse for his absence. It wasn't until after a half-hour of trying to reach him on his radio that he realized he was gone; seriously injured, most likely, if he wasn't able to answer. He would have searched for him, if he thought there was any chance of finding him in the dark.

Later, in the black of an overcast night, the sounds of bawling wolf cries woke him from a restless sleep. Their growls and yelps were excited and frantic, and they were uncomfortably close to his position. The pack had made, or found, a kill and they were feeding ravenously.

As the hours passed, and the noisy feast of the wolves continued, he listened and tried to think of the various large mammals that could provide such a satisfying and hearty meal. Probably a deer, he reasoned, or maybe a bear. It could even have been a moose, he thought; anything but the most likely possibility that he'd rather not consider. That was an image he fought desperately to keep out of his head.

More wolves joined the chorus throughout the night, their ravenous snarls and grunts daring Meyers to risk sleep. In the early hours of the morning, the growls became more threatening and more ferocious and he listened as the pack fought over the remaining scraps of meat.

CHAPTER 13

They kept on the water, paddling in the dark until they reached the far southern shore of White Iron. Josh suggested, insisted actually, that they *not* use a public campsite. Instead, they found the thickest stand of trees they could and hid the canoe deep in the woods. The tent was forced into a space too small to accommodate it and there was no campfire that night. Josh also suggested that one person stay awake to keep watch.

As Josh unzipped the tent flap to go out for the last turn at watch, Gib stirred from his semi-lucid sleep. Through his groggy thoughts a daunting and disturbing question suddenly popped into his head. 'Maybe they were after the stone?'

The question surprised him and brought him more awake. 'Was that what the two men wanted from them?'

"No." He countered, his lips mouthing the word even though no sound came out. "No one seriously searches for the stones any more." He breathed. "Its over. Let it go."

He forced his attention to Gerald's cabin and possible clues for the second stone. He wanted to stay focused on the positive.

His suspicion wouldn't let go and butted in again. 'It seemed funny that the men just happened to show up right after they had the stone.'

'Well,' He reasoned back, 'not right after. The two men had all of last night to come for the stone if they really wanted it.'

'Who knew they were looking for them? Had they been followed? If so, for how long?'

The last question lingered and he began visually retracing their journey from Pipestone bay backward. Fall Lake, the bear, the eaten trees, Garden Lake, the resort on White Iron; could those men have been there when he was walking around alone at the old resort? Had they been that close to danger since then? Before? The thought so unnerved him that he sprung up from his sleeping bag and he ran his hand through his sweaty hair.

Now completely awake and alert, more rational thoughts prevailed - safer thoughts. Only trusted friends and family knew that they were here. People had given up on the stones long ago. And why would anyone be so sneaky about it anyway? Why be so threatening?

If he wanted, if he were to allow his mind to do so, he could come up with good arguments against each of these points. But they were safe now and the mystery of the Gerald's cabin was far more pleasant to think about.

He closed his eyes again and this time he stubbornly kept his concentration on the second stone. Back on Basswood he'd had several ideas on what to look for. There were patterns to be considered and possibilities to be explored. Now each possibility seemed hazy and each pattern insensible. Numbers seemed important and also… He fell back into a restless sleep before any answers came.

Down at the shore, Addison jumped when she saw Josh standing beside her. She was surprised to see him already and surprised that she hadn't heard him approaching. He had been completely quiet and that was unsettling. If he could do it then so could the men that had been chasing them. "What time is it?" She whispered.

"About two-thirty." He answered.

"You're early. Why aren't you still sleeping?"

He took a seat beside her. "Did you actually manage to sleep when you were in there?"

She hadn't. Her mind raced each time she heard a noise outside. Even familiar sounds sparked her suspicion. "Good point." She said.

"Gib's doin' a pretty good job of pretending, but I heard him jolt awake each time he started to snore."

Josh looked for the lake. A cloud front had blown in, hiding the moon and stars and limiting his sight to no further than ten feet. No rain though, he thought, and at least that was something.

"I don't think I've ever seen a night so dark." He offered casually.

She responded only with a disinterested "a-huh."

"Looks like it might rain. You think it'll pass on through?"

"Prob'ly burn off by mid-morning." She mumbled.

They sat quiet then, comforted in each others presence, but still awkward with the events that brought them here. Addison kept a watchful eye on everything around them, or at least on what she could in such blackness. It was different now, the forest she'd always known. The darkness that never bothered her before now hid the burn of stocking eyes, watching her from the shadows as they plotted and waited.

"What do you think those guys really wanted?" She finally asked, confronting the real topic on both their minds.

"I'm not sure." Josh answered soberly.

Addison picked up a small rock and lobbed it out in front of her. Two seconds later came the "plunk" of it hitting the water. "I've never run into trouble out here. I know a few people that have, but it's never happened to me."

She was arguing really, though to Josh it sounded more like she wanted someone to prove her wrong; to tell her the whole thing was just some greatly exaggerated and over-blown misunderstanding. He was willing to help. "They were probably just trying to scare us."

"Chasing us half way across the boundary waters seems like a lot of effort just to scare us." She said sarcastically. Her exaggeration was bitter and more; there was sadness to it as well.

She was right, but he didn't think she was really looking for truth. She was looking for a way to feel safe again in this place she loved. "Well Addy, they couldn't have been *that* dangerous." He started. "People who are really dangerous carry guns – real ones. And they don't let you get away. If they were really *that* dangerous, the guy on the shore could have killed us. I mean, we were less than seventy yards from him. It would have been easy. So he couldn't have been that dangerous."

There was sense to his justifications and that was all she needed. Her demeanor took a slight turn of confidence and the gloominess of her words lightened a little. "Musta been dealers – they had to be. Or maybe poachers. Whoever they were, I think you're right; we just got too close to whatever they were doing and they wanted us to know it."

"Poachers, hmmm." Josh said. "I never thought of that. It's a good possibility. Like I said, there is a lot more they could have done if they really wanted to."

He didn't really believe that. They had been smart and cautious. If the guy did have a gun, and had he shot at them, he would have probably only gotten one of them before the others dove in the water. They would have been able escape and get the police. Not taking a shot, if he did have a gun, was smart and cautious as well. Josh kept that to himself though, because Addison was framing it into something easier for her to accept. She was finding her strength again and he would let her.

They sat talking about the encounter and continuing to play it down until the first light cracked over the horizon. Gib joined them as soon as it did and Josh was glad for that. It saved him the trouble of making an excuse to wake him so early. It saved him the trouble of trying to come up with an excuse that wouldn't alarm Addison. Twenty minutes later they set out for Bear Island River.

Years pass quickly under the weight of anticipation; the promise of future so favored over today. Faces grow ever distant with the turn of each generation and surely we forget. Some will hear the call of home and they will return.

Harris sat at the table by the lakeside considering this passage from Kearny's book. There wasn't much more for him to do at this point. It was already ten a.m. and Meyers was still not back. He radioed in earlier and estimated his return at around eight-thirty, but managing a canoe by himself, against the current of the Shagawa River, proved more difficult than he expected.

Walsh strictly held the other men to the task of breaking camp. They finished packing the tents and all the gear two hours ago. Now they sat farther up the shore trading guesses on what happened to Deek.

Harris overheard them in their hushed chatter. Two were certain that Deek had done something stupid. The third, the one they called Ritter and the only one Harris ever recalled being congenial with Deek, tentatively offered weak defenses for his character. Harris did notice, however, that Ritter was careful to never completely disagree with the others at the risk of jeopardizing his own standing among them.

Temple, sitting across from Harris at the small table, was at his computer again, smugly disinterested in the passing time as he took care of other business interests.

"They could be heading to Illinois." Harris thought out loud.

Temple continued typing, silently refusing to break his concentration.

"Where Kearny grew up." Harris added.

Temple sighed, rolled his eyes, and relented. "And how have you come to this idiotic conclusion?"

"It's an idea, really; not so much a conclusion." Harris corrected. "In this section Kearny speaks of returning home. It comes right after this section on…"

"We've done so." Temple interrupted bluntly. "Have we not? We're here, at the place Kearny called home."

"*A* home." Harris clarified. "Only *a* part of their history. There was history aside from this place, before it, and after. Kearny's legacy would certainly encompass more than just this."

"In fifty years of searching by hundreds of people, not one person has ever seriously suggested Illinois as a possibility. You, however, in the face of all the expert knowledge, have come to believe they are wrong?"

"Well…those experts weren't so successful in finding the stones, sir." Harris said rather smartly.

Temple recoiled with a scathing look for his bold comment. Harris immediately turned his head, but he did not let up. "I'm not saying the other is definitely there, just that home could be the key to finding out where the other one is. Also, Gerald lived a good part of his life over in Hibbing, just west of here. Certainly, that could be worth checking…"

"Harris!" Temple snapped. "I told you I have a plan for reacquiring them. Right now I have more pressing matters than your insensible ramblings."

Harris stopped. He should have known better. Rarely did his boss show patience for sharing ideas and building on creative thoughts. He did it though, knowing that he was on to something and he continued trying to follow this line of thinking without sharing any more theories. Temple's insults, the shattering of his confidence, kept him too distracted to really think clearly.

Gib's arms and shoulders ached, but his strides with the paddle never broke. His concentration on the elusive clues to the next stone was deeper than any sensation of pain. Addison had a hard time matching his swift strokes. They arrived back at the outpost on Bear Island Lake by early afternoon. Expert time, Addison acknowledged, honoring them both for how well they had picked up the art of paddling and portaging.

Gib and Josh unloaded the canoe and Addison went to the wooden box at the end of the dock to radio Ben for a ride. When he arrived, Addison wrapped her arms around his shoulders and kissed him hard on the cheek.

"Ungh." Ben grunted in her strong grasp. "Well, that musta been some trip."

Addison, realizing her emotions had gotten the better of her, let go and retreated to a more formal distance. "Eventful." She answered with a suggestive raise of her brow then a wide smile stretched across her face as she anticipated showing him the stone.

Ben's face flushed and the hair on his neck tingled. "You found them."

"Gib…" She said and stepped away.

He was right behind her, ready for the presentation before Ben had even landed his boat. He held out a balled-up shirt in one hand while with the other he carefully pulled back each fold of cloth until the stone was fully revealed.

Ben's eyes widened with amazement and disbelief. Light twinkled off the gold lines and crystal surface and in that moment he didn't even realize the difference of the gem stone from Kearny's book. "Wh-where?" He mumbled.

"Newton." Addison answered. "You won't believe it."

Gib moved the stone closer to him, offering it for him to hold. Ben was still hesitant and careful not to overstep the courtesy extended to him. He only touched it with the tips of his fingers.

"Feel the weight." Gib invited. "It's heavier than you'd think."

Ben gently wrapped his hands around the stone. "You got it from Newton?" He asked with gaping curiosity. The obscure lake had no significance to Kearny's life as far as he knew.

"Well," Gib corrected. "we didn't get it until it came out in Pipestone Bay, but it came up from Newton by the start of the falls. It was in a big plastic ball that went over."

"There were others, too." Addison jumped in. "You've gotta see the family tree Gerald carved. It's beautiful."

Later, he would be interested in what else they found. Now, he was only focused on the stone – the one stone. "Where's the other?"

"They were separated." Addison said. "We're heading up the north shore to Gerald's old cabin. Gib thinks it might be there."

"The Kearny cabin?" Ben confirmed. "Connie will be awful jealous. She loves it up there. When 'ya goin'?"

"Today…now - as soon as we get back." She answered.

Josh stepped in quickly with that opening, "Which we should probably start doing." He said with a quick look back across the lake.

"Can't wait to find the other, huh?" Ben said as he handed the stone back to Gib.

"Well that," Addison explained, "and we ran into some trouble with a couple guys on our way out. Don't worry Josh, they couldn't have made the time we did."

"Just two?" Ben asked her, thinking about the group he warned her of earlier.

"Yeah, we picked 'em up on Fall Lake, but lost 'em going through Old Ely."

Not really, Josh thought as she said it. Those guys had to know where they were heading. She continued on and he kept quiet, even though he really wanted a chance to talk to Ben about it alone.

"It was no big deal, Ben. We figured they were dealers or poachers. They just didn't like us being too close."

Ben dropped it. The danger was behind them and it didn't sound like his group anyway. Still, it reminded him that he hadn't yet talked to his friends about going with him when it came time to pick that bunch up.

CHAPTER 14

By three-thirty they were already past the small town of Silver Bay and the Split Rock light house as they drove up the northern coast of Lake Superior. Addison sat in the passenger seat nodding in and out of sleep as she quietly watched for glimpses of the lake through breaks in the trees. The frequent bays and rocky peninsulas provided an ever-changing landscape with rolling waves of blue-green water crashing against the base of jagged, black cliffs. She would have liked to have fallen into a deep sleep, but she loved the drive up the north shore and her admiration for its sights wouldn't allow her eyes to stay closed for too long.

Gib was torn between the view of the big lake and the gorges cut by the many rivers cascading down the side of the stunted Mesabi mountain range on his left. This early in the summer the run off was still heavy and powerful. He didn't say much either as the peaceful scenery lulled him into a serene hypnosis that might have been dangerous had there been more traffic.

Sprawled out across the back seat, his hat pulled down completely over his face, Josh had drifted off almost as soon as they got in the truck. He didn't wake until they took a sharp turn off the highway onto a bumpy gravel road with a perilously steep incline.

"Hey, princess." Addison jabbed when she noticed his head pop up behind her. "Nice of you to join us."

"Where are we?" He asked, rubbing his eyes and shaking off his sleep.

"Almost there." Gib answered, more alert now that they were so close to their destination.

The truck kicked up clouds of dust behind them as the road zig-zagged back and forth up the modest mountainside. The higher they climbed, the narrower the road became and the steeper the incline. A small bridge of wooden planks, that Gib wasn't entirely sure was wide enough to hold the big truck, took them over a fast moving stream of tea colored water.

"Where does that come from?" Josh asked.

Gib looked at Josh in the rearview mirror, his eyes twinkling. "You'll see. It empties into one of the main rivers west of here."

The road ended abruptly just half way up the mountain. "This is it." Gib announced.

Josh looked around. There was nothing there but rows of towering blue spruces. "Um, I don't see any cabin."

Gib pointed to a small dirt path cutting through the crowded trees. "It's through there."

"Of course it is." Josh muttered under a tired sigh. "God forbid any part of this trip be easy."

"It's just a short walk." Gib said as he and Addison got out of the truck to unload the gear and several bags of groceries from the back.

Josh had slept through their stop at a road side market and didn't even know they had bought the food. He stumbled out of the truck and stopped to stretch. "I suppose it'd be too much to ask for a little electricity at this place?"

"It's got power." Gib assured him.

Addison grabbed Josh's bag and tossed it at him. "Don't worry, Josh. You'll be able to plug in your curling iron."

He caught the bag, but only barely as it bounced off his chest. She then tossed him her bag too. He wasn't quick enough to catch that, but he was quick with his response. "Hey, I'm not your butler. Quit throwing things at me."

"I'm carrying the groceries." She replied.

"We bought groceries?"

"No," She said. "Gib and I bought groceries while you caught up on your beauty sleep."

Josh headed off for the trail. "It is exhausting looking this good all the time."

"Not as exhausting as it is for us to look at you." He heard her call back.

Under cover of the needled trees, little light broke through to the forest floor, making it seem more like dusk than a sunny afternoon. After a hundred yards of walking, and still in the dark trees, Josh realized that Gib was only pacifying him when he said it was a short walk.

When the spruces ended, he came out from the shade and into a sea of white-trunked birches bathed in bright light. There were thousands of them, he judged with distracted awe and he stopped to take it all in. The canopy of fully leafed branches above him, unseen since he first arrived up here, shone brilliant with the soft glow of emerald green illuminated by yellow sun.

"Whoa." Addison gasped when she came out behind him. The sudden contrast between dark and light and green and white struck her just as deeply as it had Josh and she walked right into him.

He didn't have a smart response for her this time. Right now, he was amazed by the trees. "The worms haven't been here yet."

Gib had seen it before, eleven years ago with his family. But the memory didn't hold the crispness of the contrasting colors nor did he recall their overwhelming number. "They won't come. The border of spruce trees keeps them out. It tricks them."

Josh continued on still staring at the tree tops and thinking that this must be the way Gerald intended it.

He saved this piece of unspoiled land for all visitors, but perhaps especially for those that had come this far on his journey.

Focused mostly on the vibrant leaves, he often veered off the twisting path as they walked. It didn't matter. Even with its many curves, it was still going in a generally straight direction and he always came back to it. This little hike would be much shorter if the trail was one straight line, but he realized it also wouldn't have been as much fun.

Eventually, the randomness of the trees came back into the forest mixing both the leafed trees and the pines. Addison heard the sound of running water. "How much farther?"

"Right up there." Gib answered, pointing up the hill.

The view was as picturesque as any she'd seen in post cards or paintings. In the foreground, spanning the shallow gorge cut by the stream was an arched foot bridge made of mortised stones. Old gray wood provided the railings while thicker, vertical beams supported an eaved roof. Behind it, and further up the hillside, the upper half of a humble cabin was settled between two giant red pines. Their sprawling branches hung over the roof as if protecting it from the elements.

"I thought it'd be bigger." Josh commented.

"It's got three bedrooms." Gib defended. "What did you expect, a castle?"

"No. I don't know…something grander, I guess."

Addison disagreed. It was grand, but its grandness was in its complete integration with nature. In it she found more of herself in the Kearny legacy. It was in the building's construction with its unique structure and underwhelming size. And it was in its placement *among* the trees and land instead of *aside* from them; leaving them instead of clearing a swath of land to flaunt the wealth of a trophy home.

"It's perfect." She muttered.

The stream tumbled down the hillside, appearing and disappearing between the mature cedars lining its banks. Cedars had always been her favorite of all the trees. They were ageless and aromatic and their flat, fanned needles actually looked a lot like leaves. It was the best of both types, year-round green with a touch of softness.

The water pooled in a small flat just in front of them before continuing on down the hill. A sheared wall of exposed rock lined the back side of the pond while on the closer side there was a cozy sitting bench in a patch of grass. The water, though even browner in this concentrated area, wasn't at all muddy and she could see that it had a pretty good depth. It was the perfect place for a summer afternoon of relaxing and reflecting. And when the day turned too hot, you could simply take a quick dip in the cool, fresh water. Gerald must have spent many afternoons doing just that, she thought, and certainly many more people since then.

The path split there, one went right following down the hill. The other went left, up the hill to the bridge. "Where does the river come from?" Addison asked.

"A private lake at the top." Gib answered as he led them up. "Good crappie and walleye fishing."

"Private lake?" She gawked with a sharp tinge of jealousy. "Why didn't Gerald leave this place to someone in the family?"

"No one really knows. He never mentioned it and I'm told it was a bit of a shock to everyone after he passed away."

Josh offered his own best guess. "Well, how would he choose?"

Addison didn't quite follow his question. "What do you mean?"

"How would he choose who to give it to with so many people in the family?"

Addison thought about possible ways to split such an inheritance. There was no simple answer, but she thought there must be a way. "I don't know - some kind of joint agreement or something."

"Which would be fine for that generation," Josh countered. "But by the time it got to us, there'd be hundreds of people involved. Could you imagine coordinating vacation times with that many families? And how many more in another hundred years? Doesn't seem feasible to me. Also seems like a good way to cause a fight."

"But why wouldn't he just explain that, Josh?" Gib said. "Why leave it to speculation?"

"Like with the stones?" Josh asked back sarcastically, but smartly.

"Well," Addison interrupted, "whatever his reasons, it's too bad. Superior below, your own private lake up above, and a stream; it would have been nice to have unlimited access to this place."

When they came off the covered bridge, the cabin came into full view. The stained glass replica they'd found on Pipestone was almost insulting in its comparison. The brown walls were sided with cedar shakes and the chimney on the far side of the house was of round stones of varying colors instead of red brick. Only the front wall was close to being correct. Made almost entirely of windows, it too was dominated by a large curved glass column running all the way from the floor up to the peak of the roof.

As they got closer, Addison saw a platform sitting halfway up the length of the columned windows. On it sat two chairs with a small end table in between – a spectacular view of the lake and another great place for reflecting, she thought. The foundation of the building, the same multi-colored stones of the chimney, had an arched opening just below the viewing windows. The stream, she saw, actually ran right under the house before its course turned. Now, she was a little resentful that Gerald had given this place up.

A deck attached to the cabin's side took them up to the entrance. Inside, Addison felt at once relaxed and comfortable; at home really, like she'd lived here her whole life. The wall of windows pulled the outside scenery in and it blended almost seamlessly with the natural wood finish covering the other walls.

The great stone fire place on the far wall overwhelmed the crowded living room, though it worked well with the height of the vaulted ceiling. Beside it, a spiral stair case of black iron led to the loft and the main bedroom. With only a rail of pine logs to section it off, she guessed Gerald valued the view of the lake more than his privacy from guests. She would have chosen the same.

To her left, under the loft, was a tiny kitchen. Next to it were two more bedrooms and the bathroom. On her immediate right was a small dining area, still with the window view but cut off from the living room by the short stair case that went up to the viewing platform. Up there, she saw the two chairs and recognized that they were made of twined willow branches.

Addison dumped the bags of groceries on the counter and ran up the stairs to check out the view. "Is this good enough for you, Josh?"

Josh weaved his way around Gib and looked around with an exaggerated cursory glance. "Eh…it'll do, I guess."

"But it's still not the castle you were hoping for." She added right after.

"Well it could use a tower or maybe one of those round thingies with a cone top." He answered back.

"A turret." Gib clarified though he was quieter now, distant and withdrawn and not really paying that much attention to them.

Addison leaned backward against the railing of the platform and tilted her head back to let her free flowing hair hang down. "You mean a place where you can really let your hair down."

Josh was already heading for the first floor bedrooms and completely missed her fairy tale reference of his prudish expectations. "I'm taking the back bedroom."

Gib carried his bag to the living room. His free hand was deep inside fishing around for the first stone. At the fireplace, positioned above its large opening, was a three dimensional woodland scene jutting out a good sixteen inches from the wall. Made of metal, the makeshift mantle held dozens of green painted pines of various shapes and sizes surrounding a lake of silver. A mirror set against the chimney behind the sculpture brought it depth even into the stone wall and in the back was a ball of frosty white glass that sat as a moon coming up in a distant horizon.

Gib found the stone and let his bag fall to the floor. He flipped a switch on the thin pillar holding the moon and a light underneath the glass ball filled it with a soft glow. It was effective in its purpose, but it wasn't quite right. Gerald had created this mantle and the moon was much smaller than what the scale called for. It was Gerald's clue to let him know the other was here.

This he knew. He had figured it out when he was younger, just as he had figured out the secret of the eaten trees before this trip began. The next step was still a mystery. He had been on the right path back on Newton when he recognized the fake stone, but now he felt as if he was missing the bigger picture. His focus was too narrow. There was something in his periphery that he should be seeing.

He replaced the glass bulb with the stone and watched as it lit up from inside with prismatic colors. Reds, yellows, blues, and greens twinkled off the gold lines and against the mirrored back drop. "What's next, Gerald?" He mumbled.

Above him, and not at all noticing what Gib was doing, Addison stood enveloped in the semi-circle of glass. No part of the structure prohibited her view. She was outside again. Below her, the ground sloped away with the stream as it wound its way down to the waters of Lake Superior. She could hear its water rushing clearly - a little too clearly, when she was indoors and louder as if it was running *inside* the cabin. She looked around curiously for the open windows that let the sound in, but found that not a single one was open.

"What is that...where is...?" She asked, starting questions with obvious answers until finding the right one to ask. "Why is the creek so loud?"

Gib broke his concentration, as he remembered one of the more fascinating features of the cabin. "It's coming from here." He said as he walked over to the middle of the room and a three foot square column of the chimney stones.

On its top was a plexiglass lid with a small knob on one edge. From her vantage point above Addison could see down the hollow shaft that went even below the floor boards. "What is it?"

"It's an echo well." Gib answered as he flipped up the top.

The stream, already clearly heard, tripled in volume once the lid was lifted. The entire cabin was filled with the loud sound of trickling, bubbling water. Even Josh heard it from his bedroom and he came to see. He joined Gib at the well and bent over to see how deep it was.

"Now that is cool." He gawked.

A screen was set in below the lip of stones and through it he saw the water flowing over smooth reddish rocks on the stream bed. His most youthful inner voice tempted him with the foolish idea of climbing down and he found himself looking at the screen's frame to see how it was attached.

"Don't even think about it." Gib said as he went off to the kitchen.

"Think what?"

Gib took the bags of food and began filling the cabinets. "What you're thinking - don't."

"What do you think I'm thinking?"

"You want to climb down in it."

"I wasn't thinking that." Josh lied.

"Yes you were. You're a powder keg of disaster waiting for a match. That thing is a blow-torch."

"Give me some credit. I wouldn't actually do it."

Addison leaned over the railing of the platform, her right eyebrow arched up skeptically as she chimed in. "Yes, you would."

"Well…" Josh started, but stopped when he realized his persistence was futile now that Addison was on him too.

"Gib." Addison interrupted and turned her attention back to the view outside the window. Further down, nestled in the trees, was a second, smaller structure off to the left. "What's that building down there?"

"It's the guest house." Gib yelled back.

Josh scurried up the stairs to join Addison. "Can we go see it?"

"Sure." Gib answered. "The key is over here on the wall behind the door. Why don't you guys go check it out while I put the groceries away?"

Gib stretched over the counter and pulled the key off a hook. Behind it, also on the hook, was a small laminated map. He took it off too, but this he discreetly slid behind a toaster. Addison and Josh trotted down the stairs and Gib tossed the key to Addison as they headed out.

"Don't be too long." He said and turned away to hide his smile.

"I'm not so sure, Josh." Addison answered as she turned down yet another fork in the trail. "He doesn't have that same subtle smugness he had with the eaten trees. I don't think he knows where to look."

Josh followed her relying on her sense of direction even though they'd already circled back on their current route twice. The spruces lining the trail were thick and left them at the mercy of the foot path. "I think he does. The other stone is around here somewhere. He's sure of that. There still might be something he hasn't told us yet."

"Oh, I'm sure he's right about it being here. I just don't think he knows where."

"You don't think we'll find it?" Josh asked.

"Well, I think he's the one to do it, if anyone can."

Once again they came to a crossing they had already passed and Josh groaned. "First he's gonna have to find us."

"He knows exactly where we are." Addison shot back sourly, her frustration mounting as she stopped to remember which way they had turned the last time. "And when we get back I'm gonna rip his arms off and beat his head back and forth with them."

Josh laughed, though more at her annoyance than her colorful threat. Gib had done this to them on purpose. He'd been just a little too encouraging when he sent them down here. Josh didn't think much of it at the time, but now he was certain. Gib wanted some alone time and letting them get lost in a maze of trails was the perfect way to accomplish it.

"Come on, Addy. It's kinda fun - mysterious."

"The first thirty minutes were fun. This is overkill."

"It's an adventure." Josh said. "Lighten up woman. Enjoy the ride."

"Where are we!?" She demanded in an exasperated huff then she pointed to the left trail. "Let's try that one."

As they headed down to the next fork, Josh's comment finally registered. "Hey! I like the ride just fine." She protested.

"Oh yeah, you're really lovin' it. You've got the wind in your hair and a smile on your face."

"Wait a minute. I'm out in the woods enjoying the ride all the time."

He further qualified her statement, "As long as you know exactly where you're going."

"Of course." She said. "That's just good sense."

"Yeah, but good sense can be so boring. Sometimes you just gotta let things go and see where life takes you."

Around one more bend, and finally they came out of the trees to the front of the guest house. Josh smiled.

Much smaller than the main cabin, this building was made entirely of square gray stones. Brown, wood-paned windows held thick glass with geometric shapes created by lines of gray lead. And, on the far front corner, was a turret. It was the castle they had teased him about and though it was only the size of a cottage, it was still stately in its appearance.

The feel was completely different from the main cabin even though the layout inside was much the same. There were only two bedrooms, again a master loft and one bedroom below. The kitchen and dining areas were combined and the view of the lake was let in by only a large window instead of a wall of glass.

Hidden behind the eastern wall, where a fire place should have been, Josh saw the opening of a staircase. The hall leading up was barely two feet wide, and though obvious and unmissable he thought of it as an entrance to a secret room where one could hide away.

The tiny round room felt surprisingly open. A small area rug provided the space with a little color and warmth and upon it sat a single rocking chair and a floor lamp. Three thin windows provided a little light and Josh pushed open the middle to let the air in.

Certainly this was a favorite spot with the kids. He thought of the Kearny grandchildren, his nearer ancestors, playing games inspired by such a medieval setting. They were kings and queens and knights ruling over an untamed land.

A breeze rushed in carrying with it the squealing sound of a rusty metal hinge turning. Josh looked down to a courtyard sunken six steps into the ground. A few pieces of patio furniture were scattered around and an iron weather vane sat atop a tiered platform. The wind came again and so did the squeaking. The cross piece designating the directions wheeled slowly around. The wind was from the south east, if such an old relic could be trusted.

Addison came up the stairs and joined Josh at the window. "I knew you'd be up here. What's out there?"

"Huh...oh just a patio."

Addison squeezed him away and leaned out the window to look around. The courtyard was nice, as was the view of the lake, bus she was looking for something specific. "There's the river over there." She said pointing eastward. "Come on. We're heading back."

The raining sky, Gib thought, the earth with its secret chambers, and the confused river. These clues from Kearny's book had already helped him once and now he was looking to them again for guidance.

He sat in one of the willow chairs on the platform and stared at the stone as he held it up to the window. In his lap, opened but placed upside down, was his tattered copy of the book. He hoped Gerald's words would help him find some direction. They hadn't so far, but he hadn't really spent much time reading.

There was something in Kearny's heart that he couldn't fully see, even now when he was so close. There was the second stone, of course, but that wasn't it. There was something deeper about the man that he needed to understand. Right now he felt more distant from him than ever.

He snapped out of his distraction, dropped the stone in his lap, and redoubled his effort to concentrate on the book. He flipped forward through the pages to the one passage that always managed to keep his attention:

Archer folded his arms against his chest, digging his fingers into his ribs and holding himself still as he tried to contain his overwhelming excitement. It swirled inside him, this passion for the quest that had taken him, bubbling and building to the brink of explosion. One crack, one tiny fracture, and it would let loose; a geyser of exhilaration spewing out torrents of uninhibited emotion, threatening and dangerous if not released carefully.

The section came from the finding of the stones and it worked. He'd found his focus and was able to keep his undivided attention on the book. Unfortunately, five minutes later, from the corner of his eye, he saw Addison and Josh coming up the path. She had an especially foul look on her face.

The door burst open and Addison stomped in. Gib expected that, but he didn't expect the squishing sound her shoes made as she walked across the shiny hardwood floor.

"Hey genius," She shouted as she kicked her shoes back to the door mat. "Is there something you forgot to mention about getting to the guest cabin?"

Josh added, "Yeah, that was a good one, Gib. But if you wanted to be alone you could have just told us to go fishing. At least we would have gotten to see the lake."

"True," Gib answered. "But that wouldn't have been nearly as much fun. Well, not for me anyway. I didn't think you'd be back so soon. I was lost for hours the first time I went down there."

Josh pulled off his shoes and began peeling off his wet socks. "Addy isn't much for patience. She made us wade the stream back up instead of fighting our way through the maze again."

Gib put the book down on the table and came down stairs. He was the rolling the stone back and forth from one hand to the other. "You are a clever one."

On his way past her, Addison latched onto the lobe of his ear and sharply twisted it. The tug wasn't hard enough to really hurt, but Gib yelped anyway.

He continued on to the fireplace. "Left is right and right is wrong, remember this in a happy song. That's the secret. At every turn you go left."

Addison glared at him sternly. "That would have helped a lot."

Josh picked up a box of crackers from the counter, headed to the living room and plopped onto the couch in front of the fireplace. "So, do you have it figured out?" He asked.

Gib returned the stone to the sculpture above the fireplace. "What?"

"Where the stone is, did you figure it out? Addy doesn't think you know where to look."

"I don't." He said plainly.

"Told 'ya." She gloated.

Josh looked up to the scene above the fireplace. The light glowing from the new rising moon looked perfectly in place. "Is that where that's supposed to go?"

"For now." Gib answered.

"Is it a clue?" Josh asked.

"Only that the other stone is here."

Addison joined Gib at the fireplace and stared at the moon. The bright colors of the prism danced around each time she moved her head.

Josh saw the colors as well, pouring through the stone and casting long and distorted reflections onto the back mirror. They moved more slowly for him as his gaze unintentionally wavered from the movement of his munching. The colors floated up and down, reminding him of a docudrama he once saw about the aurora borealis.

Addison broke away and turned to Gib. "Is there something we should keep our eyes open for?"

Gib shrugged his shoulders. "Something with fours is all I can think of."

"Why fours?" She asked.

"It's a recurring number in how we found the first stone." He explained. "Probably based on the four siblings. There were four birch trees at the Pipestone falls and four balls that came up from the lake. The fake rock that unlocked the balls was a perfect pyramid – four sides."

Josh was listening, but he was still watching the stone and the colors it gave off. He thought of Gerald's book and the description of their origin. He couldn't remember it exactly, but he knew it said something of the northern lights as part of their creation. There was something about the southerly seas, too. And east and west were also a part of it, although he couldn't remember how.

A passing thought drifted through his head. Not emphatic or at all certain, he blurted it out. "The weather vane."

"What?" Gib asked.

"The weather vane in front of the guest house - it shows the four directions."

'The beginning.' Gib thought, knowing Josh was right. He felt even more frustrated for missing that. He remembered the weathervane with its rusty hinges. Had Gerald planned that? Was its creaking an announcement that it called for closer attention?

Of course it was, but most likely that attention would have come in the form of an oil can by those that didn't know better. He'd probably be the first to grease the clue away without a second thought, if Josh hadn't suggested it. "Let's go." Gib said.

"Oh no." Addison protested. "I'm not getting lost down there again."

"Left is right, Addison." Josh answered. "We'll be down there in ten minutes."

"Over there." Josh pointed as they came out of the maze of trees.

The round courtyard was sunk five feet into the ground and was lined with light gray paving stones. The weather vane sat atop four tiers of smooth white cement. Josh didn't pick up on that clue right away, but Gib did. The four tiers, the four arms identifying direction, the four-masted sailing ship serving as the ornament to catch the wind and, at the bottom of the post, four legs supporting its weight, these were no mere coincidences.

Josh grabbed the pole and gave it yank to test its sturdiness. "It must be sunk pretty deep."

Gib didn't think so. The pole and its legs were attached to a round metal base set into the top tier. The seam between the metal plate and the cement was wide and filled with grainy dirt and pieces of pine needles.

"I don't think that's gonna work, Josh." Gib said. He bent over, took hold of two of the legs, and gave a hard, jerking twist. A century of water and ice exposure slowed its turn, but it did move a little. "Give me a hand with this, guys."

Addison took hold of another leg, Josh the last, and together they turned. Less than a quarter around and a seal inside released. The pole tilted over slightly and a puff of dank and musty air wafted up. Josh stepped up to the third tier, bent down, and grabbed the lower part of the pole.

"Josh," Gib said, too late to really warn him. "That's probably too heavy…"

It was too heavy, but Josh already had it up and he was already teetering backward with his feet slipping off the tier ledge. Gib planted his hand against Josh's back to stop him from falling. "See what I mean - a powder keg of disaster."

Josh regained his footing and together he and Gib lowered the weather vane to the ground.

Addison would have had a sharp comment for Josh and his brashness, had she not been so intrigued by the hole he revealed. It was only a foot or so wide, but it was deep and there was just enough light from above to show her the faint outline of something deeper in.

"Something's down there." She said, her last word echoing deeper into the chamber.

She reached her arm in all the way down to her shoulder and even then only the tips of her fingers touched the object. It was some kind of thin wire mesh. She felt around the sides until she found a metal handle. What she pulled out was a wire basket with nothing more in it than a large folded piece of paper double sealed inside a two plastic bags. She handed it right over to Gib.

The paper showed a hilly terrain with hundreds of concentric circles. Small numbers marked the heights and depressions of the represented landscape. "It's an elevation map, but I can't tell for where. I thought it was for here, but it can't be."

Addison grabbed one edge of the map and pulled it over for a better look. "Can't you read a map? Yes, it's for this area." She answered confidently. But as she studied it more, up at the top, one obvious thing was missing. "Oh...wait." She recanted.

"Can't you read a map?" Josh mocked as he forced his way between them to see for himself. "Of course it's for this area. Look, there's the main river to the west and there's the road leading up here."

Gib and Addison could have chided him back, but they didn't. Instead, they waited to see if he would figure it out for himself.

"Hold on." Josh scowled. "Didn't you say there is a lake up behind the cabin?"

"Yes." Gib answered. "And the creek through the property isn't on there either."

"Maybe this is more east of us." Addison said. "Maybe that road is a different road."

Gib didn't see how. "Then where is the road leading here. There's the highway at the bottom. Maybe it's only the lower half of the mountain."

"No. Those are the ridges of the mountains at the very top." Addison countered.

As they speculated, Josh continued studying the map. He was certain he was right. Images of the peaks and valleys floated around his head until finally he understood it. "He made it. Gerald made the lake - and the creek."

"What?" Addison asked skeptically. "How would you know? We haven't even seen the lake yet."

"I don't have to." Josh said. He took the map and laid it on the ground to show them. "He left this map to tell us what he's done. If the cabins are half way up the mountain, that would put us right about here. Now look up here, at these two points."

There, toward the top of the map, a wide ravine was cut into the mountainside. Gib, who did know the lake, was starting to see it as well. "He dammed up these two high points of land."

Josh moved his finger further up. "That main river actually comes over pretty close up here. Maybe he diverted it to fill up his lake."

"You can't do that." Addison said. "That's illegal. He would have gotten in big trouble, and he of all people would have known it."

"Why?" Josh asked. "It joins back up with the river. It doesn't hurt anything."

"You can't just split off a river to come through your property and make a lake, especially when that river is part of a state park."

"There *is* a river that comes in at the back of the lake." Gib clarified. "It has to come from that main one."

"Then I'm guessing he got in a butt-load of trouble for doing it."

Gib thought for a moment. "What would they do?"

"Fines - big fines." She answered. "And of course you'd have to undo whatever you did and restore the river to its original route."

Gib stopped to think again. It was starting to make sense. "If he did that then the lake probably wouldn't stay as high and the creek wouldn't come down the hill."

He was leading them to something, Addison knew, but she didn't know where. "Yeah, so?"

"Well, if you built a cabin that incorporated a creek into its structure, wouldn't you do anything to keep it."

Now she caught on. "You think he negotiated a deal for them to take over the property after his death as long as he could keep the property the way it was. That'd be tough. Environmental laws are incredibly strict and always have been. Maybe, I guess - if he knew the right people."

"They've made a lot of money from this place over the past century." Gib said. "It wasn't such a bad deal for them. And like Josh said, it joins back up with the river so it really doesn't hurt anything."

Josh didn't see why they were arguing about it. He was absolutely certain. "So he made the lake. Does that tell us anything about the other stone?"

Gib looked again at the map and the area that was now the lake. "He had access to the land before it was underwater. He could have done anything he wanted before filling it up. Do either of you know how to scuba dive?"

Josh jumped up from his knees and announced, definitively, that he'd be skipping the water adventure this time. Then he went over to get the weather vane. "Help me put this back on top."

"I've been a couple times." Addison offered. "I'll go down there with you."

"Alright." Gib said. "We'll go down to Silver Bay tomorrow and rent some diving gear."

CHAPTER 15

By Temple's order, they were up before the sun the next morning. Meyers' late return yesterday hadn't allowed them enough time to make it all the way back to Bear Island Lake. They did get as far as One Pine and with today's early start they were already closing in on Ben Jurick's home by ten a.m.

"Approach from the north; under the cover of those trees." Temple ordered. "We don't want Mr. Jurick to see us coming."

The three canoes veered over. Harris squirmed in his seat. He knew what was about to happen and why Temple insisted on canoeing all the way back to the Jurick's house instead of calling for a ride. He took out the book and started reading again.

At the kitchen window, swabbing up the last bit of runny yellow yolk with a piece of toast, Ben saw the canoes suddenly pop out from the left and approach his dock. Fishermen, he dismissively noted at first then he recognized one of the men. The large man with the tattooed face was impossible to mistake.

"And people say country folks are dumb." Ben chided, nervously wondering why they couldn't follow simple directions. "Damn fools paddled all this way across the lake for nothing."

He took one last sip of coffee before heading out, thought for a moment about calling one of his friends then decided there was no way anyone could get over here fast enough.

The first canoe landed just as Ben left the house and started his way down the hill. The other two canoes stayed out in the water while the first men got out. Meyers lead the way with Temple behind him. Under cover of the big man, he screwed on a silencer to the tip of his pistol. Walsh followed after.

Temple was still sixty feet away from Ben when he stepped out of Meyers' shadow. He raised the gun and squeezed off two shots, putting one bullet in each of Ben's thighs.

Ben cried out and fell hard against the ground. The pain was more intense than anything he had ever experienced and he rolled around pressing his hands on the wounds. Blood oozed between his fingers and waves of nausea flooded over him. His breakfast turned over in his stomach.

Temple and Meyers continued up the hill to the fallen man while Walsh jogged past them to the house. "A pleasure to see you again, Mr. Jurick." Temple said cheerily. "The bullets in your legs are meant to demonstrate just how serious I am. You have information I need."

Ben was too busy trying to keep his eggs down to face the psychotic man standing over him. Meyers knelt down, grabbed the sides of Ben's head and forced him to look up at Temple.

"What do you want?" Ben grunted.

"I want to know about Addison Gethold and her friends. Where are they?"

It was these men who had chased her, Ben realized, and this had nothing to do with drugs. "Who?" He hissed between gritted teeth. "I don't know anybody named Gethold."

Temple drew back his foot and gave a swift, hard kick to the bullet wound in Ben's right leg. Ben screamed out and his eyes watered. Temple then pushed the heel of his foot against the wound and began grinding it back and forth. Shards of metal tore deeper into Ben's flesh and with each twist he cried out.

"Of course you do, Mr. Jurick, and I have little patience for liars."

Walsh returned from the house and shook his head "no" to indicate that there was no one else home. He then handed a framed picture to Temple. The photo showed the Jurick family against a snowy winter backdrop.

"Nice looking family." Temple said as he squatted down to share the picture with Ben. "Now let me clarify your situation. I need to find Addison Gethold and her friends, but I have no idea where they are. That means I will have to stay around here until I find someone who can help me. If not you, then the next obvious person would be your wife."

Ben's head shuddered uncontrollably between Meyers' hands, partly from the pain, partly from the hopelessness of his options, but mostly from anger. Addison or his family; it was an impossible choice. Tears began to spill from the corners of his eyes.

"Chances are she'll be with at least one of your three adorable children." Temple continued as he gently traced an outline around the face of Ben's youngest. "Of course, it would be stupid for us to leave behind any witnesses. Even if one or two of your children lived, what would life be like for them without any parents? On the other hand, finding this woman is obviously very important to me. As soon as I know where to look, I will be on my way and you can be assured nothing will happen to them."

Temple paused, drew in a deep breath, let it out then leveled his most serious and deadly stare into Ben's eyes. "Now, I'm sure you realize that you will not live to see another sunset, but you can still do this one last thing for your family."

He could lie, Ben thought. He could send him in the wrong direction, somewhere far away. But this maniac would come back and he would not be around to warn his family. The best option, the only option he could see, was to tell him and hope that Addison could somehow escape.

"They went up the north shore!" He screamed out. "But that's all she said. My family's been gone for a week. They don't know where she is!"

"Thank you, Mr. Jurick." Temple said and waved Meyers away.

Ben's head fell limply to the side. He'd done it. He hadn't told him everything, but he had told him enough to figure out where she was. He'd betrayed Addison. He had betrayed her parents. He flashed back to the day his friends were buried. He had stood at the caskets swearing to watch out for their daughter and to keep her safe. Stronger, unrestrained tears now poured from his eyes.

"Forgive me." He whimpered softly through his sobs and he repeated it over and over, stronger and stronger until, before the sixth plea, a bullet pierced his skull and quieted the grief that tormented him.

Meyers waved the other men up from the shore and called for them to bring some rope. He instructed Walsh to tie up the body and find some heavy rocks. The body, he said, was to be taken out as far into the lake as they could go without crossing the line of sight of any other cabin.

Harris came up as well. He walked slowly past the fallen man and tried his best not to look at his face. Such business was not for him. It was not his responsibility. But the dead eyes were still open and they wouldn't let him pass without at least one quick look. Staring, though not at him, they suggested some hint of life deeper in. Harris' look lingered and he waited for some movement or maybe a blink.

"He's dead, Harris." Meyers assured him.

Of course he was. The bullet wound in his head showed him that. It leaked fresh blood that trailed down the man's brow. Harris still could not stop looking. He could not stop seeing the possibility of life within. "You'll at least close his eyes before you sink him, won't you?"

Meyers, knowing full well that Harris wouldn't, dared him to do it. "Go ahead."

He thought he should. Certainly no one else would. Meyers wouldn't, especially not after being requested to do so by him and the other men would not give such care either. The man would spend eternity staring at the cold dark bottom of the lake. It wasn't right nor was it fair. But this was not his business and touching the dead body would imply too much responsibility.

Harris was still looking at the man and his open eyes. Meyers stared at Harris with a contemptuous sneer. "He won't bite. I swear."

"Harris!" Temple called from further up the hill. "The north shore of Lake Superior, does that mean anything?"

"Huh…oh yes." He snapped out of his trance and hurried up to Temple. "Kearny had a cabin somewhere up there." Bolder then, especially for him, and also with a particularly cold look, he added, "A home."

Temple understood the reference to their earlier conversation, but he didn't dismiss him with a scornful look this time. This act of insubordination was more instinctive and from deeper in. This time Temple needed to use more finesse. "You're a little old to start growing a spine, Harris."

Harris' eyes drifted down to Temple's chest, but he did not turn away. "I'm just saying that we could have avoided that man's death if you'd listened to me earlier."

"Does that make you feel better, Harris?" Temple asked evenly. "Will that help you sleep tonight? Because I've often wondered how you do so with all that guilt you carry."

Harris stayed quiet as he considered Temple's words and his gaze eventually fell all the way down to the ground.

"I've never asked you to kill for me, Harris and I never will. I have always known that is the line you won't cross. But you decided long ago that the life I offer you is worth your complacency in my actions. I don't begrudge you for that, but I despise the way you beat yourself up over it.

"But if I'd had more time," Harris said, almost pleading, "if you had let me follow the logic…I could have figured it out."

Temple paused for a moment then spoke gently and almost pleasantly. "Had you told me about this cabin earlier I would have gladly followed your logic. Had you given me all the facts instead of senseless blurbs, I would have listened. Had you done that, perhaps we could have spared that poor man's life."

Confused thoughts reeled through Harris' mind. "I, um…well everyone dismisses the place in the search for the stones. Kearny left it to the state after his death. General consensus by experts on the stones and even the general laymen is that…"

Now that Harris had returned to his defensive rambling, Temple returned to his more condescending intonations, "Where is the cabin, Harris?"

"I, um, I'm not sure."

"Don't you think you should find out?"

Harris jumped and started down the hill, back to the canoes and the pack with the laptop.

CHAPTER 16

Josh saw Gib and Addison off after a late breakfast. He walked with them until they came to the bench by the small pond. There he decided to sit for a minute. An hour and a half later he was still watching the creek flow into the pond on one end and flow out at the other.

After that he went back down to the guest house to checkout the weather vane again, and the turret. Two hours after that, he strolled back up to the cabin and started thinking about lunch. He tried putting it off until the others got back, but by one o'clock he was already starving and he couldn't wait any longer.

Beside the dining table, on a bookshelf built into the half-staircase, he found a spiral book of depth maps for all the major lakes in the county. Folded and tucked between the pages was a cruder, hand-drawn map of another lake. It wasn't named, but Josh knew it was Gerald's lake.

He studied it while he ate and he even went to find the elevation map in Gib's room so he could compare the two. The lines marking the drop-offs of the lake matched up almost perfectly with the lines showing the different elevations. Now he was even more anxious for them to get back.

The afternoon dragged on and his impatience for their return eventually gave way to tiredness. He still hadn't caught up from the night before last. He flipped open the lid of the echo well, dropped onto the couch in front of the fireplace and drifted off to the peaceful sound of rushing water.

Later, he woke to the sound of muted voices chattering outside the cabin and the loud clanking of metal. He jumped up from the couch just as the door opened. "What took you so long?"

Addison rolled her eyes at him. "The sports store didn't even open til one. Then they made us watch an hour long video on scuba safety. We also had to demonstrate our knowledge by putting on all the gear and answering a bunch of questions on the bends, even though we're not going that deep. And, he showed us three times how to care for his crappy equipment."

"Honestly Gib, those tanks have got to be about as old as Gerald's book. I wouldn't be surprised if they exploded on us while we're down there."

Gib shrugged off her concern. She had asked the attendant three different times if the tanks were safe and each time he had assured her that they were properly licensed and regularly tested. He looked into the kitchen and saw two pots sitting on the stove. "Couldn't wait for lunch, huh?"

Josh looked at him, a little guilty and defensive. "It's almost time for dinner. You were supposed to be back three hours ago."

Addison went to see what he made. Inside the first pot was a gooey orange blob of noodles. "Macaroni and cheese? That was your lunch?"

"And hot dogs." He chirped, pointing at the smaller pan.

"You hardly left us any." She said. On his white t-shirt she saw several crusty stains of orange. "Did you manage to get any in your mouth?"

"I didn't want you guys to get too full. It's not good to eat right before swimming." He answered.

Addison went to the refrigerator, pushed around some jars and cartons, and reached all the way to the back. "That's an old wives tale." She responded as she pulled out a package of sliced deli meat.

"Hey," Josh gasped with widened eyes. "I didn't know we had roast beef."

"That's because I hid it so you wouldn't eat it all."

He couldn't blame her for that, though looking at the bag he didn't think he could actually eat all of it. Then he remembered the cheese he had seen before. "Ooh, gimme that cheese in there."

She shut the door instead. "What do you want on your sandwich, Gib?"

"Just mustard, thanks." Gib answered. He saw the elevation map Josh left on the table and the smaller map beside it. "What's this?"

"It's a depth map of the lake." Josh said, going for the cheese himself then hurrying over to him. "And I think I found your starting point."

Gib looked at the map and found the place *he* thought was best to begin. "I figured we'd start at the deepest part of the lake…over here toward the back east side."

"That's what I figured too, but check out this trench in the middle."

Gib saw it and noted the depth; also deep, but not the deepest. Then Josh pushed the elevation map in front of him and pointed to a ring of concentric circles getting smaller and smaller within each one before it.

"It looks like a high point." Gib said.

"I don't think so. All the other peaks have numbers marking their height above sea level. I think it's a depression, or maybe even a cave. And look at the depth map – it's not even shown on it."

Addison stood over them now, holding two plates of food while she checked out what Josh had found. She agreed with him. "See Gib, I told you the city boy would be good for somethin' eventually."

Josh responded with a sharp elbow to her ribs that sent half the chips from Gib's plate flying through the air. The sandwich she managed to save and as she passed the plate over to Gib she deliberately clunked Josh in the back of the head with it.

Behind the cabin, the steepest part of the mountain had slate colored stones cut into the ground for a more stable walk up to the lake. The trail followed along side the stream and in some places there was even a log rail to hold on to.

As Addison lugged her tank and diving equipment up the stairs, she inspected the erosion of the stream's banks. In its short life, only a century or so old, the trail of water had already carved a deep rut into the earth. She pictured its beginning as a gentle flow over grassy land that was quickly washed away with the powerful spring runoffs. She would have never guessed that it was engineered.

At the top, the trail turned right to follow along the shore of the lake, but Addison stopped. To her left was a line of large boulders that held back the lake. Jets of water poured through the small spaces between them to feed the stream. The disguise had been carefully constructed, but the rocks sat just a little too precariously on this extreme slope to completely convince her. Something beneath them was holding them in place. She might have noticed it even without knowing it was man-made.

The lake was wider than she expected, even after seeing it on the map, and it was more oval than narrow.

She estimated its size at around two hundred acres or so. "We're not swimming out there, are we?" She called over to Gib.

"No." He answered as he waved her to follow him. "There's a boat over here."

Around a slight bend in the shoreline and back to a shallow cove, they came to a beach of light brown sand. Certainly this had been engineered as well, Addison thought, and she marveled at the enormous effort it had taken to bring all this together.

Josh perked up instantly when he saw a white wooden row boat sitting on the beach. "I'll get the boat."

This kind of boat he knew, or at least remembered well enough from his time at the public beaches when he was a kid. He kicked off his shoes, lifted the front and slid the boat into the water.

"You know Gib," Addison said as she slipped her legs into the wetsuit. "if there is a cave down there, and if it is real deep, we might not be able to go all the way down with this equipment."

"I thought about that." He answered. "I'm not sure Gerald would make it that hard."

She hoped so. She was barely confident enough in her diving ability to do a deep dive. Cave diving, especially if it was a small cave, might be more than she could handle.

Josh grabbed their air tanks and hoisted them into the boat. When he saw Addison, covered from neck to toe in a bulky blue and black wet suit, he couldn't help snickering out loud. "They didn't have anything a little more modern? Or...stylish?"

Addison pulled her scuba cap over her head to complete the look. "The water down there is probably about forty-five degrees, Josh. I'm not gonna be too upset if the fish don't find me sexy."

He vaguely recalled the extreme cold of the deep, but didn't remember it being that bad. Of course, that was the least of his concerns during his time at the bottom of Pipestone Bay.

Addison climbed in the boat with Gib ready right behind her. He stopped and offered Josh one last chance. "Now you're sure you don't want to go down with us. It doesn't seem right to get the second stone without you."

Josh shook his head with an unequivocally firm no. "I'll see it when you bring it up. Gerald almost killed me once already."

"You almost killed yourself." Addison corrected. "Don't go blaming Gerald for your exceptionally dim light bulb."

Josh waded the boat out to deeper water then he jumped in. He crawled over to the middle seat, took hold of the oars and began rowing. His technique with these wasn't much better than with a canoe paddle, but Addison didn't see a reason to comment. Their line was fairly straight and their speed well enough for the short trip. Only once did she think about offering her help, when they came out of the cove and crossed the current too close to the falls. The water took the stern around and started to turn them. Josh pulled harder when he realized it and they passed over without losing too much distance.

He handled it fine and there were no other areas to cause the same problem. Besides, she was more interested in the shoreline. She looked for distinctive trees and rocks and lined them up with the reefs shown on the depth map. They'd surely be fishing this lake later and she, as any good guide should, would be ready to hit the best spots.

"That's good, Josh." Gib said as they approached the middle.

He and Addison lifted themselves up to opposite edges of the boat. Josh held the gunnels on both sides, leaning more toward Addison to balance the weight. "Don't tip me."

"Ready?" Gib asked as he pulled his dive mask over his eyes. Addison, already with her mask on and already with the regulator in her mouth signaled back with an upturned thumb. They tilted back slowly, tipped back further, and finally splashed in.

Just ten feet down, the stained water blocked out all traces of the sun above and the lights attached to their dive masks cut only narrow beams through the darkness. They came first to a barrier of dead branches and the remains of a drown forest of trees Gerald left standing.

Their lights reflected flashes of silver and gold lures hooked on their spindly fingers. Addison marked it as good structure for fishing, though she wasn't sure if the time taken to retie lures was really worth it.

Gib was more worried about finding a way through the trees. He wanted to avoid them, but a quick scan around showed more of the same in all directions. He snapped off the top of the closest tree and let it float away; easy enough for the higher up branches but as he continued making a hole down the trunk the branches became thicker and more resistant.

Addison stayed close behind, thinking less and less about the habitat of the fish and more about the increasingly tangled web of branches they were weaving themselves into. Each small turn in their route was another one she'd have to remember for the way back up and each tree limb they snaked around was another unbreakable obstacle to keep her from the safety of the surface. If she lost her head now, if she panicked and needed to get up fast, she'd have to fight these trees to do it.

Her brow, under the snug fit of the wet suit, felt hot and slick despite the cold of the deep. Gib's flippers kicked just inches in front of her face and she made sure they stayed just that close. She need only grab one with a firm yank to get his attention and abandon this.

Forty feet down they found the bottom of the lake. They pulled themselves from one trunk to the next, twisting around them and turning in different directions.

There would be no going back the way they came and the reality of that made Gib more nervous as well. Behind him, Addison tried to keep her mind off it. She convinced herself that the sunken forest would eventually thin if they just kept going. The lake's pretty small, she told herself, though she had a hard time believing it. Down here, right now, it felt every bit as big as the giant lake just to their south.

The lake bed sloped down and the deeper they went the steeper the slope became. The sharper angle did thin out the trees as Addison hoped. When Gib looked back to check on her, she gave him another thumbs up. Her eyes told a different story. They darted from side to side and up and down, apprehensive and anxious. He waved her up to swim along side him so he could keep an eye on her – and she on him.

In the dark, their lights gave a greenish tint to the brown water. They saw only illuminated particles of algae and silt. Gib realized this entire effort might be futile. Everything needed careful inspection; each rock they floated over, every dip, and each hump. An actual dive light would help, or maybe an underwater camera they could use from the safety of the boat. Surely the sports store had those as well and he wondered why he didn't have the foresight to think of those things earlier.

As he kept pressing on, going deeper and deeper, Addison began to slow and lag behind. She had reached her limit. Gib was close to his too, but with just a few more kicks the lake bed abruptly flattened out. He turned back to Addison, flashed his lights at her mask to get her attention, and signaled five more minutes with his hand. She nodded her agreement and swam up beside him.

This flat had none of the humps or dips that they had seen so far. It was covered in fine silt and there were no rocks. To Gib, its perfect evenness looked more like the bottom of a swimming pool than a lake bed.

They swam along the edge where the steeper drop met with the even ground and followed it around until they came back to the place he thought they entered. It was circular, just as had been shown on the map, and Gib guessed it was only about thirty feet in diameter. To Addison, he pointed across into the middle of the circle. They both kicked off from the edge to make a straight line across.

Addison's lights slashed back and forth as she turned her head from side to side to carefully watch for what might be ahead. Gib's lights scoured the floor with the same pattern as he looked for some kind of opening.

To Addison's right, just as she was passing by, she found another, thinner tree standing all alone. She scanned up its trunk until she saw two arms jutting out at right angles that were too perfect for anything natural. She reached over and tugged on the leg of Gib's suit and pointed it out to him.

Gib saw it and also recognized that it wasn't a tree. Three feet out, on both sides, the arms curved up sharply.

They curled back toward each other and rejoined at a sharp peak about ten feet up. He swam over and scratched at the pole's bumpy surface. Thin flakes peeled off and wafted slowly away. It was rust. To him it was obvious; the lock to the final stone would open with the turn of this key.

Addison watched his inspection. Her fear was fading and excitement was taking over. Attached to the bottoms of the two arms were square handles. Gib took hold of the closest one and motioned for Addison to go take the other. She swam over and let her legs drop down to secure footing. The bottom was harder than she expected and without the normal give of a mucky lake bottom. She showed Gib an okay sign and motioned that she would push while he pulled.

It turned surprisingly easy, as if eagerly waiting all these years for someone smart enough to find it, and one small turn was all it needed. The key jerked and twisted farther around, yanking Gib and Addison along with it as they held on. The unusually flat lake bed, four separate square slabs of cement, suddenly fell away into a deep chasm below and a crushing rush of draining water flooded over them.

———

"It's too big." Harris complained.

Temple continued to hold out his camouflage jacket to him anyway. The bright yellow of Harris' shirt made him too easy to spot and right now, standing among the trees below Kearny's cabin, they needed discretion.

Harris didn't want it, even if it would have fit him. Wearing it brought him too close to the sneaky act of covert surveillance. It brought him too close to being one of them. Besides that, it was really rather pointless. It didn't do anything to cover his blue jeans or white sneakers.

Above them, Meyers eased away from the windowed wall of the cabin, hopped over the stream then slipped back down the hill to where Temple and Harris stood. "No one is in the house, but someone is here. There are used dinner plates on the table."

Temple nodded and touched the receiver on his ear. "Walsh?"

"We disabled the truck, sir." Walsh answered. "We're about to head down to the second cabin."

Just as Walsh finished, another voice broke over the radio. "Tucker here, sir. I've got 'em…well, one of them anyway."

Temple frowned at the off-handed comment. "What do you mean?"

"It's one of the guys." Tucker answered. "He's sitting in a boat in the middle of the lake at the top of the mountain."

"Is he fishing?" Temple asked.

"No, he's just sitting there looking at the trees."

Temple gave Meyers a curious look. "And there's no sign of the others?"

"Not that I can see, sir."

"Stay there." Temple ordered. "We're coming to your position. Walsh, you and Ritter meet us up there."

At the top of the hill, Meyers held Temple and Harris back just before they got to the dam. Ahead of him, within the branches of a scraggly looking balsam, Tucker was holding up a halting palm. He kept them there for a moment then showed one finger to allow Meyers up when he was certain it was safe.

Temple looked over to Harris while they waited. He was still carrying the jacket in his hand. In a light, jovial tone, Temple said, "If my advantage is spoiled by your obstinacy, I will put a bullet in your head as well."

Harris' skin turned cold and clammy. He was accustomed to threats of his job, but this was the first time his life had been threatened, even jokingly. He put the jacket on and tried to dismiss the comment with a nervous laugh and a mumbled "Sorry."

Meyers' voice whispered over the radio and in it there was hint of satisfaction. "It's the rookie." He reported, happy for another chance at the kid who dared to stare him down back on White Iron. "There's something else. Bubbles keep breaking the surface of the water beyond the boat."

Temple thought for a moment then understood exactly what was going on. "They're diving."

"I'd say that's a safe bet." Meyers confirmed. "What do we do know."

"We wait." Temple answered.

―――

Josh sat in the middle of the lake whistling the song of the chickadee and listening for a reply. At first, he wished he'd brought his fishing pole. Not long after, he realized it probably wouldn't be a good idea to have a hook dangling in the water while Addison and Gib were down there.

When he grew tired of whistling, he passed the time by tracing an imaginary line with his finger to connect the tops of the trees on the far shore. He was just about to start outlining the other shore when he realized that the boat, that had been completely stationary for the last fifteen minutes, was now moving backward.

The current, he thought, even though he was reasonably certain that he hadn't been moving before. A sprig of birch leaves floated past him to the right. It was faster than he thought it should be and it was traveling in the *opposite* direction of the out-flowing falls. He followed its path across the water with a puzzled look. Ten yards out it began circling around in wide loops. With each pass its circle became smaller and smaller until it simply dropped out of sight.

Josh shook his head and slowly blinked his eyes twice to make sure he wasn't seeing things. It was as if some large fish had sucked it down from below. As the boat inched closer to where the leaves disappeared, he saw a weird depression in the water's surface. Slowly it dawned on him what could be causing such a disturbance.

The boat was picking up speed and Josh stood up to verify what he knew shouldn't be possible; what he hoped wasn't possible. A giant, swirling whirlpool had opened in the water. It looked bottomless from his vantage point and it was growing bigger.

'Addison…Gib." He thought solemnly, knowing they must have been at the hole that created this. He stood there wondering what he could do to help them until he realized that the hole wasn't getting bigger so much as he was getting closer to it.

He fell back onto his seat and fumbled with the oars while the gaping mouth pulled him around into a wide circle. With the oars in position, he beat frantically against the water to escape and tried directing the boat across the current to break free. Instead, the whirlpool spun the boat around and brought its bow forward, positioning it and him for an easier gulp. Josh switched his strokes and began rowing forward.

With each revolution, the circle became smaller and the trees lining the lake began to spin around faster. "Oh come on." He huffed, sounding more annoyed than frightened that his uncle's games were about to send him to the bottom of another lake.

Upon hitting the rim of the opening, the front of the boat hung in mid-air until its weight shifted. The boat fell over with its nose plunging straight down into the funnel's throat and Josh was dumped to the side. For a moment the whirlpool slowed and shallowed as it swallowed down it first big meal. Josh surfaced just beyond the mouth and swam as hard as he could to get away.

Growing again to its full size, the whirlpool's lip finally drew him in. His body slipped into a spiral that twirled him in tighter and quicker circles as he descended. For a split second, he marveled at the cone of water that surrounded him then his stomach churned from the dizzying rotations. Faster still, he turned and turned until he was practically spinning in place. He was about to go under. This time, unlike his experience at the Pipestone falls, he managed one good gulp of air.

This was his fault, Gib thought as they dangled from the metal handles under a barrage of flooding water. In his eagerness, his blind following of the clues to get the other stone, he forgot about Gerald's vision and the wondrous things he had shown them; that he still had to show them. This situation couldn't be avoided, but they could have at least been prepared for it. They could have been ready.

His grip started to give and he dropped his head to look below, to see where he would go when his hands finally gave out. His dive lights showed only a large cross shaped brace spanning the chasm that supported the giant key. Beyond that was the blackness of a deep abyss. He thought of Addison and forced his head up against the current to make sure she was safe.

She was still there, holding tight with both hands and looking up to the surface. She was watching the cone of clearer light that reached down to them. Once the initial confusion had cleared, she figured out what was happening. They were at the bottom of a giant sink filled with water and they had just released its plug.

She was thinking about Josh on the surface and if the row boat was close enough to get caught in the pull, or if he was even aware of what was happening down here. She envisioned a miniature version of him swirling around in her kitchen sink, his arms flailing wildly as he was swept away with the dirty water.

A large dark form dimmed the light above. The row boat, she assumed, and probably Josh as well. She turned her head toward Gib and focused her lights directly into his face. She wanted to warn him of what was coming, of the boat that might crash into them and of Josh disappearing into the seemingly bottomless pit below. The bright light shining in his eyes did catch his attention, though not soon enough.

He didn't see Addison with her single finger pointing up to something above. He didn't see the boat rushing down to them. He only felt the sudden jolt when its wooden hull slammed into the key with the pointed top, when his grip slipped to just a finger tip hold. Then he saw it, impaled through the front side with its back end tilted nearly vertical. After that came a flood of sickening guilt as he thought of Josh.

Still spinning, Josh came down right after, crashing into the boat that saved him from being impaled himself. Had he been able to think clearly, had his senses recovered from the swirling cyclone, he might have been able to react quickly enough to grab for some part to hold on to. Instead, he bounced off and passed the boat, past the arm of the key and past the shadowy figure that was Addison, down to the giant gullet waiting to take him down.

He stopped with a jerking snap. The water pulled harder on him and he slipped a little further down. Only his t-shirt held him up, bunched around his neck and choking him. His legs dangled into the black cave and they fluttered freely in the water's flow.

Addison slowly and carefully cinched more material into her grip to keep the cloth from ripping. The seam of the neck had already torn once and she nearly lost him just as soon as she caught him. Only her left arm kept them both from being flushed away and her grip was loosening. The endless flood of water continued to flow over them. Her shoulder throbbed from the pain and now her muscles started to twitch under the increased burden.

Gib saw the strain in her face. She wouldn't last much longer and if Josh slipped away into the dark below, without an air tank and without a light, he would be lost forever. He knew his next action was foolish, but he couldn't just wait for the lake to drain. He looked down at the crossbeam below and stretched his left leg as far out to the side as he could.

Addison was watching him and she knew what he was about to try. Even if she could speak, she wouldn't have told him not to. She couldn't hold on much longer. She watched as he let go of the handle and she watched as his body was whisked away.

His leg slammed into the beam and curled around it. The flow spun him upside down and left him dangling into the chasm from his bent knee. In the onslaught of rushing water, he panned his dive lights around to watch for Josh. His feet were dangling just above him, or rather, below him now from his upended perspective.

Addison's grip on the rung failed and Gib grabbed hold of Josh's shorts. He didn't need to. Josh was close enough to the cross bar to catch it with his arms and Addison was quick enough to catch Josh's shoulders.

She was about to try giving him air from her regulator, but as suddenly as the current started it simply stopped. The cave below filled, the pressure equalized and the flow of the water reversed. The three of them were thrust back up to the surface. None of them expected the shift in current and all of them were snatched loose from their holds. Their bodies were thrust upward about twenty feet before the ebb subsided. Josh, now underwater for almost two minutes, found himself once again swimming madly for the surface.

The gray light above him, blurry and distant, came clearer and crisper with each frantic kick. His arms paddled in large arcing loops, pin wheeling around as he pulled through the water as fast as he could. His lungs burned, but he did not panic. He hadn't even started to black out yet. He broke the surface with a speed that lifted him nearly waist high out of the water and he filled his lungs with a loud, raspy swallow of air.

Addison and Gib popped up right after. Addison spit out her regulator and swam to him. "Josh!" She called, concerned only, but sounding just as harsh as she did at Pipestone Bay.

"That one wasn't my fault!" Josh defended between breaths. "He really did try to kill me that time."

Addison pulled off her scuba cap and stuffed it under the strap of the air tank. "That time – yes, he was trying to kill us."

"No," Gib sighed, frustrated that his foresight had abandoned him and that it almost ended in disaster. "I should have realized that was going to happen."

Addison scoffed, "How could you possibly know *that* was going to happen?"

"Not that specifically, but I should have known something was coming. I should have been prepared."

Gib knew better than to chastise himself with the easy judgment of hindsight, but the setup was almost obvious. The unusually flat bottom should have tipped him off and the handles on the crossbar were there for that very reason. He just missed it.

"You were really moving down there, Josh." Addison said more lightly. "I tried to catch up to give you some air, but you were like a torpedo."

"Yeah well, circling around the edge of death has a way of inspiring that." He answered. He laid back and began regulating his breathing, deep enough to recover, but careful not to let out too much air and lose his buoyancy. He was an expert at it now.

Addison looked over to Gib. "So I guess we're going to have to dive that cave after all." She said and she didn't sound all that thrilled about it. In fact, she doubted she would be able to do it.

"Maybe." Gib mumbled in agreement. Right now he was more interested in the new, lower shoreline. "The lake looks like it dropped about three feet."

Addison circled around to see it and was amazed by the changes. The tan sand of the beach now sat higher up from the water, the trees seemed taller, and dozens of boulders had popped through the surface where they hadn't been before. Also the shape of the lake, its line, had changed. The careful study of the waters that she had done earlier was now worthless.

"Why would Gerald do that?" She wondered out loud. "Why would he have rigged it to drain so much?"

"I don't know." Gib answered. A moment later he added, "With the water this low, the stream won't run anymore."

Josh floated silently, a little bitter still about his experience, but mostly calm and relaxed. His head was half submerged with his ears just below the water level. Outside noises were muffled - the voices of the others, the trees rustling in the wind, and a dull, distant rush of water. Gib's comment didn't register at first, but after a few seconds he realized the contradiction in what he'd said.

Josh exhaled the deeper breath he'd been holding and let himself float upright. "Well, at least not until the incoming river fills it up again."

Gib and Addison then heard it, too. The background noise of running water, constant since they'd arrived, still announced its presence. It was quieter now and more distant, but it was still there. They turned to the back of the lake and saw a small waterfall dropping off an abrupt rock ledge.

"That's it!" Addison cried out excitedly. "That's where we need to go." She began kicking a long side stroke in the direction of the falls.

Gib was hesitant. He wanted to be more careful this time. He wanted to think it through. "Hold on a sec, Addy."

"It has to be, Gib." She said. "It makes perfect sense and you said you didn't think Gerald would make it that hard."

She started swimming and Josh went off after her. Gib followed, though at a significantly slower pace. He kept looking around the lake, checking out the shoreline and trying to see what else he could be missing.

Forty-five minutes later they arrived at the far shore. If it hadn't been for Gib calling for them to slow down and dragging way behind, they could have done it in thirty. Addison waded up from the lake slipping off her flippers and unbuckling the heavy tank as she approached the falls. The water fell over in a wide, flat stream and through the clear curtain she saw an empty space behind.

Josh came up after, saw what she did, and looked back across the lake impatiently. Gib was still thirty yards out. "Get your butt movin', Gib!" He shouted.

Gib stubbornly kept his slow pace. "Just hold on, guys. We need to be careful."

Once again Josh and Addison waited to let Gib have the honor of actually retrieving the stone and he was glad they did. This time he would have insisted on it. His carelessness had already put them in danger once. He wanted to be ready.

During the long swim over he remembered the book and the passage he'd read just yesterday. He remembered the description of Archer holding himself tightly as he tried to contain his excitement and how that excitement needed to be released carefully to avoid danger. That passage most likely referred to the whirlpool, but he didn't think Gerald was done with them yet. He still had something more to show them. Gib was certain of it.

He tossed his air tank off to the side and took a long look at the new course of the river. Before, it had flowed into the lake evenly and with little disruption. Now, there was a downward slope of bubbling water pouring over exposed rocks on the riverbed.

Addison and Josh stood next to him waiting anxiously. "Gib." Addison pushed.

He knelt down, still hesitant and still unsure, and he looked around one last time for anything that seemed out of place or important, or possibly dangerous. Finally, in one sudden and decisive move he plunged his hand through the water. It was a leap of faith that he hoped wouldn't turn out badly.

There was more space than he expected. His forearm was completely inside and his hand still moved around without touching anything. He dropped down to his hip and reached in all the way up to his shoulder. His finger tips found rock far back, but just barely.

"Is it big?" Josh asked excitedly. The thought of exploring a cave sounded fun to him, as long as it was above water.

"No." Gib said as he brought his arm out. He pulled his scuba mask back over his eyes, flipped on the switch for the dive lights, and laid flat on his stomach with his arms under his chest.

The water only came up to the sides of his ribs and it lightly lapped against his chin as he inched his way through the tight opening. The whole upper half of his body was able to fit in. The back wall, just inches from his face, was the same smooth concrete as the pyramid rock back on Newton Lake. He crooked his head to the side and tilted it up to see above. Instead of more rock wall there was the darkness of an opening.

He wriggled and twisted his body around until his arm came free. His fingers slid their way up the slimy wall, up to the top and over the ledge to a shelf. There, he felt dry dusty sand. Even in its position directly beneath the river bed, this small alcove never saw a drop of water.

Whatever was up there was still out of reach. He wiggled his body further in until his face was pressed hard against the rock wall and his hand could go further in. Deeper back he felt the smooth and round shape of the stone. It sat in a shallow dip that kept it in its place. Gib sucked in a heavy breath and prepared him self for what might happen. He poked and pushed the stone with his fingertips until finally it rocked off its sunken base and rolled close enough for him to grab.

He retreated quickly from the cave, popped up on his knees and looked around to see what new wonder the releasing of this stone created. Nothing had happened. Beside him, Josh and Addison were completely unaware that anything was supposed to happen. They crowded around him to see the stone.

It had the same gold lines as the other, as well as the same core with milky shards exploding outward. It was its twin in every way except that the lines twisted in different directions and there seemed to be more of them. Addison ran her fingers over the glassy surface.

"I can't believe it." She said with detached reverence. "You actually did it."

There was a hollowness inside her along with her excitement. Besides the feeling of triumph, there was sadness and grief. It was over.

Gib felt it too, the emptiness she was experiencing. He was sure that there would be more; that Gerald would have left something else. The absence of it left him reeling and uncertain. He stuffed the stone into his scuba cap and gathered a hold around the neck.

Only Josh truly felt the sense of satisfaction for achieving their goal. He had enjoyed every minute of it and he couldn't ask for anything more. Only he truly appreciated the moment.

Gerald Kearny

———

Harris stood with his binoculars pressed firmly against his face. He had watched it all and he understood what had happened at the bottom of the lake. The whirlpool must have been spectacular to see, even in the threat of death. He thought he would have reveled in the experience. The waterfall, and the understanding of it, was also brilliant. That little clue he wasn't sure if could have figured out. That was far too clever for him and he found himself admiring these young kids.

Next to him, of course, now that he was close to getting his prize, was Temple. He had skipped watching their swim across the lake. He had grown tired of their slow progress, especially after they came up from the bottom empty handed and especially after the lake had spit up the "could-be" hero alive. He had thanked Kearny for ridding him of that potential nuisance when Josh first went into the water then he cursed him when he saw his ineffectiveness.

"Meyers." Temple called.

Meyers bounced himself off the tree he was leaning against and waved for the other men to get up from the seats they had taken. It was time for them now.

"They've got it." Temple said and he looked up to the darkening sky. An orange tinged full moon was just rising in the east. "It will be night by the time they get back here. Tell your men to be ready."

He turned back to Harris who was still watching the kids. Temple thought he saw him smiling. "Harris!"

Harris jumped and dropped the binoculars. They crashed against a rock with a loud crack and the sharp clink of breaking glass.

"I want you to go to the main cabin and find the other stone." He ordered. "Tear the place apart if you have to."

Harris didn't turn to acknowledge his order. He didn't jump at his command with his usual "Yes, sir."

Temple watched him carefully as he picked up the shattered lens. "Take Ritter with you." He amended.

Meyers nodded Ritter out of the attentive line. "Where do you want the rest of us?"

"We'll take positions just below the lake, on both sides of the trail. Until Harris has the other stone, we will keep the girl and Mr. Larkin alive."

"And the rookie?" Meyers asked.

"Eliminate him first when they cross between us."

CHAPTER 17

Josh shifted his footing, steadied his weight and carefully hopped from the big boulder he was standing on to another just ahead. His arms wavered to counter his wobbled landing and the two sets of flippers he was carrying for Gib and Addison swung back and forth in his hands. This new shoreline allowed an easier way around the lake without having to fight the trees, but the rocky bottom didn't seem any easier to him. "Man I'm hungry." He said as he picked another boulder to land on.

"Really," Addison said sarcastically. "that's so unlike you." She jerked up her shoulders to shift the weight of the air tank and pulled its strap tighter to carry the cumbersome load higher on her back.

"It's almost dark." Josh defended. "Lunch was hours ago."

Gib gave him a dubious, sideways look. "What about the brick of cheese you had before we came up here?"

"Well…that was just a snack."

"And the chips? And the candy bar?" Gib said again.

"Yeah, but they were part of the snack." Josh countered then he leapt to another rock. "It wasn't an actual meal. I need something more substantial."

Addison watched his landing, expecting the inevitable fall but holding her tongue for now. "Hey Gib, Josh and I were talking yesterday and we were wondering what you're going to do with the stones now that you've got them."

He thought for a moment, though he wasn't sure why. He'd considered that question many times without coming to any definite answer. The few more seconds he was taking to respond wouldn't change it. "I'm not sure. What do you guys want to do with them?"

"Oh no." She said right back. "That call is on you. I don't want the responsibility. If we don't agree it will just end up in a big fight."

He reconsidered his approach and tried again. "Well let's say it was your decision. What would you do then?"

She looked over to him with an irritated and exasperated glance. "Funny, that seems like just another way of making us responsible."

Gib laughed. He didn't really expect her to fall for that, though he half-expected Josh to chime in. "I used to think I would keep them, but I let that go a long time ago. It seems kind of selfish and I wouldn't want my family fighting over them when I'm gone. I'd really like them to be shared among the families, but I can't see a way for that to work."

Josh jumped again to another boulder but this time he wasn't so careful, or graceful. His body rocked wildly and his arms flailed to counter his unstable landing. The flippers in his left hand whipped around and hit him in the face, stunning him and causing him to slip off the wet, mossy rock. He was able to keep his feet under him and he danced a few awkward steps on the smaller sharper stones covering the exposed lake bed.

"Josh," Addison finally snapped. "just walk on the ground! You're making me crazy. You're gonna fall and bust your head open."

"Hey! You guys have water socks on. I don't have anything. Those little rocks are killing my feet."

Addison didn't accept his excuse. "A gash in your head is gonna hurt even worse. And if I have to haul your unconscious butt back to the cabin it's gonna hurt even more 'cause I'll be draggin' you by your feet."

Gib gave a low chuckle as he pictured Josh's limp head clunking against each of the stone stairs on the hill. He laughed again, and a little louder, at the image of a frustrated Addison dragging him along, grumbling and complaining under her breath.

Josh defiantly hopped across two more boulders before heeding her advice. They were just about to the dam of boulders anyway. On the more stable and rockier ground, his toes curled upward with each step and his feet arched and twisted to find the least painful placement.

"What about a museum?" Josh asked, continuing the topic Addison had started as he tried to keep his mind off the irritating little rocks.

"Maybe." Gib answered thoughtfully. He'd considered that solution before, but it seemed somewhat detached from Gerald's legacy to just ship them off to some far away museum in a big city. "I just don't want them sitting around collecting dust without meaning something."

"Well," Addison said. "It's not like you have to decide right away. Keep 'em until you figure something out." She stopped when they came to the dam and once again shifted the tank on her back before stepping up on the first one.

Josh came up behind her waiting for her to cross over and pick up the trail leading back down to the cabin. He couldn't resist this opportunity. "Oh no! How are we ever gonna get across the boulders without busting our heads open?"

Addison shot back a scathing glare for his excessive exaggeration. She was about to argue. She was about to explain that the tops of these boulders were never under the water and weren't covered in wet moss. She thought about it then realized that was just what he wanted. Instead, she extended her hand and gave him a mischievous smile. "I'd be happy to help you across."

Josh pushed Gib ahead of him to avoid her and to avoid possibly tumbling back down to the cabin by way of the creek bed.

Through the cracks, as she led them over, Addison could see the smooth surface of the cement mortar holding the boulders in place. It was easier now that the water wasn't flowing, but not too easy and still too disguised from anyone who didn't know to look.

"Hold up." Josh called wincing as he stepped off the last boulder and finally back on the trail. He didn't expect any of the sharp little rocks on the dirt path, but they were there too. He lifted up his foot to inspect a particularly nasty pebble imbedded almost completely under the skin. "I've gotta get my shoes." He said and gingerly trotted down the trail to the beach.

"Just meet us down there." Gib shouted back.

With the darkness of night already taking over, Josh picked up his pace despite the pain to his feet.

Across the path, from their hidden positions among the trees, Temple and Meyers exchanged questioning looks as only Gib and Addison passed between them. Neither dared even a whisper to ruin their silent advantage. Meyers was waiting for orders. Temple expected him to make the call - it was, after all, his area of expertise. That is what he was paid for.

Temple shrugged his shoulders with annoyance and Meyers got the message that he was now in charge. He pointed a finger to Temple and then to Walsh and simulated a walking motion with his fingers. He wanted them to follow the first two kids down the hill after they passed. He then gestured that he and Tucker would go up the hill for the rookie.

Once Temple nodded his understanding, Meyers gave the go ahead signal. His own first step was careful and quiet, but his awareness of his surroundings was not. A dried and broken branch from the tree that covered him was snagged against his shirt. As he rolled back around the trunk, the stub of wood snapped off with a loud crack.

In the quiet transition from the busy daytime forest to the waking nighttime creatures the sound traveled through the trees clearly and crisply. Meyers froze and melted into the dark background hoping the telling noise would not reveal them.

Both Gib and Addison heard it and both assumed they would see some larger animal accompanying them through the woods. Even in the darkness Gib recognized the human face. In fact, the darkness helped him remember. It was the ghostly, floating head from White Iron and that face meant danger. He dropped his air tank and yelled at Addison. "Run!"

She was already a half-step ahead of him, dropping her tank as well and leading their full sprint down the hill. One shot rang out from Walsh's rifle. The bullet splintered off the bark of a tree trunk that Gib had just passed.

"No!" Temple screamed. "I need them alive." He touched the radio piece in his ear. "Ritter, they're coming to you. Be ready. Meyers, take care of the rookie. Walsh, you're with me."

Gib and Addison beat down the trail leaping three and four steps at a time until they were back at the cabin. Addison grabbed the rail of the porch and was about to turn up the stairs when she suddenly skidded to stop. Her legs slid out from under her and she fell to her side. The cabin was lit up and they had left no lights on.

"No, no, no." She huffed and scrambled back to her feet. A man suddenly appeared in the windowed door.

Gib pulled her up by the arm and they started again down the path at full speed. Ritter opened the door with his gun drawn. Temple and Walsh came down soon after. "They took off before I could get them." Ritter reported.

Temple, now frustrated that his clever back up plan had failed, hissed back at him, "You've found the first stone?"

"No." Ritter answered cowering slightly behind the door when he saw the anger in Temple's eyes.

"Find it!" He ordered sternly.

Addison leapt off the bridge, turned toward the pond and began to slow again. They had a choice here and she really didn't know what to do. The parking lot and the truck was the smarter option, but that was almost unthinkable. "What about Josh?" She called back to Gib.

"Down to the guest house. We'll lose 'em on the trails."

The echo from the shot rang out across the lake just as Josh was slipping on his other shoe. He had to think for a moment to recall the vaguely familiar sound. When he was seven, a friend of his father's had taken them to Iowa for a turkey hunt. It was the last year real bullets were allowed to be sold for old fashioned guns. Josh was brought along so that one day he could tell his children how he had gone hunting when it was "done the right way."

That day his father's friend shot just about everything that moved in the field they walked. Nothing was safe from him; squirrels, rabbits, gophers and a variety of birds fell before the man that was hell-bent on cramming a lifetime of real hunting into just one day. Josh was too young to remember it very well, but he could recall the sound that rang in his ears even hours after they'd gone home.

His heart raced as he envisioned one of his friends falling like the prey of that maniacal hunting spree. But he'd also heard someone shout "no" and "I want them alive." The shot had missed and that gave him some hope that Gib and Addison could have gotten away.

His next thought, his instinct, brought him back to Old Ely and to the men that had chased them; to the persistence and tenacity in their chase. They were carrying real guns. They had tracked them here somehow and surely they knew where he was too.

There was only one reason why they would still be after them. Gib's interest in the stones may be altruistic, but there were plenty of other people with more self-serving intentions. There was money to be made from the stones and these men were willing to kill for them. He hoped the others realized that. He hoped they would have the sense to escape into the woods and bring back the police, though part of him knew they wouldn't leave him behind. He also knew that these men had been waiting for them and that at least one of them would soon be coming for him.

He darted across the beach and into the cover of the woods, crouching and creeping from spruce to balsam. He shed his white t-shirt for the duller color of tanned skin and he carefully kept hidden among the twilight shadows. At every sound he stopped. The mosquitoes fed unchecked, but he didn't move until he was sure the way was clear.

Meyers passed him first, on his way back down from checking the beach. Not three feet from him, Josh stayed perfectly still within the dense, needly branches. Even his recognition of the camouflaged clothing and the marked face didn't cause him to stir.

Twice more the two men crossed his path as he made his way down the hill and both times he was the silent monster in the trees, blending with the forest and keeping its dark secrets. He followed them even, with a discreet distance as he stepped lightly around fallen twigs and low-hanging branches. He watched their signals to each other and he looked for the pattern in their search. Their sweep of the woods was methodical and symmetrical, even when they doubled back in arcing loops to check behind them. He watched it and he committed it to memory.

The two men split at the cabin and signaled to meet up on the other side. Once they were out of sight, Josh crawled into the creek bed and slid on his belly under the arch of the cabin's base.

He refused to dwell on what else was down there with him; the many-legged insects and hard-shelled beetles that took comfort in this tight, dank space. Surely he was crushing some of them as he slid along the ground and more were probably falling onto him from above. Even with the fluttering sound of a bat taking flight, the tousling of his hair by one of its leathery wings, he did not lose his focus. The light from the echo chamber was just ahead.

There, he was able to stand straight up in the small square space and the top opening was only two more feet above him. He stretched up and forced his fingers through the mesh of the screen where the clasps held it in place. They "clicked" their release and he cringed at the potentially revealing sound. More carefully then, he pulled and twisted until the flimsy aluminum frame collapsed in half and he quietly set it on the creek bed.

Wedging his legs against the sides of the rock wall shaft, he inched his way up until he was able to peek over the edge. In the kitchen, shifting around glasses in one of the cabinets, was another man in a camo jacket. Unlike the other two in the forest, the look didn't really suit this guy; not only in its too-large size, but in its suggestion of ruggedness as well. This man's fine hair was too styled and too neat and his delicate handling of the glasses suggested a gentler disposition.

In the loft above, Josh heard drawers being roughly yanked out of the dresser and banging loudly against the floor when tossed aside. That guy would be wearing the same jacket and, judging by the sounds of his recklessness, Josh figured it probably suited him just fine.

'They're looking for the other one.' He thought. He looked over to the sculpture above the fireplace and saw the stone still sitting there – and still lit up. They expected it to be hidden and with that frame of mind they would never see where it sat in plain sight.

He pulled himself up and over the edge and stretched his first step far over to the area rug covering the hardwood floor. Two more long, striding hops and he was to the wall separating the bedrooms from the living room, flattening his body against it to stay out of sight from the man in the kitchen. From the end table next to the couch, he carefully removed a pillared candle from its thick wooden base. He poked his head around the corner, watching the man as he put the glasses back and waiting for the right moment.

Harris replaced the last glass and closed the cabinet. Behind him Josh leapt from toe to quiet toe to cut the distance as swiftly as possible. The tiny grains of sand embedded in the tracks of his shoes scratched across the bare kitchen tile. When Harris turned at the sound, he saw a muddy blur charging at him.

Josh brought up the candle holder from behind him and with one looping swing connected it with the side of the man's head. Harris' head snapped to the side, his sight went black and his legs gave out. Josh caught the limp body and slowly lowered it to the ground.

"Harris." Ritter called out from above. "Harris, it ain't up here, man." His heavy boots clanged on the iron spiral stairs as he trotted down. His last step, a leap from the third stair, announced his arrival on the ground floor with a loud thud.

"Harris?" He called again as he came out of the living room. Deeper into the kitchen he saw Harris' legs sprawled on the floor. "Har…" He began to say again then he suddenly dropped to the ground in a fit of convulsions.

Josh stood hidden in his bedroom doorway with his arm stretched out along the wall and his taser gun still trained on the man. The body jolted one final time before Josh relaxed his stance. As he walked back to the kitchen, he lifted his cell phone and said "911" into the speaker.

"Yes, I've got an emergency." Josh calmly told the dispatcher. He stopped at Harris' body and put his gun on the counter. "Josh Bertram." He answered the operator as he bent over to unbutton Harris' jacket. "There are several men trying to kill us…three of us. We're at the Kearny Cabin on the north shore. These men have guns – with bullets."

He unzipped the jacket, peeled it off the shoulders then he rolled Harris onto his stomach. "There are four that I have seen. I have two unconscious in the main cabin. Two more are searching the woods for me and I'm not sure how many more are chasing my friends."

The operator, skeptical of such malevolent violence in this rural area and skeptical because Josh's voice wasn't panicked and rambling, continued to press him with more questions. Partly she wanted to keep him on the line for his safety and partly she wanted to make sure this wasn't a prank.

Josh knew what she was doing and why. He curtly cut her off, his voice commanding and with a deep, surly boom. "Ma'am, my friends are about to die. I could be out there helping them instead of chit-chatting with you. Just send the police."

It was just the right mix of controlled anger and waning patience to get the woman's most serious attention. She told him a unit would be there in twenty-five minutes. He expected that this far out in the woods, but he answered that she'd better send three. Just as she was telling Josh to find a safe place to hide, he clicked the phone off and slid it into the pocket of his shorts.

He took Harris' jacket for himself then he went to the other man and took the radio piece from his ear. He couldn't chance leaving by the door and opted for the echo well again. He took one final look at Harris in the kitchen and slid back down to the riverbed. As he crawled out to the front of the cabin, a hushed and cautious voice sounded in his ear. "Meyers, we've almost got them. Come down to the second cabin after you've taken care of the rookie."

Gib took the lead when they came to the maze of trees. He grabbed Addison by the hand and led her down to the first turn. He took them right, as she expected, but then he stopped just after and pulled her tight against the tree branches. He peeked back around the corner and when he saw the two men coming he began rustling one of the larger branches sticking out into the path.

"What are you doing?!" Addison whispered harshly as she slapped Gib's hand away from the branch. "They're gonna see us."

Gib hurried her down to the next split in the trail, turned right again, and stopped again. The rising full moon gave the night a pale, steely glow that was just enough for Gib see all the way back down the trail. He brushed his nose against the side of Addison's head and softly spoke. This he did not want the men to hear. The rustling of the branches was intentional. "I want them to follow us. Go down to the next fork and wait for me."

Temple and Walsh saw the sign again. They rounded the turn and jumped to a stop with their arms stretched out and their guns ready. They'd just missed them, but down at the next turn the branches were wavering again. Walsh waved Temple to follow and they ran down to the next.

Ahead of them, at the next turn, Gib rustled another branch then ran to join Addison at the next intersection. "We'll lead them deeper in then we'll go wait for Josh by the guest house. I know he'll go there. It's the smartest place to go."

"Or he'll try something stupid." Addison said.

Gib hoped not, but he certainly wouldn't deny the possibility. After all, they were doing something stupid as well. "He'll come here by way of the stream bed just like you did yesterday. Then we'll disappear into the woods and make our way down to the highway."

Addison pointed at the scuba cap in his hand. He had taken it from his waist band when they first started down the hill and now he kept it tightly clutched in his hand. "That's what they want." She said. Then, hesitantly, "We could just give it to them…and the other."

Gib lifted the stone and looked at it as he considered her words. "We don't know if that'll change anything. We've seen them. We know what they look like. As far as we know, this is the only thing we have to bargain with."

The pounding footsteps of the men came again and Gib and Addison quickly headed off. At the next fork, Gib waited again for the men to catch up and again he moved the branches to show they had just passed by.

Walsh led Temple down to the next turn. Further down another shaking branch and another turn. Again they chased and two more times after that. Each time they were just one step too slow and each time they knew which way to go.

Walsh slowed up before they came to the next fork. This time he stopped before taking the corner and he held Temple back as well. He kept their pause until Temple finally became too impatient and began to push forward. Walsh suddenly rushed around the corner to make it seem like they were still running, but this time he didn't even bother lifting his gun. Still there was another disturbed tree branch at the next fork. "They're leading us, sir. They want us to follow them."

Temple's face turned its deepest shade of red, noticeable even at this time of night. He touched his earpiece and quietly barked at Meyers. "Meyers! Get down here." He waited for an answer, but none came.

He could guess why. Meyers wouldn't risk revealing his position during a hunt if he was close to his prey. "Get down here as soon as you're finished."

Temple retreated back down the path they just came from. "Follow them." He told Walsh. "The guest house is their destination and I'm certain there's an easier way to get there."

Walsh understood the plan. He would be the dupe lost in the woods while Temple waited to surprise them. He picked up his pace alone, but was only shown one more turn. At the next, he looked down each trail waiting for another sign. This choice was left to him. He looked at the trees for signs of broken branches and he looked at the ground for signs of tracks. There were none, but he did notice that the path leading left was more deeply depressed than the one on the right. After two more turns he understood the trick.

"They've split up." Gib said when he got to her at the next fork.

Addison's heart skipped and her breath caught. This little game of his had her feeling optimistic, until now. "Are you sure?"

The serious and somber look in his eyes showed the same concern as she. "We need to get to the guest house - now."

Each turn, each correct turn, was made with cautious looks and blind faith. Either of the men, or maybe more if the others had joined them now, could be at the next fork. Any of them could be in the trees, waiting for Gib and Addison to pass just as they had been waiting up by the lake. For Addison, the dark of this unknown forest was even more unnerving than the woods of White Iron. With each step her head swung from side to side expecting to see someone coming for them.

Gib noticed it. "They're lost, Addison. We just don't know where they're lost."

She wasn't comforted. It didn't feel that easy.

"Come on," Gib said, trying again. "the guest house is just ahead."

They stuck close to the tree line until they came to the opening. Gib stopped her and looked around. "We'll do a sprint around the courtyard to the stream bed."

Addison nodded her agreement and readied her self for the run with a deep breath. They burst into a furious sprint for the other side, crossing the grass, past the near side of the house, and rounding the sunken courtyard.

"Aughhhh!" Addison shrieked as a sharp pain suddenly pierced her upper left thigh. She stumbled and fell sideways onto the ground, skidding across the grass while clutching her leg.

"Addison!" Gib called sliding to a stop and turning to see what happened to her. He could see dark liquid oozing through the fingers pressed against her leg. She turned over to her side to right herself, but through the waves of pain she didn't realize how close she was to the drop into the courtyard. "Addison no, wait!" Gib warned.

She tipped over the stone lip and fell five feet to the stone floor below. Her upper arm and shoulder absorbed most of the fall, but her head took a good crack as well and now her whole body shuddered in pain.

Gib rushed down the stairs, past the weather vane, and dropped to his knees where Addison was trying to fight the daze of pain and disorientation.

"Hold still." He said with a gentle hand to her head. He looked at her leg and saw a frayed, round hole in the leg of her wetsuit. A bullet hole, he thought, even though there had been no gun shot.

"Gib." A man called out from behind him; what would have been in front of him had he not turned back for her. They had been outsmarted.

Josh found the two men during one of their back-tracking loops not far down from the cabin and close to the covered bridge. Or, at least, he'd found one of them. The ugly one with the scarred face was still out there. He hated that face. In those long seconds that their eyes had connected, he saw the coldness of a man without conscious or caring. He saw the face of a killer. He wanted to know exactly where that man was before taking out this one.

He was waiting for them to cross again, waiting for them to come back together so he could take them out at the same time. If he took one out now, if he interrupted their pattern, he would lose the other and his advantage.

Suddenly an angry and aggravated voice called through the ear piece telling someone named Meyers to "get down here". To the guest house, Josh assumed, and the maze. It was the most logical place for Gib and Addison to go. Well, it was the second most logical. He was right - they wouldn't leave him, no matter how much he wished they had.

This man didn't answer, nor did any other. A moment later the voice came again, calmer but also colder. It told Meyers to "get down there as soon as he was finished".

Finished with him, Josh knew. Gib and Addison were running out of time. He had to abandon his plan to wait these men out. He raised his gun and fired two quick shots at the man he was tracking.

Tucker's body jerked and convulsed then the muscles in his hands went limp and his gun dropped. It cracked loudly against a rock before Josh could catch it.

"Tuck?" Meyers barely whispered. "Tuck?"

Josh heard the voice in his ear, but he was trying to hear it from the woods so he could pinpoint the man's location. The scar-faced man was too careful and too clever to reveal himself that easily. Josh looked up to the lit windows of the cabin. Time for plan "C", he thought.

CHAPTER 18

Harris' eyes blinked open and they rolled big, lazy circles in their sockets. The left side of his face felt like it was glued to the shiny wood floor and his head felt like it had been split in two. It started with a sharp, stabbing crack in the back of his skull that dulled as it pulsed outward. He let it come again and again until he pinpointed the exact spot where his head had been cracked open. He reached up to rub the ache and drew his hand back to see how much blood was coming out. Surprisingly, there was none.

This is what he got for his involvement with men of questionable means. "I can't do this anymore." He said under his breath. He pulled himself up onto the kitchen counter. His sight was fuzzy and his legs wobbly. He'd have to shake that off along the way. He couldn't afford to rest now.

He hobbled shakily as he guided himself around the counter then he stumbled out the door, down the stairs of the deck and onto the dark path. His head was still pounding and his blurry vision struggled to adapt to the moonlit night.

He plodded along the path with clumsily steps until he saw the bridge and he pushed himself to move faster. In the shadows of the night, with his sight still blurry, he didn't see the dip in the ground ahead. His right foot stepped in, breaking his stride and twisting his ankle over. He fell down to one knee then his momentum lurched him farther forward. He crashed his chin into a corner post of the bridge.

"Ungh." He groaned as his teeth clunked hard together. A dull ring echoed in his head and it throbbed harder. Looking down into the ravine of the stream, he realized it was better to wait to regain his stability before continuing on and risk a more serious injury. He stood up and braced himself steady with one hand on the bridge rail. A loose chunk of his left eye-tooth was floating around his mouth. He hocked up all of his saliva and spit it out.

Below him, further down the slope from the cabin and sneaking through the trees, Meyers saw the light colored shirt crouching beside the covered bridge. "Stupid." He mumbled as he leveled his rifle for the easy shot. "You should have run away, kid."

He first sighted the kid's head for the quick and painless death, but then he moved the gun barrel down to his back. The rookie had been more trouble than he was worth and Meyers would make sure he had several long and agonizing minutes to think about his stupidity before dying. The shot rang out sending a flurry of birds scattering from tree tops, screeching their anger at the booming noise that disrupted the otherwise peaceful north shore evening.

The bullet tore into Harris' back, clipped two vertebrae in his spine, passed through his stomach and exited just below his sternum. A warm gush soaked his shirt, slickening it and matting it to his body. It was so quick and so unexpected that at first Harris didn't even realize what had happened. He only felt an intense burning in his torso.

He ran his hand across the wetness on his stomach and lifted it to his face. It was too dark to distinguish the color, but the thickness and warmth was enough for him to know. It was blood and the burning sensation was from a bullet. He stood motionless still looking in horrified awe at his bloody hand as the wetness spread further down the front of his shirt and into his pants.

He'd done nothing, he thought. Life had brought him to this when he had done nothing. He was no angel, but he was definitely no devil either. For this cruel and gruesome fate, he'd done nothing wrong.

His vision doubled and the dark trees surrounding him started rocking from side to side. He instinctively shifted his weight to adjust for this swaying reality and tilted far to the side until his balance was lost. He crashed to the ground, hip first then shoulder then head. He didn't feel this fall. There wasn't any pain. His sight rocked faster, nearly spinning fully around in dimming circles.

In his final moments of consciousness, Harris searched for some reasoning for his violent death. He had never harmed another human being, he rarely spoke negatively about others and he always did as he was told. There seemed no justification for his murder other than his poor choice of associates. It wasn't fair. He thought of Ben Jurick at the bottom of Bear Island Lake and he squeezed his eyes tightly shut.

Meyers cautiously approached the body with his rifle still held ready and his sight fixed on the back of the kid's head. He had underestimated him and friends from the beginning. He would be ready for one final burst of life if it came. With the heel of his boot he pulled back on the shoulder. The body rolled and Meyers gasped in confusion at the face he recognized too well.

Behind him and to his right, Josh stood up from the trees that covered him. His gun raised, he took two quiet steps closer to assure his shot. Meyers didn't hear him at all and the sting of the dart in his neck was barely felt before he passed out. Josh pulled off two more shots just to be sure.

Addison posted her hands and raised her upper body off the ground. Her long damp hair had fallen over her face and through the fan of blond strands, her fiery hazel eyes watched with a hateful stare as her shooter, a stylish and graceful man with a refined and relaxed gait, half-trotted down the stairs.

Gib, his back to the man as he helped Addison steady herself, kept careful watch of him as well with quick, nervous glances over his shoulder. "Are you alright?" He mumbled.

Her jaw clenched tighter until the muscles in her cheeks bulged. Her eye lids narrowed to mere slits. All of her pain and all of her anger shot out from the hard stare that stayed fixed on the approaching man.

The loud crack of rifle fire suddenly reverberated through the forest. Temple came off the stairway and crossed to the middle of the courtyard. "You're friend Josh, I would assume." He said lightly.

Addison's stare didn't break. She refused to give in to this man's taunts. Only Gib saw the change in her. The green tint that gleamed brighter when she was angry had softened and gave way to the more soulful brown.

Above them, Walsh had found his way out of the maze. He hopped into the courtyard beside them, aimed his gun at Gib and waited for the next order.

"Give me the stone." Temple demanded.

Gib slowly stood up and turned to face Temple. These were the men that had chased them - maybe not the same men, but definitely with them. This was only about the stones; the chase on White Iron was only about the stones. Somehow he had known even back at Old Ely. He had known it and ignored it in his naïve and unmindful focus. He handed the scuba cap over to the man beside him. Walsh pulled out the stone to verify it and took it to Temple.

Under the light of the moon, Temple inspected his prize. "What type of gem is this?"

"Quartz." Gib answered.

"Quartz?" Temple confirmed with a disgusted and disbelieving look. He then huffed an exasperated little laugh for all his trouble. "They're worthless."

"Then let us go." Gib challenged carefully.

"I think not." Temple answered. "Their worth may be less tangible than I hoped, but I certainly cannot go home empty handed. Where is the other?"

Gib didn't answer, not to antagonize him, but more to give him self time to think of a possible escape.

"People know we found them." Addison blurted out. "They'll know you stole them from us."

Temple looked down at her with a twisted and evil grin. "People…or you're friend Ben?"

Finally Addison's defiance melted into shock and horror as she stared longer at his face. That smile, with its certainty and its casual indifference, showed how little he was concerned about the threat of Ben Jurick. The reason was obvious.

"Ben?" She gasped. Her bottom lip lightly quivered and tears filled her eyes.

"Only dead men keep their secrets." He said callously. "Words to live by, I've found. And dead men lying somewhere on the bottom of a dark lake are especially good at keeping their secrets."

The arm holding her upright began to tremble and her blurry, broken stare drifted past Temple to the cold gray stones of the courtyard. "Ben…" She rasped softly.

Temple breathed out another little laugh. He expected a scream of anguish for the old man and a stream of curses for himself. Gib did too. But the news was only slowly seeping in; the finality of it, of not seeing Ben again and of losing a second farther, was still foggy and distant and her anger hadn't surfaced yet.

Gib dropped his head and gave a gentle stroke across the back of her head. Temple stayed with his pleasant grimace, watching her face as the pain spread through her and ate away her strength, watching as her burning eyes turned to watery pits of sorrow and he delighted in it.

Gib let out a long heavy sigh that he hoped sounded like genuine defeat. He stole a subtle look around in the darkness behind him. "It's in the car, back at the parking lot." He lied, trying to buy them some time and hoping that maybe Josh was somehow still able to help them.

Temple lowered his gun to Addison, the barrel sighted at her head, and he clicked back the hammer to bring

Gib's attention back to him. His patience had expired a long time ago. "I have no time for liars, Mr. Larkin. And there is no one left to save you."

Gib shifted and looked around again, his mind now racing desperately for an answer. "I put it somewhere safe." He fumbled. "Will you let us go?"

"This is not a negotiation." Temple replied coldly. "And one way or another I will get its location from you."

No, this wasn't a negotiation, Gib realized. There had been no implication of safety in return for their cooperation. The second stone, the bargaining chip he thought could save them, was only worth the difference between a quick death and a slow agonizing one.

"It's not worth it Gib," Temple continued. "all this running through the woods for something with only little more value than the earth beneath our feet. You're holding out for nothing."

Not for money, but certainly not for nothing, Gib thought distractedly. It was the things Gerald showed them that were truly valuable. His legacy, so carefully constructed and so imaginatively folded into the land around them, was more about the journey than the stones themselves. It was more about what Gerald could manipulate within this environment – what he could show them and the memories he could give them. It was about potential and the unexpected wonder to be found in the simplest of things.

In this anxious moment, this deadly moment, a surprising and peculiar thought popped into his head. It was the book again and again the last passage he read. There was an answer beyond finding the second stone; something spectacular for accomplishing Gerald's task. He understood its complete meaning now. There was still more to see.

"Is it worth her pain?" Temple prodded.

Gib looked down at her and she up to him. Already she was burying the grief, putting it away for a more appropriate time when they were safe. The green of her eyes flickered brighter once again. She wasn't ready to give up. His own eyes twinkled with a reassurance he hoped she understood.

"Gib!" Temple shouted.

"The weather vane." He answered solemnly, sounding defeated and deflated. "The base of the weather vane is hollow. I put it there to keep it safe."

Temple nodded Walsh over to the metal ornament.

"The legs at the base turn to unlock it." Gib added. "Turn it counter clockwise."

Addison didn't flinch at his lie. She knew one was coming. It was a gamble, but it wasn't without reason. He certainly wouldn't risk her life before the stones. He had a plan. There was confidence in his words underneath the fear and dejection he tried to convey. It was the same confidence he had before with his secret knowledge of the "been eaten" trees. She trusted it and she would be ready. She pulled her good leg underneath her body until her weight rested fully on her knee.

Walsh went to the weather vane and grabbed the legs. One quick twist was all he needed then a high pitched whistle screamed through the open seal. Walsh paused. In a split second he recognized what it meant, but that split second was more time than he had to react.

With the seal broken and the pressure released, a jet of water shot through an underground tunnel below, propelled by the weight of the lake high above them. It rushed through the tunnel with blinding speed and the weather vane exploded upward. Its iron base cracked against Walsh's forehead and knocked him back. The blow launched him into the air and he landed, unconscious and limp against the far stone wall of the courtyard.

The geyser spewed over a hundred feet into the air; a spectacle demanding to be seen by anyone who wasn't prepared for it and Temple was not prepared for it. Gib knew it was coming. He knew it from Gerald's book, he knew it from the whistle, and he knew it was his best opportunity. He was there in two bounding leaps, striding through the shower of water then slamming his shoulder into Temple's stomach and tackling him to the ground.

"Addison, go!" He shouted as he fought his way up Temple's torso to secure the gun.

It was no longer in his hand. Stunned by the suddenness of Gib's action and the breath-stealing blow to his sternum, Temple's hands went loose. The stone had fallen to the ground and his gun had bounced off across the courtyard. Gib began hitting Temple with quick, short jabs to his gut, over and over and faster and faster until Temple brought up his hands and slammed the heels of his palms into the sides of Gib's head.

Gib's vision crossed and clouded and his head swayed. The jarring of his equilibrium was all Temple needed. He quickly rolled Gib over and climbed on top of him, bringing a wide swinging right hook across the side of Gib's cheek and nose. Another came right after and one more just to be sure. Now Gib was too dazed to really think of anything but the pain.

Half-sitting on Gib's chest, his other leg posted out to secure his balance, Temple pinned Gib's right arm to the ground while he used his other hand to grip his neck. His fingers dug deep into the flesh tightening around his windpipe and close to crushing it.

Gib wheezed a throaty gulp of air and heaved his body up with high kicks and sudden jerks as he tried to buck him off. Temple's stance was too effective. He swung his free hand at Temple's head, but his position on the ground, and Temple's slight turn away, kept him from landing a punch with any force. Finally Gib tried digging his nails into the skin on the back of Temple's neck. The killing eyes looking down on him only became more focused and more intent as he realized he was about to win.

It was a chance he took, thinking that the element of surprise gave him an advantage. It did, but only at first. He had underestimated him. As the grip squeezed harder around his neck he felt regret for his failure. He felt regret for Addison because this man's determination would never allow her to escape.

In his last moments of blurry consciousness, Gib saw the white light of the moon above him. Then, suddenly, he also saw the twinkling of gold and crystal. Addison was standing over them with wet strands of hair hanging over her face and thin streams of water pouring from her nose and chin. Her arm was raised high over her head with the stone in her hand. She brought it down in one swift motion and she cried out as the torn muscle in her wounded leg tensed with her movement. The stone connected to the side of Temple's head and he crumpled in an unconscious heap on top of Gib.

"Gib!" Addison shouted. She fell down to her good knee and rolled Temple's body away.

He choked and coughed then managed to speak. "I'm alright." He said as he wiped away a trail of blood from his nose. "I'm alright."

Josh arrived just as Gib was getting to his feet and he was struck by the sight; the fountain still spewing water into the air, the courtyard filling like a pool, two of the bad guys unconscious on the ground and his friends safely recovering from whatever had happened. "You guys okay?"

Gib and Addison exchanged quiet smiles of relief when they saw he was still alive. "She's been shot." Gib called as he tried to help Addison to her feet.

Josh jumped into the rising water and waded over to take her other arm. Together they brought her up the stairs and over to the ledge, still under stray sprays of rain, but safe.

"There were more than just these two." Gib said between heavy breaths. "The man from White Iron with the tattoo was part of it and more in the…"

Josh flashed his gun confidently. "I got him, Gib. And the others."

Gib looked at the filling pool and the water level that would soon cover the fallen men. "We have to pull them out of there. They'll drown."

"Noble, Gib." Addison said coldly. "But I'm a little more concerned about them waking up."

Josh casually lifted his gun and squeezed off a shot into each man. The bodies jolted and twitched from the surge of power then fell motionless again. Gib and Josh dragged them up the stairs and dropped them on the ground.

"We need to call the cops." Addison said when they'd finished.

"Already done." Josh answered. "I'll go wait for them in the parking lot."

Addison, with one eye constantly watching the unconscious men called out before he disappeared into the woods. "Leave us your gun."

Josh smiled at her dryly, silently gloating once again at her change of heart about the "toy gun".

CHAPTER 19

The engine of a metallic blue car whirred to a quiet stop in the parking lot of the Ely Historical Museum. There was no truck for Gib this time. He had driven in with his family. A large group of people were waiting at the doors, huddled closely together as they watched some spectacle. Most of them were different branches of the Kearny line and with them they carried memories and mementos to donate to the new exhibit. There was a wedding ring that had been passed down through the Kearny women, family portraits, baby books, quilts, and anything else that could be considered a keepsake.

Gib slung a green and brown back pack over his shoulder and walked right through the mass of people without being noticed. Even as he politely excused his way through the tightly knit group, no one paid him much attention. At the front of the crowd Addison was standing at the entrance to the building, forcing a smile as she spoke with reporters from the Duluth television stations. After a year of such interviews, she'd learned to disguise her dislike of such formalities fairly well. Gib knew better.

Beside her, wearing a floral patterned summer dress, her nana Alise sat in a wheelchair. Addison stubbornly refused to give the reporters any more than short, one or two word answers to their questions and after each one Alise prodded her to shed her humility and enjoy the moment.

It wasn't until Addison saw Gib and called his name that he was finally recognized. The reporters began shouting questions at him until Alise sternly dismissed them. "Now you folks just give us a minute to say hello."

She hadn't seen Gib since the day he came with the others to show her the stones. The reporters heeded her command and even the crowd backed away to give Gib and his family more space.

"Alise," Gib greeted and bent over to kiss her cheek. "I'm glad you were able to come."

"Well where else would I have to go?" She answered with twinkling sarcasm.

Gib was talking about her health and was about to clarify that when he realized she was goading him. He and Addison exchanged a warm hug then Gib presented his family to Alise.

Gib's father Sam was especially interested in meeting her. "Did you know my grandfather, Michael Larkin?"

Alise didn't have to think hard to remember that name. "Oh I remember Mikey. That boy was born for destruction. God bless your parents if your apple didn't fall far enough from his tree."

Sam laughed. "Well my own dad was no picnic either from what I was told."

Gib left them to their conversation as he looked around. The news crews were still filming and now the reporters began calling for he and Addison to stand together for a photo.

"Where's Josh?" He asked Addison.

She turned and shouldered up to Gib for the pose. "He's already inside with his parents. The newspaper wants some pictures of us in the exhibit before they open the doors."

"You're hating this." He softly said from the corner of his mouth.

"With all my heart." She answered through a gritted smile.

The usher at the door interrupted the photo session and invited Gib, Addison and their families to come in. He then told the crowd it would only be a few more minutes before the museum would officially open.

Inside, Gib was speechless at the incredible effort put into this tribute. Artificial trees, the most realistic looking he'd ever seen, had been placed all around to simulate a forest. The floor was uneven and hilly and covered with tamped dirt and rocks of all sizes. An automated moose, life-sized, stood peeking out from the trees moving its head and giant rack of antlers back and forth to watch the passing guests.

On the other side of the room there was a black bear standing on his back legs with one of his forepaws against the trunk of a tree. The other arm was swiping upward at a pack dangling just out of reach. A walking path, a black tar road identified by a green road sign as The Old 169, wound through the landscape. It was even painted with intermittent yellow stripes to better simulate the highway that once brought visitors to the town of Old Ely.

The first stop on the route was a sixteen by twenty foot video monitor displaying a map of Old Ely and the surrounding lakes. A computer generated voice invited onlookers to call out a name by one of the many red dots on the map. It promised a magnified image and a historical account of the site.

The towns of Ely and Winton had their own dots of course, and also most of the lakes. Miner's Lake had been left off this version too, though only Gib and Addison knew that. In the numerous recountings of their adventure, they never mentioned crossing the dead lake, or Old Ely, to anyone. They, and Josh, agreed to omit that part of the story so as not to pique the interest of anyone who might follow their journey.

"Winton." Gib's sister Emelia said loudly. The map dissolved to an inset of the town and the computer began talking about its founding. There were more red dots showing more points of interest within. Emelia wanted to continue, but the usher moved them along before she could call out another name. They were running behind schedule, he told them, and people were waiting.

Further along, they came to a model of Gerald's north shore cabin. Scaled down, but still standing at least five feet high, it was incredibly detailed. The mountain had been recreated and real water flowed down its side to show the creek. Addison was especially impressed and pleased that the artist had remained so true to the source. He even included the sitting area by the small pond that she hoped to spend time at someday.

The tarred road ended, but a smaller dirt path lead on between two rows of trees. All their leaves had been stripped. A wooden sign nailed to one trunk identified the new trail as "The Beaten Path". The rows of bare trunks curved and twisted through a sprawling forest of green firs.

The wind blew and birds chirped and there was a strong scent of pine combined with the musty odor of damp dirt. Gib breathed it in with the blissful warmth of nostalgia. As Addison pushed her along, Alise looked up to the ceiling of a bright blue sky. "Beautiful day." She said.

"And no bugs." Gib added cheerfully. He looked around for the one thing he was especially excited to see. "I wonder where the Kearny cabin is."

"We're coming to it." Addison answered. "Just wait." Her lingering inflection hinted that she had some big secret. She hadn't been in the exhibit yet, but she had helped the curators with the basic lay out when they designed it. She knew just where everything was supposed to be.

The path wound in a tight ess curve then met up with a wide wooden dock. Suddenly, a recreation of the Kearny cabin popped into view. Gib jerked back from the abrupt appearance of it and his head swam in a dizzying, disorienting stupor. There was no way he could have missed seeing it before. It was the only thing he was looking for. He turned around and right behind him, what just a second ago was the forest they were walking through, was now the long open waters of Garden Lake.

"Oh, my." Alise gasped and her face lit up.

Gib reached toward the water, realizing what the illusion was, but still not completely certain. Where his hand should have gone through, his fingers instead brushed against the same fiber-optic curtain that he had seen at the Duluth airport. The scene of rolling water wafted slightly and slowly from his brief touch.

"Wow." Sam breathed as he came up behind. He walked backward, back into the forest, and looked at the curtain from the other side. It still showed the forest scene.

The dock served as the only access over a large pool of real water. The breeze, simulated by vents, had changed direction and was now coming off the lake. Before them, the front wall of the Kearny's Garden Lake cabin stood among the trees. Every detail had been painstakingly recreated from the pictures Gib had given the historical society. Even the ground sloped up almost as high and with the same sharp angle of the original site. They had included the front deck and also the mangled swing.

He was there again, as they were last summer; closer even, now that it had been brought back to life. It was better than any image his mind could conger up. "Amazing." He whispered, thinking his long held disdain for technology in the northland was perhaps unjustified.

"Come on, Gib." Addison said as she dug in her feet and pushed Alise's wheelchair up the hill. "They remade the whole thing. You gotta see it."

The interior looked just as he'd expected. He wasn't surprised. They had requested even more photos from him for just this purpose. Though the experts had certainly gotten the dimensions right, the cabin was smaller than he expected. He wondered how the Kearny's were able to fit so many people into such a tight space.

The only change, the only difference he could clearly see from what he knew should be there, was the addition of Gerald's carved family tree from Newton Lake. It was displayed on the kitchen table and that was really the most appropriate place for it. He was glad he decided to give that to the museum as well.

The back door through the kitchen showed the way out and led to a large room filled with vintage photos of Ely both before and after the restructuring. Every decade of the town's history was represented, demonstrating its growth from its founding in the late 1800's to the present day. Nearly a quarter of the display was dedicated to the time of the relocation.

In the middle of the room sat a large glass case lit up by a tract of glowing yellow bulbs at the top. Inside was the old cedar chest gifted to the Kearny parents by Gerald. The lid was open to display the tray with golden grooves and the two holes sat empty.

"Gib!" Josh shouted from behind him as he walked away from his own crowd of reporters. "It's about time you got here. What took you so long? You left the resort before we did."

Gib nodded over to his father, standing with his vidcam and capturing every moment. "My dad had to stop and get new batteries."

A tall, lanky man dressed in a neat black suit came up right after. "Mr. Larkin." The curator greeted with an extended hand. "Are you sure you don't want to change your mind?"

Gib didn't hesitate for a moment, nor did he feel any regret for his decision. "No." He said as he dropped his backpack off his shoulder. "I can't think of a better home for the stones."

He took them out and the reporters began shouting for Josh and Addison to stand next to him while they took pictures. They only got off a couple before Gib, Addison and Josh insisted that their families be included. They were relentless though when it was time for Gib to put the stones in the chest. That was to be done by him alone.

Standing at the glass case, he placed them both in at the same time as a steady clicking of camera shutters sounded off all around him. He rolled the stones around in the tray as he looked for the perfect setting. He didn't stop until he'd found a match for each flowing line on the stone to a corresponding one on the tray. Only then was he satisfied and he offered the press a broad smile.

―――――

Finally the doors to the museum were opened and the people poured in. A symphony of "oohs" and "ahhs" filled the room. The replica of the cabin was the biggest hit, even ahead of the stones, Gib thought. All of the descendants wanted to experience the place that had shaped their lives in at least some obscure way. They stayed for hours enjoying what it had to offer and more people came as the day went on.

On the deck in front of the cabin, Alise sat in her wheelchair welcoming all visitors and telling them things she could remember of the Kearny family. The museum hadn't planned this, but they did nothing to stop it either.

The line continued filing quickly along until a woman with tightly curled wisps of pure white hair, thick glasses and a copper cane prepared to make her way up the stairs. She was heavy set with a round cheery face and a gentle smile. At her side, a young man held onto her arm as he patiently helped her up each stair. She easily matched Alise's age. Beneath the wrinkles surrounding the woman's deep set eyes and the low sagging skin of her jowls, Alise found something familiar in her; something vague and just beyond her failing memory.

"Are you Alise Gethold?" The woman asked, her voice cracking softly. She shuffled her feet across the deck almost forgetting to rely on her cane as carefully as she should.

"Yes." Alise answered.

"My father was Frank Barrister, your second cousin on your mother's side."

Alise gasped and her eyes teared. "Maggie?" She asked, remembering immediately once she'd heard the surname.

"Why, yes." Maggie crooned with a glimmering smile. "I didn't know if you'd remember me. I haven't seen you since my parents moved us to Colorado."

Alise stood up from her chair and carefully leaned forward with her arms stretched out to welcome her long lost relative. The picture was clearer now. The warm memories of her childhood and of holiday traditions were coming back to her. Maggie was closest to her in age and during those reunions, from the ages of four to eleven, they were inseparable.

Alise kissed her on the cheek. "I haven't thought of you in years."

The young man assisted Maggie down onto a bench. The wind pushed around her fine hair and she looked out to the lake. "Well, life has a funny way of pulling people in different directions, I guess - my, isn't that a beautiful scene. Reminds me of Uncle Thomas' house on the fourth of July."

"Mmmhmm." Alise agreed. "All we need is Uncle Thomas and cousin Martin drinking too much beer and fallin' off the end of the dock. Then it'd be just like old times."

Maggie burst out with a raucous howl and doubled over in a fit of laughter. Alise giggled and cackled along with her. When they regained themselves, they started spouting off other happenings that were just as memorable. One would bring up fragments of certain memories and the other would add various important details. Together they filled in many of the blanks from a childhood long lost. Gib stood behind them, his arms folded across his chest and leaning against the wall as he eagerly waited for the next story.

Printed in the United States
207795BV00001B/2/P